Finders Keepers

By Kate Cheasman

ISBN: 9798699638345

DEDICATION

This book is dedicated to my mother, who introduced me to the magic of words at a very young age. It has never left me.
And to my sister, Margaret, who has always supported and encouraged me, even when others had given up on me.

ACKNOWLEDGMENTS

I would like to thank Ruby Ormerod, my writing tutor for several years, who saw something in me and encouraged me to write a novel. Thanks also go to my author friend Natalie Meg Evans, who has been an inspiration and has kept me going when the ideas stalled. Without her, this book would never have been finished.

And to the Cutting Edge Creative Writing Group who suffered reading it chapter by chapter – and helped me refine the prose and produce this final version.

To Simon Watts for helping me to prepare Finders Keepers for publishing.

And to all my family and friends who have continued to encourage me and have put up with my determination to see the novel in print, however long it took.

Chapter 1

That day changed her life forever. Such a small thing to happen, but one that led Mel on a totally different course. A bin bag of all things!

Mel had slowed to pull in to the layby to take a phone call but was so startled by what she'd just seen that she slammed on the brakes without a thought for the furious motorists on the road behind her. Embarrassed, she waved her apologies. 'Sorry,' she mouthed.

This time, she took more care before easing into the lay-by. There was the bin bag that had attracted her attention. But the possibility that she'd seen it move? That was something else. And yet she was consumed with the need to make sure.

Climbing out of the car, she crossed to the bag. Briefly she hesitated, heart thumping, afraid of what she might find, wondering if a heartless person had dumped some defenceless kittens or puppies. She was a sucker for animals, especially young ones, and she knew she'd have to take them home. Heaven knows what Tom would say when he returned.

He'll just have to get used to the idea, she thought. I'd never forgive myself if some poor scrap suffered, or even died, because I didn't have the courage to do something to help it. Brushing away the frost that coated the bag, she cautiously peered into the sack. It might just be a snake after all, and she was terrified of them.

Thankfully, there was no snake lurking there, but what she saw was surreal. She must be obsessed, like Tom said. But she could have sworn she'd seen a tiny baby, before she'd jumped back in disbelief. She must have made a mistake. No one would dump a new-born in a lay-by on a freezing March morning. She was shaking now, not only because she thought she was seeing things, but also because, though angry, she had been gripped with a terrible excitement

She peeped into the bag again. There it was, a scrawny infant, a girl, blue with cold. Nothing shielded her from the clammy black bag except the well-worn woollen scarf that had been carefully wrapped around her and fastened with a safety pin. The baby made a feeble cry as Mel lifted her out. She was miraculously still alive. Mel held her close, wrapping her coat around the tiny form for warmth.

Unable to quell the thoughts in her head she whispered to the child, 'I was meant to find you, you know. I'll look after you and we'll be together forever. I love you already and I shall call you Chloe.' Her dark eyes were moist, and her long fall of blonde hair brushed the baby's cheek as she bent to kiss her.

But now Mel had to consider the practicalities of getting the child home. With one hand cradling the infant, she reached into the boot for the rug she always kept there. She wrapped it securely round the ice-cold baby. 'I'll soon have you home safe and warm,' she told her as she placed her gently on the back seat and fastened the seat belt securely across her.

She was momentarily distracted by a movement in the hedge at the back of the lay-by. Until now she hadn't given a thought to who had left the bag there but had assumed it was the child's mother. Immediately she'd written her off as being uncaring, brutally ruthless. But what if she did care? After all, she'd chosen the spot carefully, aware that this was a place where lorry drivers often stopped to take a break, and the child would have every chance of being found before it was too late. It was possible she could have waited to see that her daughter was safe.

Now Mel wanted to be a bit more charitable. There must be a good reason why the mother felt compelled to do such a terrible thing. What if she was homeless; had no money, and no family or friend to turn to? Mel knew what it was like to feel alone. Her own parents had been killed in a car crash when she was twelve. How she'd longed for her mother when all her efforts to have a baby had come to nothing. A mother's hug would have been such a comfort.

Her own loss made Mel think about how close the poor little scrap in her arms had come to going through life without knowing a parent's love. Suddenly she felt compassion for the mother, wanted her approval even. She wanted to tell her that her child would be safe and loved.

Hastily unclipping the safety strap, she scooped Chloe up again. She went over and peered through the sparse hedge, just in time to see a jeans-clad figure, thin coat flapping in the wind, disappear into a nearby thicket. Mel wanted desperately to talk to her, but if she didn't get Chloe home and warm very soon, she... might die. There, she'd forced herself to acknowledge the painful truth. She couldn't let that happen. Not again. She had lost too many babies. Reluctantly, she turned away and soon they were on their way.

Arriving at the house, Mel stowed the baby carefully in her empty shopping bag away from the neighbours' prying eyes and hurried indoors. The shopping would have to wait.

'Come along little one. Let's get you upstairs.' She sang softly as she sponged Chloe with warm water and saw a pink glow creep into the child's skin. As gently as she could she removed the grubby-looking rag that bound the crudely cut umbilical cord and bathed the stub with diluted antiseptic, before re-dressing it with a sterile bandage.

Chloe was now screaming. Mel worried that it was her unskilful handling that had caused the baby pain but calmed herself with the thought that it was probably hunger. Gently she dried her on a soft towel, and carried her to the spare room, the room that had once excitedly been prepared for their longed-for child. The child that had never been brought home, even though one pregnancy had lasted seven months. It had broken Mel's heart.

After a while Tom had insisted they redecorate the nursery as a guest room, but Mel still saw the pale yellow walls and the colourful farmyard frieze that had paraded round them, and not the sophisticated coffee and cream décor that covered her hopes and dreams.

She placed the baby carefully on the bed, before diving underneath for the suitcase she'd hidden right at the back against the wall. With her arm at full stretch, she located the handle and pulled the case out. Not for the first time she clicked it open and lovingly stroked the tiny garments. She pulled out a vest and a disposable nappy, then selected a fluffy pink sleep suit and snuggled the infant into it.

All the time the unfocussed blue gaze never left Mel's face. Damp tendrils of baby-fine, dark hair clung to her tiny cheeks. And she had the longest eyelashes, and lips that seemed to be set in a permanent kiss. She was quiet now, soothed by the warmth and Mel's gentle crooning.

Mel felt her heart melt as tiny fingers clasped her own. She studied the minute fingernails and planted a kiss in the palm of Chloe's free hand. She might be tiny, but she was perfect and Mel sent up a silent prayer for the gift she'd received that day. A day that had started out as drab and mundane as any other.

Once again, she thought of the baby's mother, wondering what could have made her so desperate that she'd had to give up on her child? Mel just hoped she'd seen her retrieve Chloe and had some consolation from seeing how much she cared for her.

Brought back to the present by a burst of urgent crying from Chloe – there was nothing wrong with her lungs it was clear – Mel hurried downstairs with her. She reached into the back of the cupboard where she had secreted the microwavable sterilizer and bottle, afraid to admit to Tom that she couldn't give up completely on her dream of being a mother. What would he have said if he knew she'd kept clothes, and nappies, too?

She punched open a can of evaporated milk and diluted it with water according to the instructions. She'd read that new babies tolerated it better than cow's milk. She offered the bottle to Chloe, but the little scrap had no idea how to suck and screamed even louder. If she'd had her own baby, and God knows she'd tried, she would have been taught how to handle a new-born, but right now she realised how lacking she was. On the edge of panic, Mel tried the bottle again and again. In desperation, she sprinkled a few drops of milk onto her little finger and touched it to Chloe's lips. Suddenly Chloe clutched it and started sucking. Mel gently withdrew her finger and replaced it with the teat. Soon the baby was sucking away enthusiastically at the warm milk and Mel relaxed.

For that moment she forgot Chloe was not her flesh and blood and cherished the feel, the smell, the warmth of the baby's body against her own. She longed for Tom's promised phone call and imagined telling him about the miracle that had happened. After all the years of pain and disappointment, he was going to be as thrilled as she was. At last their life was going right.

When Chloe seemed satisfied, Mel winded her, changed her nappy and settled her in a drawer that she had padded with a soft blanket. She began to grow more confident and stood watching as the child, her child now, slipped into sleep. A warmth, born of excitement and fulfilment, crept over Mel then, so that she was startled by the intrusive shrillness of the phone. She snatched up the receiver, concerned that the noise would wake Chloe, but she was too late. Loud wails echoed across the room.

'Hallo... Mel?' Tom's voice was hesitant; as if he thought he might have the wrong number.

Mel picked Chloe up, rocking her to soothe the frightened cries.

'Yes, it's me. You'll never guess what's happened, Tom. I've found a baby. She's gorgeous.' There was no way she could stop her excitement spilling out as soon as she'd heard his voice.

'What on earth do you mean? You don't just find a baby, are you mad?'

In that moment the aura of happiness that had enveloped Mel dulled a little and immediately she was defensive.

'No, I'm not mad. It happened,' she snapped. But as she told Tom about finding the child in the lay by and bringing her home, she experienced again all the elation, the feeling that it had been meant to happen, that they deserved this gift. She tried to convey all this to Tom.

He was silent for a while.

'Tom, are you still there? Isn't it wonderful?'

'Mel... I don't know what to say to you. You must know you can't keep the baby. She's not yours.'

'She is. The mother was there. I'm sure she saw me pick her up and she didn't stop me. She meant me to have Chloe.' Oh God, she hadn't meant to let that slip out. But suddenly, it had seemed like only yesterday that she had spent hours poring over books of names, eventually settling on Dominic for a boy and Chloe for a girl.

'Chloe? You've named her? Oh Mel. You need help.'

'What do you mean?'

He ignored her question and carried on, 'I'm sorry but we have to hand her over to the authorities, you know that. We'll sort something out when I get home.'

Mel felt the colour leach from her face as she fought the fear that had settled in her stomach. She struggled to suppress the threatening nausea. He meant it, he really meant it. All the promise, all the hope, annihilated in a couple of sentences. She tried again, pleading with him. 'Tom, this is our last chance. You know my age is against me now. They have made that plain. Can't you stop being a policeman just for once? This is our life we're talking about. Not some hypothetical case.'

But he had said ''When I get home.'' Quelling her fear Mel asked, 'Are you going away again? Straight away? You haven't even been home from this one ...'

'Fraid so. They want me in Germany.'

How could he be so callous, so dismissive of her feelings?

As a DCI in the Met, Mel knew there would be times when he was called away without much notice. But did it have to be now? And did they have to send Tom? To Germany of all places? It would have been so much easier to discuss this face to face. Mel was full of resentment that once more his job had come first, taking him away when she needed him as never before. She was only vaguely aware that he was still speaking.

'We still have to do what's right,' he said. Plainly, he wasn't giving in.

'When are you due back?' she asked him in a voice that was as flat and colourless as a blank manuscript.

'We've nearly done here, just a few ends to tie up. Then I need to go straight to Germany. I'll catch the 2.30 plane home tomorrow. Should be home by teatime. We'll talk about it then. But we do have to hand her over to the authorities ASAP. You know that. We have to sort this out. Promise me. Bye.' There was finality about the click that signified the end of his call.

But Mel was still full of questions. Do we? she wanted to ask him. Do you really love me at all? You obviously have no idea of what I've been through. Or the guilt I felt that I couldn't give you the child I thought you wanted.

Now at last I have a chance to be a mother. But you can't see it can you? You just can't see what it means to me, to us. All these thoughts hammered in Mel's head.

Why hadn't she noticed his detachment before? He'd been much more philosophical about their inability to produce a child it's true, accepting that it wasn't to be and getting on with his life.

At the time she'd thought it was his way of dealing with it. That he was trying to keep positive for her sake. Now she realised it really hadn't mattered much to him and the knowledge was a cruel blow.

She remembered when they met. She had been instantly attracted to his tall frame, the dark hair that curled over his collar, his ready laugh and the grey eyes that had mirrored his feelings. How she'd loved him then.

Now she recognised the tell-tale signs of change. The job had sucked him in until he was a policeman first and foremost. The job always came first. It always had, but more so now that he had been promoted to DCI. Why hadn't she noticed? In that moment she could so easily have hated him.

He had filled her with doubts. Surely it would be all right when he saw Chloe? He couldn't help but fall in love with her. But what if he didn't? She couldn't take that risk. Urgency forced her into action. She settled on a plan.

She couldn't let Chloe go. At first light tomorrow she would leave to start a new life with Chloe. There was no going back. She booked her ticket and would collect and pay for it at the channel terminal. All night she tossed and turned, tormented by the decision she'd made. If only Tom had understood, but it was cruelly obvious that he didn't. She decided to confide in her close friend Caro. Before she could change her mind, she keyed in the number on her mobile.

'Hi Mel. This is a nice surprise.'

'You may not think so when you hear what I have to say.'

'Why? What's up?'

'I have to go away.'

'What? Why" Where to?'

'Best you don't know. Then if they ask awkward questions at the office you can genuinely tell them you don't know anything.'

'You're not making sense. Are you in trouble? '

'No. But I might very well be if I stick around. Of course there are reasons. But I'm sorry Caro I can't tell you why, or where I'm heading. I just didn't want to leave without saying goodbye. I hope we can catch up soon.' She quickly ended the call before Caro detected the break in her voice.

It was hard saying goodbye to her best friend, but Mel knew it would be worth it. If it meant leaving, that's what she would have to do. She'd go to the place she'd chosen, where they were not known. Perhaps she would say she was a widow.

She would bring Chloe up as her own and, if things went well, perhaps she could contact Tom later on. It had to be for the best. Even if it meant leaving Tom - for now. He'd brought it on himself after all. No understanding, not a glimpse of sympathy, just a callous statement that her last chance was over.

She couldn't let that happen.

Chapter 2

Mel took one last look at the house that had promised so much happiness. She'd loved it as soon as she saw it. Modern and clean-lined with large windows to let in maximum light and a generous garden for a child to play in safely. Tears blurred her vision as she pulled away.

Tom…Tom…If only things were different.

She imagined him reading the note, his hurt and probable anger, but she felt driven to do this. Some things were worth the sacrifice.

She turned to look at her beautiful baby, snug, and gurgling happily and knew, even through her tears, that she was doing the right thing.

Constrained by the urgency, Mel had thrown together the plan. She was going to France. Her French was fluent. With no time to spare, she had bought a new pay-as-you-go mobile in a new name and ordered her ticket for the crossing. She'd robbed her bank account to organise a baby seat for the car that would be waiting for her in Calais and a buggy for the onward journey. Having seen an ad in the paper, she had spoken to a friendly woman in Normandy who had an apartment to rent and she'd booked it for a month. Despite the trauma of the events that had triggered this sudden change in her life, and although she had acted in panic, she was now bracing herself for her new adventure.

She'd fallen in love with France on an exchange visit from school and had returned there many times to tour the country. She loved Normandy, for its historic architecture, the friendliness of the people and the open landscape that was not unlike the scenery around her Suffolk home

But when she met Tom, he introduced her to Greece and her islands. They'd holidayed there ever since, and she'd learned to love it too. Tom thought it a courtesy to endeavour to master the rudiments of the Greek language if they intended to visit the country at least once a year and they'd struggled over it for five years. In fact, if it occurred to him that she would have the courage to take Chloe abroad, that's probably where he'd look.

She doubted very much whether he would remember that France had been her favourite place before she knew him. He had an aversion to France and French people anyway. Her only worry now was how to smuggle Chloe into France, but it was a risk she'd just have to take.

Having made good time, she was soon nearing the channel tunnel terminal in Folkstone. Now all she had to do was pull off the road to feed and change her baby, before transferring her to her temporary cot in the boot. Hopefully, Chloe would sleep throughout the train journey.

Mel gave Chloe one last cuddle before placing her in the cot. As if sensing Mel's anxiety, the child was uncharacteristically fractious, working herself up into a frenzy of kicking and screaming. Aware of the time passing, Mel tried everything to soothe her. Eventually Chloe wore herself out, the hiccupping sobs eased and she drifted off to sleep.

As she drove on to the terminal, Mel thought fleetingly of how much easier it would have been if she'd been able to have a child of her own. It wasn't as if they hadn't tried. She'd worn herself out with trying.

At the channel tunnel terminal Mel presented her ticket and was told which queue to join. The waiting seemed interminable. She was aware that Chloe was still unsettled. 'Please don't cry,' she silently pleaded. As the wait dragged on, she became more and more nervous. Unable to sit still, she was so afraid that she would attract unwanted attention.

At last the queue began to move and, at the two checkpoints where tickets and passports may have been examined Mel received only a cursory look, leaving it to the attendants on the train, she guessed. It was almost an anti-climax. But the relief was immense.

Then they were boarding, and Mel was beset by new worries. She tormented herself with questions. Chloe seemed unnaturally quiet. It was purgatory to remain in her seat when she was desperate to check on the baby and Mel was tortured by visions of her choking on regurgitated milk, or whether the amateur attempt at providing airway to the boot had failed and Chloe had suffocated in the confined space. She'd be so relieved when they arrived in France and she could rescue the child from her unavoidable exile. 'I'm so sorry little one. I promise I'll make it up to you,' she whispered.

When she saw a guard approaching, randomly checking passports, her throbbing head echoed the thump of her heart. But the Gods were with her, because suddenly there was a commotion in the next compartment and he was called to deal with it.

Mel let out a shuddering breath and willed herself to relax. The rest of the journey passed uneventfully. Until, as they neared the French border tension began to build again. But once there, the bored official barely glanced at her before motioning her on. She gave him the best smile she could manage and he accepted it with obvious pleasure.

Mel had done her homework and negotiated the busy road away from the terminal and into the nearby complex that held a huge Hypermarket and the car hire office she had chosen in advance. Tucking her car away in the mass of cars already there, she seized her bag and hurried into the store. Not that she intended to do much shopping, just essentials for the journey. But she had to go through the motions.

It was almost impossible to think straight in her haste to get back to Chloe and her heart was pounding as she opened the boot. She uttered silent thanks when trusting eyes gazed back at her and Chloe gurgled happily.

Mel picked her up and hugged her close, feeling a suffusion of happiness warm her. She grabbed her bags in the other hand and made her way awkwardly across to the Hire Car Office. She sank into the nearest seat to wait her turn.

But the kind lady sitting next to her said, 'You look as though you've got a handful. Please go before me. I'm not in any hurry.'

Relieved, Mel thanked her gratefully, presented herself at the desk and produced the necessary papers. There was a moment of panic when she very nearly signed the documents with her real name. But all was well and soon she was being walked across to the waiting car. The requested car seat was in position and the cheerful assistant who had offered to carry her bags was now opening the boot to reveal the buggy she'd asked for. After strapping Chloe into her seat, they were soon on their way and Mel could breathe again.

She drove carefully, the map on the seat beside her for confidence. But she knew the area quite well and covered a good few miles in good time. Mel studied the map and drove in the direction of a web of quiet roads not far from the station at Rouen. She chose a secluded area but with a few other cars parked haphazardly here and there, not wanting to draw attention to one solitary, conspicuous car.

Then she tucked Chloe into the new buggy and gathered up her bags. Locking the doors of the hire car, she walked to a row of shops she had noticed, a short distance away. She walked into a newsagents.

'Pardonné moi, pouvey-vous un taxi pou, s'il vous plait?'

'Mais oui. Asseyez-vous.'

Chloe keeps the shopkeeper entertained until, in minutes, the car pulls up outside.

'Il est ici.'

A gesture of a hand had Mel making for the door. 'Merci bien,' she called over her shoulder.

'Portez moi a la gare, Rouen, s'il vous plait.'

The cab driver was a man of few words. He shrugged his shoulders in typical French fashion and forced himself to reach over to help her position her bags on the back seat.

Not the best welcome, but she wasn't about to let him deflate her balloon. The first stage of her plan had worked. She was on her way to a new life. Briefly, she remembered that Tom would be arriving back home about now. Consciously, she brushed aside the sudden flush of guilt. She'd made her choice. It was up to her to make the best of it.

Chapter 3

'I'm home!' Tom called as he arrived back in England from his business trip.

Only an echoing silence answered.

He'd expected more of a welcome than this, but he wasn't unduly worried, trying to console himself with the thought that perhaps Mel had come to her senses, done as he'd told her and gone to hand over the baby. He attempted to relax, but his theory was somehow not convincing. Something niggled at the back of his mind. Things were never straightforward; his Police training had taught him that.

What was it she'd said on the phone? Like a flash it came back to him. **When will you be back?** Oh God! What had she done?

He took the stairs three at a time, dreading what he might find. Every door on the galleried landing was closed. Heart thumping, he started with their room. Bed made, everything tidy.

Too tidy.

Panicking now, he continued opening one door after another. Each room vibrated with unnatural stillness. He didn't know what he'd expected to find. But, instinctively, he knew something was badly wrong. He needed time to think.

Back downstairs, he made a coffee and took it through to the lounge. Bizarrely, he registered the motes of dust floating in the shafts of late March sun and lighting the silent room. Out of habit he switched on the radio. Pavarotti's voice, full of pathos, was an intrusion and only served to accentuate his mood. He slammed it off.

Deep in thought, he hadn't noticed the pale blue envelope on the table in the window. Now, lit by a sudden burst of light, it was magnetic. He seized it hungrily and began to read:

My darling Tom,

I'm so sorry to have to do this, but I can't let Chloe go, and I know you would make me do what you see as right. But it's not right for me. I love you and I hoped you loved me enough to see that I

13

need this baby, even to help me. I was wrong. Horribly wrong. Don't try to find us. It's better this way. Mel.

Tom couldn't believe what he was seeing. He raked his fingers through his unruly dark hair. What did it mean? Think man. Think.

He'd known she was angry that he was called away at such a crucial time for her, but he didn't deserve this. She was besotted with this blessed kid. It was someone else's, for God's sake. It would have been different if it had been their own. He'd never understood her preoccupation with being a mother anyway. They had each other. So they couldn't have kids. It wasn't the end of the world.

He scanned her note again. No hint of where she might have headed, so where should he start? His first thought was to phone round her friends. He'd start with her work mate, Julie. She'd know. Mel would have had to let them know she wouldn't be at work.

He thumbed in the number. The phone rang interminably. Finally, the ansafone cut in. Thwarted at the first hurdle, he flung the phone down.

He was exhausted. It had been an exacting couple of days and he'd been relieved to be returning home. Home to a hot meal and a couple of beers. And to a warm welcome from the woman he loved.

Now this. He couldn't think straight, let alone relax. He racked his brain for where she might have gone. Devon? She loves it and has friends there. No, too obvious. Perhaps it was too simple to think she'd go to friends. It would be easy to trace her. And she would surely want to put more distance between them. Well it's not going to be Scotland, that's for sure. She can't stand the cold.

Furiously, he brushed away these irrational thoughts. He was tired and hungry. Food was what he needed. Maybe he'd be more able to think straight then.

He dragged himself to the kitchen and opened the fridge hopefully. Clearly other things had been on Mel's mind. All it yielded were a few eggs, a slab of cheddar and some slightly soft tomatoes. Looks like it's going to be an omelette then mate, he thought.

'No, to hell with that. I'm off to the Pub!' The empty room shuddered at the explosive words, and at the resounding slam of the door on his retreating figure.

A few beers, some good food and cheerful company would put him right. But it was several hours later when he wove his way unsteadily back to the house. In his stupor he half expected Mel to be there to greet him, but that dream was shattered as soon as he opened the door and the shroud of silence settled on him once more.

Unconcerned at the lateness of the hour, he lurched to the sofa and took out his mobile. Somehow, he managed to get his parents' number. Surprised, he launched into the whole bit about Mel being missing. 'I don't suppose she's at yours,' he slurred unhopefully.

'No, son, she isn't, his Father's voice replied. Alarmed at the obvious state his son was in, he continued, 'Are you OK Tom. What's happened? Have you two had a row?'

'What? No. She's gone, that's all.' Tom couldn't be bothered to prolong the call. He cut the connection and tried again.

A sleepy voice answered.

'Julie, is Mel there?' he fought to get the words out.

'Tom? It's bloody midnight. Of course she's not here. You're drunk. Go and sober up, she'll be back soon.'

Tom heard the click as Julie ended the call and suddenly he was irrationally angry. 'I've had enough. I'm going to bed,' he muttered.

Banishing the fleeting thought that he was wasting precious time, he trudged wearily upstairs and threw himself, fully clothed, on the bed. Automatically, he reached out for Mel, and was momentarily puzzled when his hand encountered only a coldness where Mel's warm body should have been. Then the truth grabbed him. 'Damn her!' he said, before the alcohol took over and plunged him into oblivion.

In the morning his head was throbbing. Involuntarily, he looked for Mel. With sick realisation, her absence came flooding back. So it hadn't been a bad dream then. She'd gone.

He tried hard to focus on a plan of campaign but, the truth was, he didn't know where to start. He drank down a stiff coffee, but it did nothing to clear his head. One phrase drummed over and over in his head. Mel, where are you? He was getting nowhere.

His job should have prepared him for this, but it was so different when he was personally involved. His heart ached. Why aren't I enough for you? The silent question reverberated around the room, but no answer came. 'I need a drink,' he said aloud. He poured a stiff whisky and downed it in one.

Maybe it was because of his restless night, or the fact that he hadn't eaten, but it went straight to his head. He flopped onto the sofa, as the unfocussed room swam around him. He must have dozed because, into his head came a clear picture of him and Mel on their last holiday in Greece. It was an answer to his prayer.

Could that be where she'd gone? Why hadn't he thought of it before? No, that was surely too easy. She'd have been cleverer than that. His mind was playing tricks. But they had been happy there. And she'd picked up the language so quickly. Better than him, he had to admit. His thoughts went round and round. He felt like he was on a treadmill. One minute he was convinced that's where Mel was, the next he wasn't convinced at all.

Anyway, if she had chosen Greece, it was a big country. Would she go to the mainland or one of the islands? He ruled out Crete where they'd holidayed frequently. She would want to lose herself in some anonymous town where she and the baby would be less noticed, he guessed. Where then?

He'd come to a dead end. It had seemed such a positive place to start his search. Now he wasn't at all sure that she'd gone to Greece at all.

With difficulty he brushed aside the seeds of doubt that had flourished all too readily, fertilized by his euphoria when he'd thought he'd happened on a plan. He had to do something though. And, he conceded, he was limited in the amount of assistance he could solicit, if he wasn't to reveal that Mel had left with a very young baby.

Perhaps the mother had had a change of heart and reported the birth. They may, even as the thought occurred to him, already be looking for the child. He didn't want to cause any more problems, for himself as well as Mel. He just wanted her back, that's all. Whatever it took, he'd do it. He *would.* But his newfound optimism was short lived, as an unwelcome thought wormed its way into his mind. He could feel it wriggling around until he could stand it no longer.

If it meant taking on another woman's child, could he do it?

Chapter 4

Mel began to relax as the train bore them into the heart of rural Normandy. The precarious pale blue of the winter sky was smudged with cloud. A weak sun turned the roads to ribbons of mother of pearl and put a silvery sheen on the turreted buildings that punctuated the villages. Fields burgeoned with the lush green of thriving winter wheat and the tracery of leafless trees that surrounded them was like a scrawled frame for a watercolour. There was a sense of calm, like a whispered prayer. If only she had Tom by her side to see all of this, then everything would be perfect.

However, Mel was calmed by the gentleness of the scenery, and suffused with a growing optimism for the future.

Soon she would be setting up home in the picturesque market town of Mortagne. She tried to visualize the apartment overlooking the busy market square. In her mind it was light, spacious and airy. The reality might be quite different. But at least the owner had sounded friendly.

She couldn't wait to see her new home and longed to visit the bustling market. There she would buy local pottery, pictures and textiles to add touches of bright colour that would make the apartment feel her own. And she would feast on the fresh produce brought in daily by the local growers.

Summer would come early there. There would be glossy peppers and tomatoes tasting of sunshine, and fragrant herbs and juicy fruits from that morning's picking. She would revel in eating seasonally, instead of relying on the year-round tasteless offerings of her local supermarket in England. What a great place for Chloe, too. She would grow fit and healthy and be a continual delight.

She startled, as her daydreaming was interrupted by a sudden loud wail from Chloe. Mel felt a twitch of alarm. Not for the first time she was aware that she had no real knowledge of new babies. Chloe had been so good that Mel had been convinced that it was due to her natural flair for motherhood. That Chloe had sensed how much Mel loved her and was happy.

But now the child was inconsolable and Mel felt a frisson of fear. Reaching into the baby carrier, she was alarmed to find the little body rigid. Aware of the disapproving looks from other passengers, she picked Chloe up and tried to hold her close, crooning soft words and gently stroking her flushed cheeks. But Chloe was having none of it. Face scarlet, she screamed and thrashed her tiny legs in anger.

Flustered, Mel endeavoured to change the sodden nappy. But the arched back and pumping legs made the result very amateur. In vain she tried to wrap the soft blanket round the protesting infant but furiously she kicked it aside. Around her, the tutts of disapproval increased until Mel could have screamed herself.

She was exhausted. The physical and emotional effort of getting this far had left her feeling drained. She struggled to retain her composure but was conscious of the fraying edges of her own temper. Momentarily, she wanted to shake the baby, and was immediately stricken with guilt as a new burstt of crying rent the carriage.

Was this what being a mother was all about? In a moment's panic she wondered how she was going to cope. Frantically, she seized the last bottle of formula she had brought with her and offered the teat to Chloe. When the fretting infant refused the milk it was all Mel could do to keep calm.

'Hush little one,' she tried. 'You'll feel better with a nice full tummy.' She began to sing a lullaby she remembered from her own childhood.

'Lulla, lulla, lulla, lulla bye-bye.
Do you want the moon to play with?'

Oh my God! I've blown it all in a moment's carelessness. She broke off, cheeks scarlet with the stain of guilt. Here she was, assuming a French identity, thinking it was all so easy, and yet she'd fallen at the first real hurdle. She glanced round at the other passengers. If they'd noticed her English words they weren't showing it. She tried to appear natural. She could be returning from a stay with English friends who'd taught her the lullaby, she reasoned. She decided to risk continuing, but this time with the trace of a French accent.

'Or the stars to run away with?
They'll come if you don' cry....'

'You speak English very well Madame.'

Mel turned sharply. Had she been rumbled after all?

But her fellow passenger, a small woman dressed simply but neatly in the dark clothes of a countrywoman, was smiling gently. 'My name is Monique D'Anjou. I've been staying with my son in London. He married a lovely English girl,' she said proudly. 'But English – it is very difficult, isn't it?'

'I worked in London for a long time. I needed to know the language for my job,' Mel explained with a smile.

'You have done well.'

'You're very kind. But I longed to return to my roots, so here I am,' Mel added.

'And, forgive me, will your husband be joining you?'

Mel looked away. 'He died,' she said. 'He had a bad accident, so now I must make a new life for us.'

Thinking of Tom brought genuine tears to Mel's eyes and Madame D'Anjou was upset at her tactlessness. She regarded Mel with pity, putting a comforting hand on her arm.

The gesture of warmth somehow gave Mel strength. 'Merci,' she said simply.

Gradually, Chloe's convulsing sobs quietened, the legs stopped kicking and tiny hands grabbed for the bottle. Bliss for them both. Mel sent up a silent prayer.

Lulled by the rhythm of the train and the warmth of the sleeping baby, Mel herself drifted into the sleep she so badly needed. But not for long. It seemed like only seconds later she was jolted back to the present by Chloe's renewed screaming.

Once again, she was unsuccessful in pacifying her. Suddenly Chloe went pale and frighteningly quiet.

'Mon Dieu!' Mel said the words out loud but was regarded with distaste by the stern-looking woman opposite. The opposite of Madame D'Anjou, she had no sympathy. It was not difficult to translate what she said then.

'You don't deserve to have that child. What are you doing travelling with her when she's obviously not well?'

There was no time to reply because, without warning, Chloe suddenly convulsed and was violently sick.

'Help me,' Mel pleaded. Tears were streaming down her cheeks and she wasn't sure if they were for Chloe or herself. But the accusing woman had no intention of responding to her plea. The woman's words haunted her. She was right. She didn't deserve to have Chloe. She'd brought her miles from anywhere, in a foreign country.

'Have you ever had a child?' Madame D'Anjou now addressed the woman. 'Have some compassion for the poor girl. Her child is unwell. She wouldn't have started the journey if she'd known, I'm sure.'

It felt good to have someone on her side, but Mel still tortured herself with how desperately Chloe needed help and how little she knew about how to get it for her. She was forced to admit that she had painted far too rosy a picture of motherhood. Her dream had been centred round her own needs, her own desperation to have a child. To her shame, she hadn't thought much about the child except that she would love her.

She'd been trying to recreate the kind of childhood that had been denied her, she admitted now, but she'd been naïve to think that love would be enough. She'd been given one last chance to be a mother and she'd thrown it away.

Still distressed, she set about cleaning them both up as best she could. Gently she sponged Chloe's flushed face, brushing the damp curls aside. She changed the baby's clothes and placed her carefully in her carrier, before mopping at her own clothes with another wet wipe. Chloe's cries became whimpers, then hiccups, until finally exhausted, she fell asleep.

Relieved, Mel sank thankfully into her seat. She couldn't think of dozing now. She wanted to be alert to Chloe's slightest sound. But there was no need for concern. Whatever had been troubling the child had passed and she slept on and on. When she finally stirred, she seemed back to her normal, placid self.

Excitement began to edge its tentative way back into Mel's mind as, glancing at her watch, she realised they must be nearing their destination. Soon they'd be settled in their new home.

The train had made good time and, when it drew into the station Meg struggled with baby, buggy and several bags towards the door

'May I help you, madame?' a soft, accented male voice asked.

Mel looked round in surprise and flushed as she met the dark eyes of a well -dressed and very handsome Frenchman. 'Merci,' she replied, flustered. She was only too aware that she looked a mess and smelt of baby sick. But there was no time to dwell on it. Her Good Samaritan took both buggy and bags in one hand as if they weighed nothing and, with his free hand helped her down the steep step on to the platform.

'Where are you staying? Do you have a car?

'I'm staying near the market. I can walk there. Thank you for your help.'

The smile that lit his face would have had her weak at the knees in other circumstances. 'Alors, au revoir madame. A bientôt,' he said. His voice was softly enigmatic.

Till we meet again. Had she imagined she'd heard a touch of regret in his tone? Of course you didn't, she told herself firmly. It was highly unlikely she would meet him again.

Chloe was smiling as they turned to go, but Mel realised she had been too hasty to decline the offer of a lift. It wasn't easy trying to juggle the bags and push the buggy with one hand. With each step, they grew heavier and heavier. She glanced at the scrap of paper in her hand though she already knew the address by heart. Dix-sept Place du Marché. Surely it couldn't be far now.

Just when she thought she could go no further, she saw a smiling, slightly plump woman waiting by the entry to an imposing block of apartments. Seeing Mel struggling towards her, she rushed to meet her. 'Madame Dubois? she asked. 'I've been expecting you.'

'I am Amelie Dubois. Vous êtes Madame Zoubiron?'

'Mais oui. Bienvenue' Smiling, she planted a kiss on each cheek in typical French fashion. 'Give me your luggage Madame.'

She turned and led the way up the stairs to Mel's apartment, talking non-stop.

Mel endeavoured to keep up, both with the pace and with the interrogation. Arriving outside the apartment, with an expansive gesture Madame Zoubiron opened the door with a flourish. 'Voila,' she presented Mel with her new home. 'You like?'

'It's beautiful. Thank you, Madame,' Mel replied.
'Please call me Odile.'

'Amelie.'

Madame Zoubiron's nose twitched. 'You are unwell, Madame?'

Embarrassed, Mel explained, 'Not me Madame...Odile... the baby. But she's better now.' They smiled shyly at each other. Madame Zubiron seemed more than satisfied with her new tenants. Her gaze lingered on Chloe, who was cooing happily. She reached out to take the baby's tiny hand in hers, stroking it gently. She seemed reluctant to let go. Suddenly self-conscious, she made for the stairs. 'I'll go downstairs,' she said, already heading for the door.

In the French way, she was soon knocking on the door and carrying a tray of coffee and a selection of tempting nibbles. Mel knew the French were renowned for their effortless hospitality, but she'd never felt so grateful 'Thank you so much, Madame – er – Odile.' Mel was exhausted but managed a smile. 'Shall I pay the rent now? A month, yes?'

'Later, Madame – Amelie,' she said, returning the smile.

Mel watched Odile disappear downstairs and then, pouring herself a coffee, sank wearily into the nearest chair. Chloe was still in her carrier but was happy enough. Mel watched as the little eyes gradually closed. It seemed she too was exhausted after the horrendous journey.

Relieved to have a few moments to herself, Mel looked around her. The apartment was as light and airy as she had imagined but, tired and dispirited, she couldn't take it all in. Instead, she allowed her mind to parade its one weakness.

Oh Tom, I miss you so much. Her heart ached. She longed to feel his arms around her, but had she hurt him too much by leaving? She clung to the hope that he still loved her enough to try to find her, refusing to accept that he may not want to now; that she may never see him again. For the first time, she looked at the sleeping baby and wondered if she was too high a price to pay. There was a trickle of tears on her cheeks, but she felt too helpless to brush them away.

I'm so sorry Tom, so sorry.

But he was the one who had forced her into making this choice. He had to take some of the blame. She had a new life now and she must make it work. Tiredness overcame her and, when she awoke, the light was already fading.

Chloe was already awake and regarding her with the solemn look of the very young. Feeling refreshed, Mel scooped her up and together they went on a tour of the apartment. It quickly became apparent that a lot of thought had gone into making it an attractive place for Odile's new guests. Yes guests, that was what it felt like. A welcome that felt like a comforting hug.

The rooms were high ceilinged, bright and spacious. In the salon pale walls embraced a stunning armoire, hand painted in cream and gold and housing a fine collection of the blue and white china so beloved of the French. A further selection of cupboards and shelves would be more than adequate for their needs. There was a small table and several dining chairs, as well as comfortably upholstered armchairs. There was even a high chair for Chloe, though she wouldn't need it just yet.

The large windows overlooked the ongoing activity in the market square. The remaining produce was being packed away, awnings dismantled. Voices were still animated and friendly rivalry floated up to Mel as she stood hidden from view by the intricate lace blinds that were a feature of this area of France.

On the other side of the square, beyond the busy market, there were shops with attractive living quarters above. On the balcony of one, an elderly lady with her silver hair impeccably styled and expensive looking clothes sat watching the bustle below. It was great to be in the hub of things, and Mel looked forward to becoming part of this thriving community. She couldn't wait to start exploring.

Odile must have crept in while she slept for there was fresh coffee on the table next to a large rocking chair. This simple act made Mel feel that at last she had someone to care for her like the mother she could barely remember might have done.

Restorative coffee to hand, she cradled Chloe, rocking and talking softly to her as she marvelled at the tiny fingers and toes and the delicate bloom of the baby-soft skin. For her part, Chloe showed no sign of her previous discomfort, but sucked lustily at the bottle of milk that Odile had warmed for her. She seemed unfazed by her new surroundings; her attention caught by the colourful curtains blowing gently in the breeze from the open window.

Mel began to hum an old French song as she went into the pretty flower-sprigged bedroom to begin stowing away their clothes.

Il était un petit navire ...There was a little boat ...

She felt just like that little boat, setting sail into a whole new world, not knowing what the future may hold. Glancing round the room, she was drawn again to the elaborately draped cot that stood in one corner. She fingered the silky fabric of the soft covers and wondered about its previous occupant. Was there a history attached to the cot or had Odile in her kindness prepared it especially for Chloe?

Scooping Chloe up, she was on her way downstairs to thank Odile when there was a loud knock on the door. Mel's blood froze. Immediately she panicked. Surely they haven't caught up with us already, no one knows we're here.

Heart pounding, she crouched in the bend of the stairs and listened as Odile opened the door.

'Oui?'

'Bonjour Madame. I am Sophie Piquet. I am from the Mairie. I'm looking for Monsieur Guillaume, Monsieur Paul Guillaume. Is he here?'

'No, he is not. He left without paying. Four months,' he owed. Her voice was curt.

'Where did he go. There has been a complaint.'

'I don't know. I can't help you. Good day.'

Mel heard the door close and breathed again. A false alarm this time but she couldn't stop herself thinking if it would always be like this from now on. Living on a knife-edge, suspecting everyone. Not for the first time she wondered if it had all been worth it.

Chapter 5

Mel's nerves were on edge. She couldn't help wondering who this Paul Guillaume was. He must be wanted for something more than non-payment of rent, but that left her pondering what he'd done that had the police chasing after him.

She didn't have time to dwell on it now. Chloe was beginning to get fractious. It had been a long and tiring day for both of them. 'What is it little one?' she soothed. 'Are you hungry? Mummy will make you some warm milk. You'll feel better then.'

It came so easily and gave her such a thrill to be able to say it at last. Chloe was well and truly hers, no matter what anyone said. She'd felt an immediate connection with her in that lay-by, and knew they were meant to be together.

Soon the child was fed, changed and full of smiles again. Tucking her up in the cot, Mel sang softly to her as her eyelids began to close. Gathering up the scattered baby clothes, she realised for the first time that she was hungry herself. Mulling over what she would have to eat and how good it would be to slip across the road for a light supper in the café opposite, she breathed in the appetizing aromas drifting through the open window.

But I'm a mother now, she thought. I will not leave my baby, not even for a moment.

In the tiny kitchen she dug into the welcome hamper a thoughtful Odile had left and offered up silent thanks for the generosity of her new landlady. There was a crusty loaf from that morning's baking, a selection of local cheeses, some olives and a bottle of red wine. A small bowl held a couple of rosy apples and a banana. A simple meal, but her mouth watered in anticipation.

Mel set it all on a tray and carried it through to the salon. Just as she was beginning her feast there was a sharp knock on her door. Annoyed at a further interruption, she grudgingly opened the door. 'Oh Madame, it's you. Come in please.'

'Pardon Amelie, you are eating. I shall come another time.'

'No, I'm sorry. What is it you wanted to say?'

'I just wanted to apologise for the disturbance earlier. Quelle nuisance. And you'd only just arrived.'

'It's not your fault Madame – er – Odile. Who is this guy they want anyway?'

'He's not a nice man. He was here six months and always forgot to pay. Now they say he owes money everywhere, and he can be violent when threatened. Not a nice man at all.'

Mel's expression must have revealed her concern, because Odile hastened to add,

'I don't want you to worry. He won't be back. And I've told them not to trouble you.'

Mel knew Odile's outburst was as much to reassure herself as to calm her tenant. But now Odile delved into the capacious shopping bag she carried. Out came a sturdy casserole. Lifting the lid, she released an earthy fragrance that had Mel's taste buds working overtime. 'A dish of rabbit and chanterelles - I picked them myself this morning very early, from a special place I know,' she confided.

'Thank you. You are very kind. But I was just starting the bread and cheese you left.'

'Pah! You can have that any time. This will be much better.'

Mel couldn't help smiling. 'I'm sure it will,' she agreed. 'Will you join me?'

'Not today, merci. You need to rest.'

Mel thanked her again and settled down to eat. The bread and cheese were side-lined as she tucked into Odile's offering. The savoury warmth seemed to seep into her very core and at last she began to relax.

She felt optimistic for her new life in this friendly town and knew she would enjoy her visits to the local shops and the vibrant market. Shopping would be a joy. Perhaps tomorrow.

The following day she showered and, after a breakfast of fresh fruit and yoghurt, set out with a smiling Chloe to wander through the market. Finding it was accepted here that you handled the goods before buying, Mel loved smoothing her fingers over the silky fabrics and holding the filmy lace curtains up to the light, the better to appreciate the intricate patterns. On the produce stalls, under the brightly striped awnings, the fruit and vegetables were still warm from the morning sun, the flowers fresh with dew.

It's true the locals were inclined to be inquisitive, in the open way that continentals adopt. But Mel had her answers to their many questions well-rehearsed.

'What's your name?'

'Amelie Dubois.'

'Where are you from?'

'Lyons.'

'That's why your accent is different. We thought you weren't from around here.'

So they've been discussing me, Mel acknowledged with amusement. Now they were ready with the next question.

'Are you staying with Odile Zoubiron?'

'Yes.'

'Ah bon. You will be happy there. She's a good woman.'

'Yes. I'm lucky.'

'But are you not here alone with your child?'

'Yes.'

'You have no husband?' There was no embarrassment in asking these personal questions, just a genuine curiosity that made them totally inoffensive.

'He died in a car accident.'

A sympathetic hand touched her arm. 'Ma pauvre Madame. I'm so sorry.'

Mel was quiet and composed as she answered their questions, as if she'd really suffered a bereavement. It didn't seem like lying. She'd rehearsed it all so well in her mind that she had almost convinced herself, never mind her well-meaning neighbours.

Chloe drew lots of attention and Mel enjoyed showing her off, dressed in the cute French outfits she bought in the enticing shop in the square. She was a beautiful baby, but Mel knew she must curb her spending. Such money she had brought with her was not a bottomless pit and she didn't want to have to find a job while Chloe was so small.

Continentals love children and regularly, small gifts were tucked into her buggy: a fluffy toy animal, a tiny teddy bear, a rag book. And often when she opened her door, Mel found an offering of fresh produce; perhaps half a dozen new-laid eggs, some freshly gathered mushrooms, some preserved fruits or a bottle of homemade wine. Mel wished she could repay these kind people in some way, but still loved these tokens of the usual French welcome when someone new arrived in the neighbourhood.

This was further demonstrated when Odile frequently invited her downstairs to eat with her. Mel suspected she was lonely but, nevertheless, the food was delicious and she enjoyed the company just as much as her hostess apparently did.

She tried to reciprocate whenever she could, with a posy of flowers or a treat from the patisserie where the beautifully arranged window display couldn't be ignored. Fruit tarts, glossy with a coating of jelly, tiny blushing meringues oozing vanilla flavoured cream, rich almonds croissants and fragrant pastries scented with cinnamon.

Odile accepted her gifts with effusive thanks, never for a moment revealing that she was a trained pâtissiére herself.

It was all so calm here, no deadlines, no over egged egos, no vying for one another's position. No, she didn't miss her job at the busy publishers one bit and wondered how she'd ever thought it was all she wanted. But she felt bad that she had left without a word of explanation, unable as she was to reveal the reason for her departure.

She could almost forget that, technically, she was as guilty of crime as Odile's former tenant, but always hovering at the back of her mind was the worry that eventually the authorities would catch up with her. A shiver would run down her spine as she thought of the consequences of her actions.

But, for the present, life was good, and it was Chloe who made it all pretty near perfect. Despite the possible outcome, she didn't regret her decision. If only Tom were here to share the new life she had embarked upon.

Every night she thought about him. What was he doing? Did he miss her? She knew she'd hurt him badly, but still hoped he'd been able to forgive her and was searching for her. Sometimes she wished he would find her. He would see for himself how happy she was in this quiet country town. She even dared to hope that he could come to love Chloe as much as she did. Surely if he saw her, held her, he would see how beautiful she was?

She missed Tom desperately: the feel of his arms around her, the scent of him, the taste of him. Sometimes the longing almost overwhelmed her.

Chapter 6

As if by telepathy, Mel's longing had communicated itself to Tom. Her presence was tangible. Even as the clock ticked relentlessly towards midnight, he felt a renewed surge of energy, a resolve to search again every conceivable avenue of possibility.

He hadn't risen to the rank of Detective Chief Inspector by accident. He had always been thorough, working tirelessly and relentlessly in the pursuit of each crime. This, together with a certain intuition, had achieved an enviable measure of success, and a rapid rise through the ranks.

But that wasn't helping him one iota with his current predicament. He recalled his shock at finding Mel gone. There'd been baby stuff all over the house and he'd been furious, tossing the offending objects into the nearest bin. Mel had put him in an impossible position professionally by taking off with that brat. What the hell could he do?

He was hurt and angry, unable to accept that she had left him and had covered her trail so successfully. He found it hard to believe that she'd put someone else's kid before him. She'd married him and he wanted her for himself. If they'd had their own kids he supposed, he would have got used to the idea. Kids of your own were something to be proud of. But other people's? That was a whole different equation. For him, a problem that went round and round in his head until he thought it would burst. He wasn't sure if he could do it. The whole idea made him feel impotent professionally and personally. *I need a drink,* he conceded.

He had every faith in the two officers he'd earmarked for the case, should he decide that's how he wanted to proceed. DS Andrew Swanton would treat it as a straightforward kidnap, and WDC Cathie Allan would act for the Child Protection Unit.

But Tom had an impossible choice to make. He had the authority to set the wheels in motion, but he couldn't make himself do it. Although he was desperate to find Mel, he had so much to lose. Firstly, everyone would know that his wife had left him and taken off with a kid in tow, a kid they'd heard nothing about until now. Secondly, and more importantly, he was well aware that even a DCI would be taken off a case in which he was personally involved.

He liked to think that he was still doing a good job. Though, if pressed, he would have to admit that his mind was inclined to wander at times. At the end of every day he couldn't wait to get home and continue with his own investigations. He began each night full of hope that this would be the night that would give him a hint of where Mel was, but always he was disappointed. Weeks had turned into months and still he had no clue to follow. He grew frustrated and irritable, wondering why he couldn't apply his work skills to help his own case.

Now, as he sat and gazed at the blank face of his computer screen, he tried again to put himself in his wife's mind. Patently her need to become a mother had warped her judgement, causing her to give up on all that was dear to her, including him. How could she do it? He couldn't understand it himself, though of course he never had fully understood women.

The familiar longing swept over him as he thought of Mel. He missed everything about her: her throaty chuckle, her glossy blonde hair, the love that had shone in her beautiful brown eyes and the feel of her body responding when they made love. He'd really thought she loved him, now he realised that he seemed to count for nothing when balanced against her need for a child. The realization was like a physical pain.

Tormented, he switched on the computer. His investigation was limited if he wasn't to expose his vulnerability. She must have known that. If only her parents were still alive, or she had other family. She surely would have confided in them.

Frantically, he tried to think where she might have gone. To picture her in places they had visited. He saw her in Crete, where they'd once been so happy. He'd been convinced he would find her there and he'd toured the island in the guise of a private detective, but all his enquiries had drawn a blank.

Defeated, he switched off the computer, poured himself another stiff whisky and retired to bed exhausted. Soon a vivid dream claimed him.

He was in a deserted cove. The cliffs rose sharply behind and, on the lower slopes, oleander bloomed. He could hear the bleating of the goats as they scampered on the rocks and feel the warmth of sun on his skin. Gentle waves lapped at his feet.

He was aware of all these things, but only one thing mattered. Mel was in his arms. They were lost in the aftermath of lovemaking.

He reached out to pull her closer; wanting to feel her skin-to-skin once more, but he could feel only air. She had vanished. Suddenly he was in a nightmare. He covered the beach, searching behind rocks and scaling the cliffs in panic.

Heart pounding, he awoke bathed in sweat. Vainly he reached for her, but her side of the bed was empty and cold.

Morning came at last: seizing him by the throat, echoing the way he had been wrenched from Mel in his dream. Like a robot, Tom showered and dressed. Remembering nothing of the drive there, he then found himself in the office. Andy Swanton was waiting for him. He sprang up as Tom entered.

'Morning sir.'

'Morning Andy,' Tom replied wearily. Out of habit he asked the usual question. 'Have you anything for me?'

Swanton seemed strangely excited. 'Well, yes. You won't want to hear this, but I had an odd phone call yesterday.'

Tom was wary. 'Go on,' he said.

Swanton was obviously uncomfortable but ploughed on. 'The caller wouldn't give a name but was anxious to let me know that your wife was seen leaving the house with a very young baby. The child was dressed in pink and he assumed it was a girl. I got the impression that this was some while ago and that she hasn't been seen since. Is it true sir? I didn't know you were a new dad. You kept that quiet.'

There was no use denying it, but Tom had no intention of elaborating. Swanton was a reliable chap. Tom would have to trust him and rely on his discretion. 'Yes, it's true. She's left with a child, Chloe she's called. But it's complicated. And it's not for general knowledge.'

'I understand sir. But I'm afraid that's not all. I don't know where my chap got his original info from, or why he was watching your house. He could be a crank for all I know. Just wanting to cash in on a bit of local scandal. Some people make a living from it.'

Tom was getting impatient. 'Get on with it man.'

'Well sir, he had someone follow her. She managed to give him the slip, but he seems to have contacts at various airports, because he said that a similar woman, also with a very young baby, has been seen in Athens.'

'So?' Hope surged through Tom's veins but he tried to level his voice.

'She fits your wife's description sir. It's believed she was making for the ferry out of Piraeus.'

Suddenly the fatigue left Tom. He punched the air. 'I knew it!' he exclaimed. 'I thought all along she'd be heading for Greece.'

'I wasn't sure what I should do sir. I thought you would want to know.'

'Yes. Thank you.' Tom was preoccupied. His head was full of questions. One was bothering him. He addressed Swanton, 'This chap was obviously on the make, why didn't he contact me direct?' He thumped the desk in frustration.

'You asked for all your calls to be filtered Sir.'

'Oh yes. I wanted to get that blasted report finished. God, I can't tell you how difficult this is for me!'

Swanton was sympathetic. 'I can understand that.'

Tom had to think fast. 'Have you told anyone else?'

'No sir. I didn't know if any of it was true. You can depend on me to be discreet.'

'Thank you.'

'I'm supposed to be on a couple of day's leave. I only came in to see you. I'll be off now.'

'Have you anything planned for your days off?'

'Nothing special sir.'

'Would you consider going to Athens and then make for the port in Piraeus to check this out, Andy? I'll cover all your expenses of course. With a bit extra for your trouble. But this is strictly between you and me. You can't even discuss it with your wife. Can I depend on you?' Tom knew he was taking a huge risk.

Not only could his personal dilemma be all over the Station, but his hard-won position could be on the line too.

'You can sir. And I'll go.'

Tom knew Andy Swanton had a great deal of respect for him. Relieved, he could hardly trust himself to speak. 'Thank you,' he said. 'Will this cover it?' He handed Swanton a cheque for £500.

'It's more than generous sir.'

'I'm very grateful for your support Andy. Please keep me informed.'

'Yes sir.'

The hours dragged by and at 7.00pm Tom was just leaving the office when the phone rang.

'I'm glad I've caught you sir.'

Tom's heart missed a beat. 'Is that you Andy?'

'Yes sir. I just wanted to let you know that, after talking to the people in the ferry ticket office in Piraeus...'

'You're there already?'

'Yes sir, and I've ascertained that the woman and child boarded a ferry to Poros. I'm afraid there isn't another one till the morning. I'll contact you again as soon as I can.'

Tom was deflated. He replaced the receiver and leaned wearily against the desk. His head was pounding from a succession of broken nights and he could no longer think straight. Pulling himself together, he headed for home.

On the way he mulled over this latest development. He wondered why Mel had chosen Poros. He knew of no connection there. She must have realised that Crete would be too risky. Poros would most probably have been a random choice, he reasoned.

Reaching home, he went straight to his study and poured himself a drink. He flicked on the computer as usual but didn't know what he hoped to find. He couldn't afford to put too much personal information out in the ether. He slammed it off again and poured another drink. He drained the glass and felt momentarily comforted as the warmth travelled round his body.

Sleep eluded him again that night and he was exhausted. Back in the office next day he waited impatiently for news. With his team he was discussing the facts of the Hargreaves case – one of fraud on a grand scale - when the phone rang. It took all his self-control not to pounce on it.

PC Bradley handed the phone to him. 'It's for you sir.'

'Stevens.'

'Morning sir. Is this a bad time?'

'Yes. Can I ring you back? OK, got that.' He scribbled a number down. 'I'll ring as soon as I've finished here.' His nerves were over-tightened violin strings, ready to snap at any moment. How he got through the next few minutes he'd never know. He could remember nothing of the summing up of the Hargreaves case.

At last, with shaking fingers, he punched in the number he'd noted. It barely rang before it was answered.

'Has there been a development Andy?' With extreme difficulty he managed to keep the tremor from his voice.

'Yes sir. But I'm afraid it's not good news. The child is a boy.'

Chapter 7

If only Mel had known the risks Tom was taking to try to find her she would have been heartened but, in the salon of the apartment in Mortagne, she was facing a challenge of her own.

'You have no papers for the child?' Sophie Piquet was back, arriving unannounced at Mel's door with an irate Odile in tow.

'I'm sorry, Cherie. She wouldn't let me...'

'It's OK. Not your fault.'

Reluctantly Odile turned away and went downstairs to her own apartment.

Mel wondered how Sophie Piquet had known that she and Chloe were here. Perhaps Odile had let something slip on her previous visit, or maybe she'd spotted the baby buggy in the entrance and had made enquiries. She had the uncomfortable feeling that Mme Piquet was trying to forge a link with the missing Paul Guillaume. Warily, she answered her question about the required papers. 'Er... no. It was a spur of the moment decision to leave.' She'd had to think quickly.

But Mme Piquet was not going to be brushed off that easily. 'Why was that?' The question was gentle.

Mel's eyes filled with genuine tears. What she was about to say might not be true, but she felt the same acute sense of loss. 'My husband died suddenly and I had a new baby, the child he would never see.' It sounded so convincing Mel almost believed it herself. A tear trickled down her cheek as she battled on. 'Everywhere I looked I could see Jean-Pierre and it all got too much. I just had to get away.'

'What made you come here? Have you friends here?'

'I have now. Madame Zoubiron has made us very welcome and everyone has been very kind. But when we came I knew no one. I wanted a fresh start and this seemed as good a place as any.'

Mme Piquet didn't seem too impressed.

'I think I chose well,' she added hastily.

'Perhaps you did, and I would like to be your friend, too.' The visitor rose to go. 'I will call again and we will decide what to do.'

'Merci.' With relief Mel closed the door after her. She had been unnerved by the visit. Although Sophie Piquet had seemed friendly enough, there was something about her Mel couldn't fathom. Some sense of a hidden agenda.

She tried to put it all to the back of her mind, and managed almost to forget about it as the days trickled by pleasantly. Mel had grown to love the busy market town. Shopping was a pleasure, a feast for the senses. Each shop was an Aladdin's cave of delights. The beautiful colours of the displays, the scents of baking, the tasty titbits that were offered before making a purchase. Add to this the pride taken in the wrappings and it became a pleasurable experience, not just a necessity.

Mel found her French improving as she gained confidence on these outings. It seemed impossible that they had been here almost four months. But the market stallholders had become used to her and usually had a little treat waiting for Chloe and she responded by giggling merrily when her chubby legs were squeezed.

Mel became expert with the gadget Odile gave her to mash Chloe's food, and Chloe thrived on all the fresh fruit and vegetables Mel bought and pureed for her. 'Thank you, it's very good of you.' The traders shrugged off Mel's thanks as if their kindness and generosity was nothing.

Odile continued sharing her meals and buying little gifts for Chloe. Mel valued the closeness that was beginning to grow between them and welcomed the time they spent together.

'You're very good to us,' Mel told her one morning as they sat over coffee in the sunny salon of Mel's apartment.

Odile looked uncomfortable and played nervously with her handkerchief.

Mel guessed she had something to say. 'What is it?' she asked softly.

Odile's eyes misted as she gazed hungrily at Chloe who lay kicking on a rug nearby. 'I had a little girl like her once...' She broke off, unable to continue.

'What happened?' Mel prompted.

'They took her away. We had hoped to adopt her you see. We were waiting for the confirmation. But the mother decided she wanted her back. It was such a shock. I hadn't known they could do that after so long and it broke my heart.'

Mel shivered as an icy spasm of fear pulsed through her. She could never let Chloe go. She would go mad. Filled with compassion for her new friend she asked softly, 'Did you never feel like trying again?'

'I thought I would be unable to bear the pain if it happened again. I regret it now.' With an effort Odile shrugged off her cloak of sadness. 'Would you allow me to hold Chloe, just for a minute?'

'Of course.' She scooped up the baby and placed her in Odile's arms. There seemed to be no sign now of the listlessness and pallor that Chloe had displayed earlier. Maybe she'd just been tired by her outing to the market.

Mel watched the older woman as she tenderly cradled the child, cooing softly to her. 'How did your husband cope with it,' she asked.

Odile's face clouded. 'He didn't. He was besotted with the child. We both were.' It was a simple statement that carried a burden of pain. But Odile hadn't finished. 'I think it was taking her from us that killed him. We'd had Francine for over a year and felt she was ours. We never thought we would have to part with her.'

'It must have been hard.'

'It was hard for us both, but *mon mari* never recovered from the loss. '

'How do you mean?'

'The shock affected his heart. He only lasted a few months after that. Then I was left on my own with all that grief. I had no one.'

Spontaneously, Mel jumped up to give Odile a hug. 'You poor thing,' she whispered. Then more brightly, 'But you have us now.' Appalled at how selfish she sounded, Mel tried to make amends. 'I...I know it's not the same. Chloe can never replace your little one...I'm so sorry.'

Odile shrugged. 'It's not your fault. I got over it eventually. I had to.' Her face suddenly broke into a wide smile.' And now I have you, as you say.' She took Mel's hand and gave it a squeeze, gently stroking Chloe's chubby cheek with her other hand before handing her back to Mel. 'You're my family now,' she said shyly. ' And now I must go.'

Mel gave her friend a quick hug and she was gone, down to her spotless apartment below.

At that moment the doorbell rang. Feeling anxious, for the sound of the bell had become synonymous in her mind with danger, Mel went to answer it.

Sophie Piquet stood waiting. 'Bonjour Madame, May I come in? I just need to ask you a few questions.'

Alarm bells rang deafeningly in Mel\s head, but she painted a smile on her face and opened the door wide to admit the caller. 'Come in, ' she said, greeting her like an old friend. She showed her into the salon.

'Would you like some coffee?

'Yes please.'

From the tiny kitchen Mel heard her visitor moving around the apartment. Immediately, she bristled. What right has she to poke her nose into my things, and what's she looking for anyway? She pondered on why someone who was supposed to be a friend was making her feel nervous, and came to the conclusion that she must be making something out of nothing. It was natural that the woman would wander around, she'd been guilty of it herself, and there was plenty of interest in the room after all.

But very soon she found her first instinct had been right. As she entered the salon with the tray of coffee, Sophie spoke.

Without preamble she announced, 'I would like to see your papers, especially the baby's birth registration document. You may need help with such a young child.' Although Mme Piquet was smiling Mel didn't feel reassured. Once again Mel explained about leaving her previous home on the spur of the moment. 'I had just given birth when my husband was killed in an accident. I couldn't bear to be in the house we'd shared. I saw him everywhere. It was all too much for me and I had to get away.' It was a consistent story and Mel's eyes filled with tears once again.

But Sophie Piquet was not sympathetic. 'Your papers?' she asked.

With an effort Mel pulled herself together. 'I'm sorry. I told you, when I feel better I'll go back for them.'

It was hard to guess whether Mme Piquet believed her story. She certainly wasn't going to be deflected from her task. 'Try to make that soon,' she said curtly. 'Meanwhile, I have to speak to you about money.'

It seemed Mel's new 'friend' was not all she appeared. 'That's my business,' she retorted hotly.

Sophie was unfazed. 'Pardon Madame, but I must know whether you can support yourself and the child? For example, have you found work?'

Mel concealed her anger. This intrusion into her life was inexcusable, but she must not antagonise the woman. 'I have enough money at the moment.' I don't want to leave my child while she is so young,' she explained. 'When she is older I will look for work.'

'We could take the child into care temporarily if that would help. Just till you get on your feet,' Mme Piquet added hastily.' She smiled, but her smile didn't match up with the calculating glint in her eyes.

Mel was appalled. Was the woman deliberately trying to alarm her?

Mme Piquet continued, 'Of course she would need the required papers. I could help you with that also. You should consider what would happen if the child becomes unwell.'

'I've told you I will get the documents you need. And when I think it's necessary I will look for work. If I needed to, I could probably work from here and still look after Chloe. I have no need of help.' Her voice was like steel.

'You will still need the correct documents. At least let me help with those. It would save you going back to that unhappy house.'

She sounded genuine, and for a moment, Mel thought she might have misjudged her. And yet she still felt uneasy. She was pretty sure Sophie Piquet had some ulterior motive for appearing to befriend her.

'Think about it. It wouldn't cost much and would give you peace of mind.'

It sounded so genuine and yet Mel still felt a resistance. This woman was an enigma. Mel couldn't help wondering exactly what was Mme Piquet's interest in them.

She certainly wasn't going to let go. She was like a dog with a very juicy bone. 'You don't have to think about it now,' she said sweetly. 'But don't leave it too long. I'll call again very soon.' The threat was barely veiled.

With relief Mel closed the door on her unwelcome visitor. She couldn't get Sophie Piquet out of her mind. There had been a real threat hovering in the words she uttered, especially her final warning. That night it was hours before she sank into an uneasy sleep. It seemed only a matter of moments later that a sudden noise woke her with a start. There it was again, a wail from Chloe, full of pain and fear. She went quickly to her daughter's cot. The deathly pale skin on the baby's face was scattered with an angry, raised rash. Mel watched as a little fist went into her mouth and, to her horror, saw blood dribbling down the dimpled chin.

She lifted the screaming baby and tried to comfort her, but every time she touched her, she cried out in pain. Mel endeavoured to quell her rising panic. 'What's the matter, little one?' she crooned. 'Have you got a pain in your tummy? Or did that naughty tooth bite your lip?' In truth she was almost beside herself with worry, but she tried hard to keep her voice calm while inwardly she queried what all these symptoms meant.

Tenderly, she carried the distressed baby to the changing mat, placing her down as gently as she could. Inch by inch she eased off the pretty blue daisy-strewn suit and felt the cold creep of fear as she saw the rash had spread and mingled with angry purple bruises on Chloe's body.

Mel snatched up her mobile, too worried to ponder on whether the call might be traced in France. There was no signal.

Fighting back nausea, she wrapped Chloe in a warm blanket and ran down the stairs to Odile, trusting her to know what to do. Without giving her customary knock, she burst in on her friend.

'What is it? What has happened?' Odile was immediately at her side.

'It's Chloe...' She couldn't go on, but hugged Chloe to her as the tears coursed down her face. Then a fresh thought hit her. Surely Sophie Piquet hadn't harmed her while she was on her own with the child? It was too awful to contemplate, and yet she had been at pains to mention the possibility of Chloe needing a doctor. Mel couldn't take her eyes off the fretful baby. She loved her so much. She reached out to smooth the damp tendrils of hair that clung to the flushed forehead, then withdrew in shock. Chloe was burning with fever.

Mel was terrified. She felt Odile's arm tighten around her shoulder and turned to her for help. 'Chloe needs to see a doctor,' she admitted at last. 'But Sophie Piquet was right. There is a problem.' She cursed her own stupidity. She'd known how hot the French were on legalities yet, so anxious had she been to get away, she'd foolishly thought it was something she could sort out later. Now her need was desperate.

'What can I do?' she sobbed. 'I've been so stupid.' She was so close to confessing all to Odile but first she must get help for Chloe.

'Perhaps the doctor will see Chloe and you can take him the papers later?' Odile suggested. 'He will see how ill the little one is and think you forgot them in your hurry to get to him. I will call the doctor now.' She moved towards the phone, but it rang before she could lift the receiver.

Mel sat cradling Chloe, distraught with anxiety and impatient at the ill-timed interruption.

Odile picked up the phone. 'Oui?'

There was a pause.

'This is Odile Zoubiron. Who – '

She was cut short by the voice at the other end of the line. Silently she handed Mel the phone. 'It's that Piquet woman. What does she want with you?'

Mel had no time to explain. She almost snatched the phone from Odile. 'This is Amelie Dubois. What do you want?' She was too anxious to bother to be civil.

'I wondered if you had come to a decision…'

Mel cut her short. Although it was totally against her every instinct she found herself saying, 'My child is very ill. She needs a doctor. I must have papers for her at once. You said you could help.'

'Wait there. I'll come. And I will bring a doctor.' Mel heard the click of the phone being replaced.

Relieved that a doctor was coming at last, Mel was still beset by doubts about Mme Piquet's honesty. 'Oh God, can I trust her?' She turned to Odile for reassurance.

Odile's eyes were on the screaming baby. 'You had no choice my dear,' she stated simply.

Chapter 8

HEALTH SCARE. MENINGITIS IN TOWN.

Mel's heart missed a beat as she read the day's headline. Who could have tipped them off? The only person who knew of Chloe's illness, and that meningitis was suspected, was the Doctor himself. She doubted he would want to alarm people at this stage. Of course Odile knew, but Mel trusted her completely. Who else then?

As if in a burst of flash photography, an image appeared on a virtual screen in front of her. Sophie Piquet! How could she have been such a fool? Mel had thought she was a friend, but she had betrayed her. It was obvious that the E1000 Mel had paid her for the necessary documents was not enough, was never going to be enough. She was out to make as much as she could from her predicament.

Mel spent an anxious few days in the local hospital, rarely moving from Chloe's side. She thanked God when at last the child began to show signs of recovery. For the moment all was well. Meningitis had been ruled out and a virus blamed. Secretly, Mel thought there was more to Chloe's bouts of illness, but she tried to brush away her fears and focus on the fact the Chloe seemed well now.

Back in her apartment, she resumed life again, marvelling daily as she gazed at her perfect little daughter. Baths were a delight, with Chloe gurgling happily at every ripple and splash and trying vainly to capture the trickle of water from Mel's hands. Afterwards, with Chloe wrapped in a warm towel, Mel would plant soft kisses on the tiny fingers and toes. Sometimes she was drawn to finger the tiny butterfly birthmark on the baby's temple. Each time she felt a sense of connection hovering on the periphery of her mind. A connection she'd felt the first time she'd held Chloe, but which lurked somewhere in the recesses of her subconscious.

And yet, from time to time a cold chill would blow across her heart as, with a mother's intuition, she knew that her child had been very ill and there must have been a cause. In these moments she couldn't shake off the feeling that it wasn't just a temporary infection.

With an effort she tried to push the whole episode to the back of her mind. It had been hard to weather the hostility of the other mothers when, knowing that Chloe had been ill, they suspected that it was she who had brought meningitis into the town. But now they had been reassured that meningitis had never been on the agenda, they were all smiles again. Chloe was once more the centre of attention and seemed the picture of health.

Always at the back of Mel's mind lurked the spectre of Sophie Piquet. She was well aware that the woman had not finished with her, would not stop her demands until she had drained every penny from Mel's meagre savings, and very probably beyond that.

But Chloe came first. She was all that mattered. Mel would get the money somehow. She renewed her efforts to find work, ideally something she could do from home. Perhaps she could do some proof reading or editing. Something would turn up eventually.

She was determined not to let her worries spoil her enjoyment of being a mother. She had never felt so fulfilled. Her poor appetite and disturbed sleep were the only indicators of her dilemma. On the surface she was happy.

At times, if pressed, she would have to admit to feeling alone with her worries. For whom could she confide in without revealing her secret? At these times she needed Tom more than ever and wondered how near he was to finding her. When she felt really low, she tormented herself with thoughts that he may not be even trying, but she shook off the heavy cloak that settled on her shoulders then.

As autumn approached Chloe was thriving. Now six months old, she was sitting up and making her first attempts to crawl. If only Tom could see her now. He couldn't fail to fall in love with her. She was an absolute charmer, with her dark curls and dimpled smile.

Some days Chloe seemed tired and listless and Mel tried not to worry. The child was growing and becoming more and more active, Mel reasoned. She's bound to get tired. And, after a good long sleep Chloe always bounced back to her normal sunny self.

Odile continued to be kind to them, helping out in any way she could. She often looked after Chloe so that Mel could pursue her quest for work, and Mel was grateful that her friend insisted on preparing their evening meal most days. Sometimes it was hard for Mel to do justice to the tasty food with so many worries in her head. She knew it upset Odile to see her pick at the food listlessly so she tried to show some enthusiasm. But it fooled no one.

'What is it?' Odile asked gently. 'Are you not well?'

How Mel longed to tell her everything. Although she had been loath to discuss it with Sophie Piquet, she was getting worried at the rate at which her money was disappearing. 'I'm getting desperate to find some work, that's all,' she confessed. That much was true. 'I have very little money left and I need to pay you and look after Chloe. Why doesn't anyone want me? I have the qualifications.' It was hard to keep the tears in check.

'I don't want you to worry about money. You will soon get work. You can pay what you owe me then. It doesn't matter.'

Mel was overwhelmed by Odile's generosity. Her friend deserved so much more. But her kind words had unlatched the floodgates and Mel's tears flowed freely as all the dammed-up fears of the last few months escaped. It was so tempting to confide in this good woman who had taken them into her heart.

She'd made one mistake with Sophie Piquet. She wasn't sure if she could risk another. Even after all the time they had spent together Mel couldn't be sure Odile would understand. She might be so shocked that she would feel compelled to notify the authorities.

Mel's head was in turmoil. Each considered attempt at getting Odile on her side seemed futile. She couldn't risk losing Chloe now. Not after all they'd been through to get this far.

Odile waited patiently for the tears to subside. Then she put a comforting arm around Mel's shoulder. 'Never forget you have a friend my dear. I'm here when you're ready. It will be all right, you'll see.'

The words were a lifebuoy and Mel clung to it with all the desperation of a drowning man. 'Thank you,' she said simply. She pasted a watery smile on her face. What else was there to say?

As soon as was polite, she took Chloe up to their apartment. They were both exhausted. She made a poor attempt at singing the customary lullaby as she scooped warm water over the squirming body, but her heart wasn't in it and Chloe picked up on her mood and grizzled in complaint.

Later, Mel sat beside the cot and gently stroked the baby's flushed cheek. Strangely, she found that Chloe was not the only one to feel soothed. As the child drifted off to sleep Mel stood watching, full of love for her child; the child who would have surely died if she hadn't found her in time. She shuddered at the thought. 'I'll never let you go little one,' she whispered.

Emotionally exhausted as Mel was, sleep still eluded her. She tossed and turned, kicking the bedclothes to the floor. When at last sleep came, it threw her into a dark pit where writhing snakes tightened around her. Overlong, pallid arms reached out for her. She struggled to curl into a ball. A cocoon to protect the precious form within. Hideous screams pierced the silence. She hurtled back into consciousness and the shocking realization that the screams were her own.

Pitiful cries from the next room performed a chilling duet.

'Chloe!' Mel shrieked as she leapt from the bed and ran to her. She was totally unprepared for what she found. Her darling baby's face was covered in the blood that gushed from her nose. Ghoulish, gargling noises clogged her throat. She was barely able to breathe. 'Oh my little love, what's happened to you?' she sobbed.

In a panic Mel seized the child and, holding her close, ran into the bathroom. In vain she tried to stem the flow of blood with a damp towel. Chloe was like a furnace and her screams increased with every movement, as though the slightest pressure caused her fresh pain.

As gently as she could, Mel stripped off the child's clothes so that she could sponge her with cool water. What she saw then made her very afraid. The angry rash of months before was back, fighting for space with livid bruises.

Mel dabbed frantically as the bleeding lessened and, wrapping Chloe in a warm blanket, ran downstairs. Odile was slow to respond to her frantic hammering, disturbed as she was from a deep sleep. Angry words died on her lips when she saw Mel's stricken face. 'Call an ambulance, PLEASE! It's Chloe. I need to get her to hospital. I think she's... dying.' The voice she heard was someone else's – shrieking, incoherent.

Odile was already making the call. 'They're coming,' she said as she put down the phone. 'Come.' She led the way into her cosy room and coaxed Mel, and the now deathly pale and floppy baby in her arms, into a chair by the dying embers of the fire.

Rigid with fear, Mel perched on the edge of the chair, holding Chloe close and saying over and over, 'Please don't let her die.' She lifted tear filled eyes to her friend and implored her, 'don't let her die. I couldn't bear it.'

At the hospital skilled medics were waiting. Gently they prised Chloe from Mel's arms and rushed her into an examination room. Mel could only watch and pray.

Tom, where are you? I need you here so badly. I can't do this on my own. Help me! How she wished he could hear her words.

Never had she been so close to risking everything to have Tom's support. If only he were with her. Her hand automatically dug into her pocket for her mobile, but stopped short, remembering that she'd decided not to use it. Now she was beset by doubts. Wasn't it worth risking being traced to have Tom by her side? Chloe was the important one here, not her, she told herself. If she had to pay the consequences to get Chloe well, so be it.

She switched on the phone, uncaring that she wasn't supposed to use it in the hospital. No signal.

In a panic she flew down to the phone booth in the hospital entrance. Her hand hovered over the receiver as she realised that this call could just as easily be traced. Furthermore, Tom could lose everything he'd worked for if this story came out, so he may not even come. Normally she would not have dreamed of putting him in the position of having to make that choice, but this was a crisis. She didn't know what else to do. And yet... the risk was too great.

Temporarily defeated, and concerned that she had been away from the waiting room too long, she left the booth and hurried back, telling herself that it had been her decision to leave England. Now she must deal with the painful consequences. Blindly, she made her way into the waiting area.

As she passed the desk, someone called her name.

'Madame Dubois?' The nurse looked concerned.

Mel's face paled. 'Yes,' she replied.

'We've been calling for you. Your baby is in Intensive Care on the fourth floor. I'm afraid she's very poorly.'

It was worse than even Mel had thought. 'Can I see her?'

'I'll take you up to the department. The Doctor will see you soon. He will want to speak with you.'

In Intensive care it was a frenzy of activity. Mel watched a machine she recognised as a heart monitor being wheeled into a side room. 'Where's Chloe?' she screamed.

'They're running some tests. I know the waiting is hard.'

'How long will it take? And that heart monitor. Oh God, it's not for Chloe is it?'

'They need to do a thorough check on everything. I can't say how long it will take but the doctor will see you as soon as he can. Your baby's in safe hands.' The nurse did her best to reassure Mel. 'Why don't you get yourself a coffee. There's a machine over there.' She pointed to the corner of the waiting area.

Mel muttered her thanks and moved listlessly away. She went through the motions of getting a coffee, but it sat in her hand untouched. She couldn't sit there drinking coffee while her mind was so disturbed.

Chapter 9

Tom thought back over the previous few days. It was not good. How could he have been so stupid?

Now he sat in front of the computer in his study clutching the whisky glass as if his life depended on it. He took another gulp. These days he seemed to be in a permanently befuddled state. He was vaguely aware that his life was falling apart, but powerless to do anything about it. His numerous searches had proved fruitless. He had no real leads. It was useless. **He** was useless. Angrily, he switched off the computer.

Dull eyes sunk in a gaunt face stared back at him from the blank screen. He shielded his view from the apparition whose lank, dark hair and soiled clothes shocked him. He whipped his head around, convinced he would find an intruder behind him.

The empty space mocked him. He looked again at the image on the screen. The hand he raised towards it moved in synchronization. With awful clarity, he knew it was him. He reached for the bottle, took a long swig, and then made for the door, unable to stay in the room a moment longer.

With an effort, he stumbled up the stairs and fell into bed. But there was no relief to be found there. He tossed and turned, fighting the bedclothes that his mind insisted were out to get him.

Suddenly he was wide awake. Irritably, he struggled out of the clinging sheets that held him fast. With a sudden flash of lucidity there was one thought clear in his mind. Mel was in France. Where that had come from he had no idea. Maybe something in the tormented night hours had triggered it.

Now he remembered. Out of nowhere Mel's voice had threaded through his fractured dreams. She was singing along with some French song on the radio and it prompted a memory. He recalled thinking that her accent sounded convincing, though he was no expert. Languages were a foreign country as far as he was concerned. He allowed himself a wry grin as he remembered how pleased with himself he'd been when he'd thought up that pun.

He hadn't thought to query her ease with the French language at the time, but now he pondered on it.

Sorting through some old photos, his eyes misted as he saw Mel smiling back at him from various vacations around the world, always with a group of friends. She'd never had a problem making friends. People seemed drawn to her. Like he was.

She looked so happy then, laughing and fooling around. Was she happy now, without him? Maybe he hadn't done enough to make her happy. It was his fault. But did she have to leave him?

God, how he missed her.

In misery he tossed the photos aside, but one of them stared back at him. There she was, with Notre Dame behind her. He turned the print over. The legend on the back told him all he needed to know.

She was an au pair. I knew it!

The only problem was he couldn't remember exactly where. He dug deep in his mind but received no inspiration. *I need a drink. Clear my head. Get some focus.*

With no great plan, but still convinced that France was his best lead so far, he threw a few things in a bag and headed to the ferry terminal. He'd cross to Calais. A good enough starting point,. He had no idea where to head after that, but he'd come up with something.

There was a merry crowd on the ferry and, for a while, he had been able to forget the quest that usually claimed his life. He'd joined in the jokes and laughter going on in the bar. There was no shortage of drinks and Tom had stood his round from time to time and spent the rest of the crossing there. Normally not a very good sailor, it was good to have something to take his mind off it.

When the boat docked, the revellers jostled each other onto the lower deck. The ground beneath Tom's feet wouldn't keep still. Up and down it went. He didn't feel very well and suddenly threw up at the side of the boat. Somehow, he'd got to his car and made it off onto the quay. Oblivious of the ever-present Gendarmes keeping vigil, Tom hadn't even left the port before he was stopped. Cursing himself for buggering up the only lead he'd had, he gave the policeman a mouthful.

Aware he'd not done himself a favour, he then compounded it by adding, 'don't you know who I am? I'm DCI Stevens from the Met.' Too late, he saw the look of derision cross the officer's face. He wasn't sure if it was disbelief of satisfaction at his big catch, but it wasn't looking good.

He didn't remember much of what had happened after that. All he knew was that he'd woken up in a gloomy cell at the Gendarmerie. Momentarily, he felt a rush of shame, and cringing embarrassment as he remembered his dishevelled state.

But the feeling had passed. He was tired. At that moment it didn't seem to matter. Nothing mattered anymore. Mel had left him. Full stop.

Furiously, he'd punched the wall of the cell until a dart of pain shot up his arm.

What am I doing in this godamned place anyway? He'd asked himself. It had to be a stupid mistake. They must have got the wrong bloke. It would all be sorted by tomorrow. All he needed was a stiff drink and a long sleep. He wasn't about to get either. Sleep had eluded him in recent weeks and there had been nothing else to do but ponder on why his life had gone so wrong.

Reluctantly, he admitted he'd put his job first. It meant everything to him, always had. That's why he'd never understood Mel's preoccupation with having a kid. Why didn't she get satisfaction from her job like he did from his? There was more to life than kids.

Now he tried hard to see how it must have been for her. losing all those babies. He hadn't given her enough attention or reassurance. He hadn't even told her he still loved her, even if she couldn't carry his kids. They were ok without kids. They had each other.

A rattle of keys, the slam of a heavy bolt being drawn and, incredibly the news that he could leave, interrupted his maudlin reverie.

'Leave France, too,' the gendarme had warned him, regarding him with distaste. 'And don't be in any hurry to come back.'

'I don't understand. Why am I not being charged?'

'While you were... er... sleeping,' a smirk hovered briefly on his face, 'we found some identification on you. We notified your chief of your offence.' The smug look gave way to irritation. 'He vouched for you,' he stated reluctantly. His expression spoke all too plainly of his private thoughts. 'But don't think you're getting away with it altogether. You will be punished in England.' A sarcastic smile twisted his face.

If Tom hadn't sobered up already those words would have done it in a flash. He shuddered as he relived the events. The journey home had been a nightmare. The choppy crossing added to the nausea he felt when he thought of the outcome of his stupid, and failed, attempt to trace Mel, all because he couldn't resist a drink.

He had to report to the Super in two days time and he feared the worst. He would undoubtedly be suspended from duty. Reaching for the whisky – his constant and only friend, he upended the bottle, felt the liquor's comforting warmth seep through his body.

He was sober enough to know that it wasn't any good in the long run. But what the hell. Alcohol had been a requirement of the job. How was he to know it would get him by the scruff of the neck and shake the life out of him?

Before the whisky sank its teeth in again, he was beset by a new worry, his thoughts turned to Swanton. He'd been loyal up to now, but would he be tempted to blab? It would be another nail in Tom's coffin if the powers that be knew the full story, especially as he'd implicated another officer. He took another long draft from the bottle.

Time to give Swanton another sweetener. Keep him on my side, he muttered before blacking out.

*****

Mel was exhausted but restless. She paced the hospital waiting room. Pausing briefly at the window she realised with a shock that it was getting light outside. Absently, she watched the stream of traffic and hurrying throngs of people and felt a surge of anger, resenting that life was carrying on as normal for them while hers had come to a premature halt.

Her body tensed with pain. Waiting had become a physical agony. Irritably, she picked up a newspaper and flipped over the pages, not really seeing anything until...

Suddenly Tom was gazing back at her from the page. She closed her eyes, appalled to be in such a state that she was seeing things. Reluctantly, she opened them again. The image was still there. Now she read the accompanying headline.

SENIOR BRITISH POLICE OFFICER HELD ON ALCHOHOL CHARGE

She read on, and then shook her head in an effort to sort out the tangle of emotions fighting for supremacy. She was puzzled as to why Tom's arrest was being reported in a French paper but elated that he seemed to be on their trail. She was well aware that being caught driving while drunk would have a disastrous effect on his position in the force, and yet elated that he would soon be with her to share her burden.

Guilt surged through her. Her leaving must have driven him to take risks that were totally out of character. Unable to read on, and tormented by questions, she threw the paper down, refusing to admit that their lives had deteriorated so terribly.

Chapter 10

The voice that cut through Mel's silent prayers was soft but insistent. She felt a hand on her arm and opened her eyes.

'Madame Dubois, the doctor will see you now. Please come with me.'

In a trance Mel followed. Desperate to see Chloe, but terrified of what the doctor was about to tell her, she negotiated the labyrinth of cloned corridors on auto pilot. Thoughts ran riot in her head. She would rather walk these corridors forever than face bad news about her child. And yet she needed to hold her, to kiss all her pain away.

At last they were at the doctor's office. The nurse knocked at the door.

'Come in.'

'Ah Madame Dubois.' He rose to shake her hand and a flash of recognition lit his face for a second. 'How are you?'

Mel knew him, too. The man who'd helped them off the train. 'Worried,' she replied.

'Ah yes.' He quickly recovered his professionalism. 'My name is François Millais. Asseyez-vous s'il vous plait. *Please sit down.*' There was sympathy in his eyes as he continued. 'I wish I could make this easier for you but I'm afraid the news is not good.'

Mel thought she'd prepared herself but, at the doctor's next words, she seemed unable to stem the tears that sprang without warning. Paralysed with fear, it was as if her heart stopped beating as she forced herself to listen to what he had to say. His voice came from far away, like a voice in your worst nightmare that is always just too faint to interpret the words. She must try to concentrate.

Dr Millais was concerned. 'I'm so sorry my dear,' he said, 'but I have to tell you that the signs are that your child is seriously ill. We need to run some more tests but I'm sure they will only confirm what I already suspect.'

Shock rooted Mel to the spot. She was trembling now. Through frozen lips she forced the question whose answer she didn't want to hear. 'Is she going to die?'

'It wouldn't be right to raise your hopes. As I said, your child is very ill...'

'But you must see seriously ill babies all the time. You have to be able to do something for her.'

'I'm afraid I can't work miracles,' he stated quietly. 'I'm so sorry.'

'But you have to do something. Are you telling me that nothing can be done for Chloe – nothing at all?' Mel was clutching at straws. She knew it, but the alternative was too painful, too final even to consider.

'Be assured we will do all we possibly can for her. But she is so very young, the youngest case I've seen.'

'You haven't told me what it is that you suspect.' Mel was shaking as she made herself face the worst.

'As I said, tests will confirm it, and we would normally wait for those test results, but I won't hide anything from you. I'm afraid that my colleagues and I think your child may have a form of childhood leukaemia.'

The horror must have shown in her face. Mel felt as if every last bit of blood was draining out of her. A terrible shivering took control of her body and she was cold, so cold. She closed her eyes and prayed, as she'd never done before.

Dr Millais was speaking again. 'We will of course be treating Chloe. There are things we can do.'

'What things? Will she be in pain?'

'If leukaemia is confirmed as we suspect, we will give her chemotherapy. It may make her very unwell for a while, but she won't be in pain. We can look after that for her.'

'Is that all you can do?'

'Well ultimately, her best chance would be a stem cell or bone marrow transplant. Has she any siblings? Or how about yourself?'

'No. I would do anything for her but...' She couldn't find the words to tell him that Chloe wasn't her blood child.

'What about your husband?'

'I'm alone.' The answer was automatic.

The nurse put her arm around her shoulders and Mel was surprised by how comforting it was. Until then, she hadn't realised how much she'd missed close contact with another human being.

Dr Millais was speaking again. 'I know you're stunned and upset, but do you feel you could answer a few questions for me? Anything you can tell us about your child's illness would help us.' His voice was coaxing.

Mel was numb. She looked at him wearily. 'I'll try.'

'Tell me, is this the first time Chloe has suffered a loss of blood?'

'No, there have been two others, though not as serious.' She thought back to those other occasions, ashamed that she'd brushed them aside so casually. 'I thought at first, when her mouth was bleeding, she had scratched her tongue, or that she was teething,' she confessed. 'I feel so stupid now.'

'Why should you have thought anything else?' He was trying to be kind.

'There were other things,' she heard herself say.

'What things?'

'Several times she seemed really unwell. She would go pale and floppy. A couple of times she was violently sick. And she had bruises; every touch seemed to hurt her. I should have taken it more seriously.'

'Didn't you get help then?'

'I did get a doctor to look at her.'

'And what did he say, this doctor?' It was clear Dr Millais didn't believe her and she couldn't blame him.

'He thought at first it might be Meningitis. Of course he didn't tell me that at the time. But when those tests came back clear, he put it down to a bug,' she replied defiantly. 'She got better, so I believed him. I don't have much experience of babies. Chloe's...' Mel hesitated.

The doctor was regarding her steadily and it unnerved her. 'Chloe is my first,' she finished lamely. 'I wanted to believe him. I was so relieved that it wasn't serious.'

'I can understand that, but...'

'The truth is, being a mother is all so new to me.' She felt compelled to explain. She couldn't bear the look he was giving her. It stripped her bare and left her soul exposed. But she forced herself to continue. 'I was worried it was my fault that Chloe was ill. That I'd done something wrong. And, worst of all, that people would think I'd been ill-treating her.'

Suddenly she felt guilty that she'd put her own feelings first. 'I truly didn't know Chloe was so ill. Please don't let it be too late to help her,' she pleaded.

The doctor was still studying her face. The silence lasted a lifetime. 'I believe you,' he said at last.

The breath that Mel had been holding escaped on a sob. 'Can I see Chloe?' she begged. She was desperate to hold her little girl.

'Of course. But not for long. She really needs intensive care.' He led Mel to a small examination room.

Horror rooted her to the spot. Foolishly, she hadn't given any thought as to how Chloe would look and was totally unprepared for what she saw. The small body was trapped in a maze of wires and tubes. Huge eyes brimming with tears gazed into Mel's reproachfully.

'Mam...ma...' The joy of hearing Chloe say it for the first time was completely obliterated by the pain in the pathetic little voice. It broke Mel's heart.

'Can I hold her? Please?'

'I'm sorry. But you can sit with her for a few minutes.'

Mel drew up a chair. 'Mummy's here darling.' With infinite care she stroked her baby's once plump cheek and smoothed back the damp curls from the porcelain pale forehead. Once again, her eyes were drawn to the tiny butterfly birthmark whose familiarity was caught in the periphery of her memory.

She struggled to find some comforting words, but they seemed locked in the flickering screens and crumpled folds surrounding the restless baby. Eyes, pooled in tears full of questions, sought Mel's face. She tried had to smile as stroked Chloe's cheek. 'I'm sorry my little one, so sorry.' She didn't know what else to say.

Reaching for the dimpled hand, she held it gently as the words of that old song she'd learnt at her mother's knee came into her mind. It had soothed Chloe many times, perhaps it would now. *Lulla, lulla, lulla, lulla bye-bye...* It was always Chloe's favourite, as it had been hers. She recalled that special feeling she'd had, gazing into her mother's face as she'd sung, *do you want the stars to play with, or the moon to run away with. They'll come if you don't cry.*

Although her mother had died all those years ago, the memory was so clear, she could feel the warmth of her mother's hand around her own and see the love in her eyes. And on her forehead a birthmark like a tiny butterfly. Oh... The revelation left her reeling. What could it mean? Was such a bizarre coincidence the reason why she'd felt such a strong connection with Chloe from the start? Heat spread through her at the possibility of another, more tangible, implication.

Did Chloe somehow feel it too?

'I'm afraid you must leave her now.' The apologetic voice of François Millais cut into her thoughts.

Mel couldn't bear it. In vain she tried to blink away the tears, before kissing the baby's rounded cheek.

The doctor's eyes were full of compassion. He spoke again. 'She is calmer, you see? But she needs to start her programme of treatment. Ultimately, the transplant will give her the best chance. You might want to consider donating some bone marrow. As Chloe's next of kin there's every chance you could be a perfect match.'

'But... you don't understand...' It was so tempting to pour her heart out to this gentle man.

'Just think about it,' he said quietly.

'I will doctor. Oh I **will.** And thank you.'

Mel had to escape. She was suffocating in that small room where she'd very nearly given herself away. The doctor's words reverberated off the walls as she stumbled along the corridor. If only it were that easy. If only love were enough.

It was all she had to give.

Or was it?

It would mean risking everything, but the answer was clear. She had no choice. She had to find Chloe's real mother.

At last she admitted it. For days she'd known it: fretted about it, tossed and turned her nights away thinking about it. And about Tom. She needed his help more than ever.

Without thinking, she reached for her mobile, uncaring now of the risk that she would be found. Chloe was the only one that mattered. Only after she'd keyed in the familiar number did the panic set in. She was so afraid. Would Tom help her after all she'd done? He had to; she had nowhere else to turn.

*****

The voice that answered was strangely slurred. Perhaps, in her overwrought state she had got the wrong number. And yet...

'Is that you Tom? It's Mel. You sound awful. Are you ill?'

'I'm OK.' He was short and dismissive.

She battled on, coming straight to the point. 'I need you Tom. Something dreadful's happened. It's Chloe...'

There was silence at the other end.

Mel tried to ignore his mood. She was crying now. 'Tom, I've made an awful mistake. You were right. She was never mine. We have to find her mother.' She was almost incoherent, forcing the words out between sobs.

'Hey, slow down. Where are you? And what's happened?'

Mel was at breaking point. 'Are you drunk or something Tom? I just told you.' Why couldn't he grasp what she'd said? She battled on. 'Chloe has Leukaemia.' The word was strange; a poor fit for the waiting silence. It sounded like someone else's story. With a supreme effort she carried on. 'She needs a bone marrow transplant if she's to have any chance at all.'

'What are you talking about?' His fuddled brain could not make sense of it all.

'Tom, please try to understand. Chloe is very ill. You know I'd give her anything, but what she needs most I can't give her.' She began to cry again. 'I feel so helpless Tom. You have to help me – please.'

At last Tom seemed to understand. 'You know the whole thing would have to come out. Are you sure you want that?'

'Yes, it doesn't matter anymore. Being in prison can't be any worse than this. We have to think of Chloe. Help me find her mother.'

'You'd better give me your address.'

'21 Rue Marché, Mortagne.

'And Tom. You can always get me on my mobile. This is my new number.'

'I'm on my way. Oh my God. It's so good to hear from you. It's been hell.'

Mel would have been shocked to see just what that hell had done to him but, for now, it was enough to know he was on his way.

*****

Dr Millais had given her a number to ring so that she could check on Chloe whenever she wanted. For now, she must return to Odile. The poor woman would be worried sick.

Guiltily, Mel thought about how she had continued to deceive Odile. It was poor repayment for the kindness she'd shown them, and Mel felt she owed it to her to try and explain.

Many times she'd longed for Odile's support, but lacked the courage to confess to the secret she'd kept from her. Now she couldn't delay any longer.

After all, Odile knew what it was like to be desperate for a child. Mel clung to that thought and prayed that her friend would find it in her heart to forgive her.

Chapter 11

Tom swallowed the whisky without thinking. It was automatic now, like breathing. No Mel – whisky. A bad night – that meant every night – whisky. Lost his job – whisky. He didn't really need an excuse. It was all he had. His only friend.

He didn't care that he needed more and more before he felt it's warm embrace. He knew he could rely on it happening eventually. He could feel it now, but it didn't give him the comfort he wanted. Even in his inebriated state, he recognised the treachery of his friend alcohol. The artificial warmth, the false bravado.

At last Mel had got in touch. He knew he'd reacted badly. The truth was, the sound of her voice was better than any amount of strong black coffee. He'd been suddenly lost for words; overcome with emotion.

Then she'd gone and blurted out all that stuff about the child. He'd had a job to make sense of it. All he knew was that Mel had erased his happiness with one careless application. He'd been angry. She didn't want him. She just wanted help in finding the kid's mother.

But still, she had given him her address – and a mobile number. He couldn't believe it. After all his months of searching she'd given them to him just like that. He should have been over the moon – and he was – but the reason for her call had rattled him and his reaction had been to reach for the bottle. Now he slumped in the chair, disgusted with himself. Somehow, he had to kick this habit.

He knew it wouldn't be easy. He'd let it get such a hold on him. But he would do it – for Mel. There were difficult times ahead for both of them. He tried to put himself in Mel's place but, although her pain was of her own making, he could still imagine how she must be feeling. It was in her voice.

 He tried to picture where she was living now, but he had no clues. He wondered if she had made any friends and whether she would have confided in one of them so that she had someone to share the distress of the baby's illness.

He still couldn't bring himself to use the name Mel had chosen for her, but he thought of the baby, so ill in a foreign country. So ill she may not make it. He tried so hard to feel compassion. It would be sad, but also an answer to some of their problems. And would the baby's real mother care if she knew? He doubted whether she even thought about the child she'd dumped. She must have known there was only a slim chance of the baby surviving the cold of that March morning.

That made him think of Mel and how excited she'd been. Never mind him. Apparently, he didn't matter. She'd convinced herself that the child had been left there for her to find. That she'd been given one last chance at motherhood. Tom couldn't help thinking this kid thing had sent her off her head. The child wasn't hers, wasn't theirs.

He would bet she hadn't told her new friends about that day. Had she even told them that she'd left him in order to keep the baby? Were they prepared for his visit? There was so much he needed to know.

Mel was desperate to track down the mother so that she could help the sick baby, but Tom doubted if the mother was still around. It seemed a hopeless task she'd set him. Still, he could get the chaps at the Nick on the case, he thought, before remembering that he didn't have that luxury anymore. It was unlikely he would get his job back when all this came out either. But he was already at rock bottom: things couldn't get much worse.

And he was anxious to set the wheels in motion. To be able to tell Mel that things were under way, to feel useful, even though his heart wasn't in it. But in truth he didn't know where to start. His hand reached out for the bottle. Just a sip to clear his head. The cap was off. He could feel the soothing warmth seeping, seeping, sending him into oblivion.

Not this time.

Angrily, Tom threw the bottle down. He wasn't going to be fooled like that. Mel needed him to be strong. He had to get to her. He was shaking but managed to shower. Mesmerized, he watched the filthy water swirl down the plughole, tried to remember the last time he'd showered, and failed, but the stench of weeks of neglect was being washed away in his strengthening resolve.

A shave – two hands to steady the shaver. Some clean clothes – did he have any? And a drink. He needed a drink. A swig of strong, black coffee would have to do. Briefly, he wondered how long he could keep this up, but he must. For Mel. It was the only chance he had of getting her back.

At last he was on his way as promised, pausing only to book his place on the channel train. His spirits rose as he drove to Folkestone. He felt his heart miss a beat when he thought of seeing Mel again. Of holding her close where she belonged.

He hoped she would still look as he remembered her; that her experience wouldn't have changed her.

For the first time in months he actually felt hungry. Perhaps he'd have time to get a sandwich at the terminal. And a cup of coffee. He knew he'd have to take things gradually after so long without food.

Catching sight of himself in the mirror, he didn't like what he saw. It still caught him unawares and made him feel he was looking at someone else. He'd been a good-looking guy once, but now his face was too thin and sallow. And his clothes, several sizes too big, hung on his diminished frame like dustsheets on an unfinished statue. That's exactly what he felt like; work in progress. He smiled wryly, comforting himself with the thought that, for all that, he looked a whole lot better than the grubby drunk of last time he was in France. He just had to keep away from the bottle.

*****

In Normandy, Mel was sitting in Odile's comfortable sitting room. It had been a long, exhausting day and her friend had been waiting for her when Mel returned from the hospital. Seeing Mel's distress, Odile put a comforting arm around her and guided her inside.

'Ma pauvre. What has happened? Where is dear little Chloe?'

Seated in the cosy room, Mel's anguish broke free. She had to confide in someone but didn't know where to start.

'Mon Dieu! She is not... Please tell me she is not ...'

Mel was nearly choking on unrelenting tears. 'No, she isn't dead, but she's very ill. It breaks my heart to see her. Oh Odile... I can't bear it.'

'But she will get better, yes?'

'That's just it. They don't know. They say she has Leukaemia, and the one thing she needs I can't give her because...'

'Because what? What is this reason you cannot help your child?' Odile's voice was gentle, coaxing Mel to carry on.

'It was now or never. 'Because she's not my child.' There, it was said. She hadn't meant to blurt it out like that. Worry and lack of sleep had made her unable to think straight.

'You mean she's – how you say it – adopted? Yes, that's it. But that's nothing. Lots of people do it. And the children become their own just the same. Je ne pas comprenez.'

'Chloe's not adopted." Mel's voice faltered. 'Forgive me Odile. I've done something dreadful but, believe me, I didn't think it was wrong at the time. I wanted a child so much and there was this poor little abandoned mite...'

The whole sorry story poured out then. How she had found the baby girl, nearly dead from cold, left at the side of the road to die. 'I was so desperate for a child I decided to keep her. She was so beautiful, and just dumped in a bin bag.'

'Oh...' Odile was appalled. 'What happened then?'

'I was so angry with the mother for discarding her child like some piece of rubbish. I couldn't understand that she didn't realise how lucky she was. But...'

She watched Odile's expression change from puzzlement to shock and it was hard to continue. 'I'm so ashamed. I haven't told you the truth. My husband was working away from home when I found Chloe and decided to keep her.'

'I don't understand. Il est mort. You said so.'

'I know' Mel buried her face in her hands. 'I'm so sorry I deceived you. You've been so kind to us, and you don't deserve it. The truth is, I love Tom so much, but he wanted me to give Chloe up. He just didn't seem to see my need to become a mother.'

'So what did you do?'

'We'd tried and tried to have a child without success. I saw this as my only chance of motherhood – as if it were meant to be – but Tom didn't even try to understand. So I left him and brought Chloe here.'

'You left him?' Odile was incredulous. 'You could do that for the sake of someone else's child?'

Mel nodded miserably. 'I had no choice. I pleaded with him to let me keep the baby, but he's a policeman and insisted that we do the right thing. I couldn't. That's all there is to it.'

'Why are you telling me all this now?'

'I want so much for you to understand that I just couldn't give her up, abandon her for the second time. So I had to leave. To make a new life for Chloe and me. I know it was a kind of madness, but I wasn't thinking straight after all the babies I'd lost.'

'Why didn't you tell me all this before? I thought we were friends.'

'We are. But I didn't want to be found. I was afraid you'd try to talk me out of what I'd done or, worse still, report me.'

'Then why now?'

'Because when they told me Chloe might die if she doesn't get a bone marrow transplant, I finally realised what a dreadful thing I'd done. I took her away from the one person who could help her now, her birth mother. The authorities could have tracked her down maybe. I have to find her and I need Tom's help.'

'You've spoken to him? Do you know what all this means for you?'

'Yes. But Chloe's needs come first. I owe her that.'

'And your husband? He thinks the same?'

'I hope so. He's on his way from England. You see I only pretended to be French. My name is Melanie, not Amelie...' Her voice tailed off as Odile collapsed into a chair.

Mel ran to her and held her close. 'Oh my God, are you all right? I'm so sorry. Can you ever forgive me?'

'It's such a shock. I can't take it all in. You speak such good French; I had no reason to doubt you. So I treated you like a daughter and all the time you were lying to me.'

'I know. I'm so ashamed. I wanted so much to tell you. I very nearly did. I really needed someone to confide in.'

'But not enough apparently.' She was clearly upset.

'I thought you might send us away. I've grown so fond of you, and you love Chloe almost as much as I do. I couldn't bear to take her away from you. Especially after you told me about losing your own baby all those years ago.' Mel knew she was gabbling.

Well, it's done.' Odile's tone was flat. 'I can't tell you how sorry I am that you couldn't trust me with your secret, but perhaps we can sort something out.'

'What did you have in mind?' Mel's worried look evoked Odile's sympathy.

'Don't look so concerned. I am hurt that you couldn't trust me, and I know what you did was wrong, but I do understand what drove you to it my dear. I might even have done something like it myself, given the chance,' she said it quietly, as if she'd only just realised it, and gave Mel's hand a squeeze.

Mel's throat constricted with emotion. The dam holding back her tears threatened to break at any moment. Never had she felt so humbled, or less deserving of such generosity of spirit.

The minutes passed, but neither of them spoke or moved, each absorbed with the myriad of unanswered questions that were beating a tattoo in their heads. So lost in thought were they, that the urgent ringing of the doorbell startled them.

Mel's heart missed a beat. Her nerves were taut. She wanted to think it was Tom on the other side of the door, but what if the French authorities had caught up with her at last? The ever-present fear pounded in her chest.

Odile struggled to her feet and went to open the door.

'Is Mel here?' The voice was achingly familiar and, though still nervous, Mel was able to breathe again.

'She is, Tom. It is Tom?' Odile's question was an afterthought.

He nodded.

'We've been expecting you. Come in.'

'She's told you about me?'

'Only just.'

Incredibly, Mel saw the beginning of a smile hover on her friend's face.

Chapter 12

As Tom came towards her, Mel couldn't disguise her shock. The voice may have sounded familiar, but the man she'd known and loved all these years had been replaced by a stranger; a ghost of the picture she'd clung to in her mind. 'Tom?' she blurted; her uncertainty born of a thousand questions. 'What on earth has happened to you?'

'Don't worry about me. I'm here aren't I? That's all that matters. We're together again and, together, we must find a way to help Chloe.' He reached for her and they clung together, each a life raft for the other in the turbulence of their emotions.

They failed to notice that Odile had tactfully left the room to give them a few private moments.

'Oh dear,' Mel said. 'We've totally ignored poor Odile. I hope we didn't embarrass her.' Then she smiled. 'More likely she didn't want to intrude. The French like a bit of romance, I'm told.'

Tom grinned.

Mel gave him a nudge. 'You haven't changed, have you.'

As they drew apart, they became aware of movement in the apartment below: the sound of cups going on a tray and the clatter of crockery. The French prided themselves on their hospitality. Soon there were footsteps on the stairs. There was a discreet knock on the door.

'Come in Odile,' Mel said, going to open the door. 'Tom, can you come and get the tray please.'

The tray bore not only a generous jug of coffee, but also some very tasty-looking snacks. Small circles of toast were spread with smooth paté and a scattering of sliced cornichons. Others cradled garlic-scented baby mushrooms. Savoury biscuits hid under their burden of cheese, and crusty bread and the obligatory bowl of olives accompanied a plate of ham. The sight and smell of these appetizing morsels had Mel's taste buds working overtime. With all the worries of the day she couldn't for the life of her remember when she'd last eaten.

Odile was hovering at the door watching their reactions and pleased to have an excuse to act the hostess.

'It's so kind of you to go to all this trouble,' Mel began. 'As if we haven't put you through enough already.'

Odile's face clouded over for a second. Clearly, she'd had a chance to think over all that Mel had been forced to disclose to her. With a visible effort she pasted a smile on her face. 'I won't be a moment,' she stated, before leaving the room again.

Seconds later she was back with another tray. 'We must have a restorative brandy,' she smiled. 'You've had an exhausting day. 'And we should celebrate us all being together again,' she continued bravely.

Mel was shocked to see Tom's hand shoot out for the glass and lift it to his lips like the first cup of water offered to a man who'd been lost in a desert. Almost as suddenly he clumsily replaced it on the tray. He was pale and sweating and his hand shook.

With an effort he composed himself. 'You're very kind, Madame but, I'll just have a coffee please.'

'Tout alors! But you are a man, n'est pas? And you cannot take a small drink of Cognac?' Odile tutted, totally at a loss to understand this strange behaviour. She was clearly affronted.

Mel was annoyed at Tom's reaction. 'What are you playing at Tom?' Odile's being extraordinarily generous, considering what's happened, and you've virtually thrown her welcoming overture back in her face. I don't get it.'

'I...' He couldn't tell her. Not yet. He was supposed to be helping Mel, not giving her more worry. Oh God, life was so complicated. He wished he'd taken that drink now. One little one wouldn't have hurt surely, and it would have avoided the scene that had nearly given away his secret.

Mel watched the conflict of emotions that crossed Tom's face and felt an unaccountable surge of anger. Where was her rock? She didn't know the quivering wreck in front of her.

So many times she'd been on the verge of calling him. Poor little Chloe had been the one to galvanise her into action eventually. She'd longed for his support but, now that he was here, it was all going wrong. Not the way it was meant to be at all.

Perhaps she'd expected too much. Now she tortured herself with the thought that he was punishing her for walking out on him. Maybe it hadn't been realistic to think that they could take up where they had left off, but his behaviour was distinctly odd. Once they'd been so close they could read each other's minds. Now she was at a loss to understand him.

And yet he still appeared to love her. She was just tired. She'd have to give it time. But time was a luxury they didn't have if they were to help

Chloe.

Chloe. She was never far from Mel's thoughts, a picture of her frail little body trapped like a caged bird in tubes and wires haunted her. Mel shuddered as fear swept through her. It was torture being away from her baby and her arms ached to hold her. To set her free from the pain she was suffering. But she'd been told not to go back to the hospital until the morning.

She tried to brush away her irritation at Tom's behaviour and turned to him. 'Tom...' she ventured, 'we have to think of poor Chloe. I know it seems an impossible task, but we have to find her mother.'

Tom was deep in his own troubled thoughts. But he pulled himself together. At least he had something to offer. 'I posted a brief message on the Internet before I left. On a missing persons site. I don't know if it will bring any results but it's a start.'

Mel was impressed. 'That's brilliant. Why didn't I think of it?'

Tom hadn't finished. 'Do you remember Andy Swanton? DS Swanton?' he said now. 'Well, he's been very supportive and has agreed to make some enquiries of his own. There's an ad going in the personal column of the local paper tomorrow. I've got a new mobile for people, including Andy, to contact me on. He's the only one who knows about all this.'

Mel felt the tiniest flicker of hope as she registered that her husband had lost none of his communication skills.

'Of course these are only drops in the ocean. They may not even get a response.'

The flicker wavered as Tom went on.

'Maybe the mother will refuse to come forward. In all probability she's made a new life for herself.' Tom was gently trying to temper Mel's optimism. 'I don't want you raising your hopes too much.'

'But surely, if she knows the child is seriously ill she'll want to do something?'

'She may not. After all, she gave up on her before.'

Tom's words sounded harsh, but Mel was reluctant to accept there was truth in them.

Watching her face Tom's expression softened. He surprised himself by saying, 'There's a slim chance that she regrets what she did and, if she is too frightened to get in touch, maybe some other family member knows something.'

It all seemed to rest on maybes. There was not much to go on, but it was all they had. It was a start that made the flame of hope burn more brightly.

All this time Mel knew that Odile had listened quietly. Perhaps she had sensed something about Tom's attitude that wasn't quite right. He was saying all the right things, but his eyes told a different story. Yet, in spite of everything, he seemed still to care desperately about Mel and quite obviously couldn't bear to see her hurting so much. Mel saw her confusion as she busied herself with the coffee jug. 'More coffee?'

'Please,' they answered in unison.

Odile's mood was still frosty as she handed Tom his cup, but Mel was relieved to see that he accepted it graciously.

'I'm sorry about before,' he said to Odile, 'but you see, I have a bit of a problem with alcohol at the moment He looked acutely embarrassed as the words slipped out. 'Sorry,' he said again, 'I didn't mean to blurt it out like that.'

'But what do you mean? Are you ill?' It would explain a lot, but Odile wasn't going to be pacified so easily.

'No, not ill as such. It's just better if I stay off alcohol for the moment. And who needs it anyway, with coffee this good.'

It was a valiant effort to appease Odile and, apparently satisfied, Odile left the room.

Mel was glad. She and Tom had things to discuss. The penny had suddenly dropped for her. She'd seen the signs of alcohol abuse before and should have recognised them in Tom. It was the scourge of the police force, especially in CID. But somehow, she'd thought Tom wouldn't succumb. He was strong and had more sense, surely. That's what she'd thought, but obviously she'd been wrong. He wasn't invincible; he was weak like all the others. The realization punched her in the stomach, leaving her winded and nauseous.

From a distance, she heard him trying to explain, make excuses. 'I missed you. I couldn't believe you'd left me for the sake of some other woman's child. Alcohol was a comfort, a solace.' He was struggling to find the words. 'It's a ruthless enemy,' he continued, 'stealing up on you, pretending to be your friend. And all the time it's eating into your brain and making you want more and more. I didn't realise it had got such a hold until it was too late.'

The rock Mel had thought him to be had crumbled in front of her. 'Oh Tom, I don't need this on top of everything else.'

'Don't worry,' Tom replied, 'I'm dealing with it. You're right, we have much more urgent things to think about.' Tom was grateful to be on firmer ground. 'Of course, Chloe is our priority now.'

Once again he was saying the right things, but Mel saw he was clearly still uncomfortable with his admission of weakness. She knew he was convinced he could cope with his addiction. But would he be able to do it? She tried to sweep her doubts aside, needing to believe that he could. She searched his face for confirmation.

As if on cue, Odile, entered the room and lightened the atmosphere with talk of supper. 'Have you made arrangements for your stay Tom?' she asked then.

Tom looked embarrassed. 'I was so anxious to get here to Mel that I'm afraid I didn't get around to that,' he admitted. 'Perhaps you could recommend somewhere nearby?'

Relieved, Mel saw Odile's expression soften. Tom had obviously done the right thing by asking her advice. Mel knew the French loved a bit of romance, but she was left open mouthed by Odile's next offering.

'I can see that you two need to be together, and I am not going to be the one to separate you so soon. We will have supper and then, if it suits you, you will sleep here.' She studied Mel's face before continuing. 'I think you will find there is plenty of room.' She winked at Tom conspiratorially, and then blushed, perhaps wondering if she'd gone too far.

Tom smiled at her. 'Thank you, Madame. You're more than kind.'

Odile laughed coquettishly. 'I know what it is to be in love, you know. And please call me Odile.'

As she made to leave, Mel called after her, 'Let me help you.'

'It's nearly all done,' she replied airily.

As Mel moved into Tom's arms she made a vow. Together they would be strong. She felt a new strength as she smiled up at him. 'We'll help each other,' she promised.

Eagerly Tom's lips sought hers. His kiss was filled with longing and passion such as Mel had never known before. It felt like coming home and for a moment she thought she could conquer the world.

They surfaced breathless. Tom struggled to compose himself before asking, 'When can I see Chloe?'

'You really want to see her?' Mel was anxious. He'd never shown much interest in Chloe before and he clearly had his own demons to face. She was desperate for him to love the child as much as she did, but what would he think when he saw the pathetic little scrap almost submerged in tubes and wires and fighting for her life? Would he think she was worth all the anguish the future would hold, or would he write Chloe off? Mel was so afraid he would try to discourage her from pursuing a happy ending.

Her worries were interrupted by Odile's call to supper. Over a simple meal of chicken and salad, followed by cheese and fruit, they discussed their plans for the next day. Together they would see Chloe. Then they must consider every conceivable way to make contact with her parents.

'Do you really believe there's a chance we'll get some feedback from your enquiries?' Mel wanted to know.

'That would be the ultimate. But who knows? I just had to do something.'

'What do you mean? What are these enquiries you have made?' interjected Odile.

'I posted a message on the internet and in the newspaper,' Tom answered.

Mel was concerned to see that Odile was near to tears. 'What is it?' she asked gently.

'You have become my family, but now you have your husband and I am not needed. I see I am going to lose you. Perhaps soon.'

Mel reached out and took hold of her friend's hand. 'We have to do what's best for Chloe. You would want that too. But we will never forget your kindness. And we will not lose touch – whatever happens. I promise.' In spite of her own inner torment, Mel did her best to reassure Odile.

The sharp jingle from Tom's phone cut through the tender moment and Odile seized her chance to leave them alone.

'Yes?' Tom answered.

Mel was at his side in an instant but Tom slammed the phone down.

'Bloody pervert!' he said.

Their conversation was punctuated by several more of these false alarms. Cranks with nothing better to do than play with people's anguish. Tom was beginning to lose his temper.

Mel tried her best to diffuse the tense atmosphere by telling him of Chloe's progress before she became ill. She described the child's sunny nature and ready smile. 'Everybody loves her – and you will too,' she said. She went on to mention all the presents they'd been given and how they would find gifts of fresh produce on the doorstep. 'To make Chloe big and strong,' the locals told me.

Suddenly the phone rang again. Tom was on the point of ignoring it but at the last moment decided to pick it up.

Mel tried to get closer in order to hear what the caller had to say, but the words were still indistinct. She watched as Tom's scepticism changed to cautious hope and then to a kind of forced jubilation.

'Yes, I've got that. I'll need to discuss it with my wife of course. Hang on. Let me write that down. OK, I'll be in touch very soon.' He snapped the phone shut and sat collecting his thoughts for a second or two. He looked bewildered. Then he thumped the table in excitement, as if he didn't really know how to react but felt this was expected of him. 'We may have a lead,' he said. 'It's possible that was Chloe's grandmother. She gave me her number. We're to ring her back.'

'How d'you know it was the grandmother?' Mel was still doubtful.

'In my message I asked for something that would identify the child. She described a birthmark, said it was like a tiny butterfly or something fanciful.'

Excitement gleamed in Mel's eyes. 'But that's right,' she exclaimed. Chloe has a mark like that on her forehead.'

Chapter 13

'I suppose we should have been prepared for this,' Tom said.

'What? I don't understand.' Mel was puzzled. Just a moment ago he'd seemed full of optimism.

'It's so easy to get carried away. You forget people can be cruel. I see it in my job all the time. They all want to jump on the bandwagon. To seize their own little bit of fame I suppose.'

'But what could they hope to gain from this? There's no financial reward, no media attention.'

'They're cranks with nothing better to do.' Tom was dismissive. 'They don't care about the hurt they cause.'

'But you were so positive. What's made you question this woman's credibility when you were so certain just now?'

'I should have been more aware. I let you build up your hopes when it may come to nothing.' Tom refused to be pacified. 'I guess we just have to be more patient,' he finished.

'Patient! You've seen how ill Chloe is. We don't have the luxury of time. We need a result and we need it now. Not next week or next month. That may be too late.' The words were out before Mel could stop herself. Suddenly the enormity of what she'd said throbbed in her mind. *Too late…Too late.* 'Oh God,' she whispered.

Tom's arms were round her in an instant. 'I know,' he said, feeling helpless. They had just returned from the hospital, where both of them had been stunned by how ill Chloe was. Even when Mel had held the once chubby, starfish hand and talked soothingly to her baby there had been no response whatsoever. She'd tried gently stroking the rounded cheek but there had been no answering smile. She didn't even seem to know that Mel was there, and it broke her heart.

'She's getting worse, isn't she?' she recalled saying to the nurse.

'I'm afraid they always react badly when they first start the treatment. But she's strong. She's holding her own.'

The reply, though kindly meant, had done nothing to allay Mel's fears. She'd looked sadly at the once glossy curls, which now lay like fallen leaves on the sheet beneath her precious baby. The beautiful, healthy child she'd cherished was now a terrible reminder of the porcelain doll Mel had had as a child. Bald, fragile and lifeless. She begged to be allowed to stay with her baby, but it was not encouraged in Intensive Care where the possible introduction of infection was deemed dangerous for the young patients teetering on the brink of death. Tears had blinded her as she kissed Chloe – perhaps for the last time. That possibility lodged a sliver of ice in her heart.

Back at the apartment, tears spilled down her face again as Mel remembered that scene. Too exhausted emotionally and physically to brush them away, she let them fall.

Locked in their shared misery neither of them noticed Odile tactfully slip from the room

'Don't,' pleaded Tom. 'Please don't.' He took her hand and massaged it gently. 'We have to stay strong.'

This last statement held more than Mel realised. She felt him tremble and, for the first time since their return from the hospital, she studied his face. Was it a shudder of apprehension for what lay ahead, or a symptom of withdrawal from the alcohol he craved? There was no way of knowing for certain, but she had her suspicions that alcohol had a bigger hold on him than she'd hoped.

There was a tentative knock on the door.

'Come in,' Mel called automatically, before continuing their conversation.

Odile had brought coffee and was just in time to hear Mel's question to Tom.

'Are you OK?' Mel asked him, impatient at his suspected weakness. He was supposed to be her rock, for God's sake, not to give her another problem. 'You said we have to be strong,' she reminded him.

'With a supreme effort he pulled himself together. 'Yes, I'm alright.' His voice held a note of resolve for Mel to latch on to. 'I'm worried about Chloe, just like you.'

Odile nervously cleared her throat before speaking. 'Pardonnez moi for interrupting you,' she said hesitantly. 'You seem to have anxiety about these people who claim to be Chloe's family. You must ask them more questions, yes? Get them to mention something that only someone close to the child would know.'

'Don't you think I thought of that?' Apologising for his abrupt tone, Tom went on, 'My training has taught me that much. But when you are so closely involved it all goes out the window.'

Odile was puzzled about the window but allowed Tom to continue.

'You just want a miracle to happen – overnight if possible,' he stated.

'I understand.' Odile was not at all offended by his outburst. 'However, you have to – how you say – weed out the impostors. How else can you be sure?'

'Of course that would be normal procedure. But we know so little. I guess they wouldn't know much either. Chloe was only hours old when she was abandoned remember,' Mel intervened. In spite of everything, she wanted to support Tom.

'But what about the child's mother?' asked Odile. 'A mother would know every little thing about her baby, even if she couldn't keep her, n'est pas?'

'It's our only hope. That, if the mother is still around, she noticed something. Something unique to her child,' Mel countered.

'Like what?' Tom asked. 'A new-born hasn't had time to develop any unique characteristics surely?'

Mel ignored his negativity. 'Like some sort of blemish perhaps,' she ventured. Her hand flew to her mouth as she remembered. 'Chloe has that birthmark on her temple. I told you. And her grandmother mentioned it too, remember? Her mother must have noticed it too.' She was excited now.

Mel mustered one of her best smiles for Odile. 'Thank you,' she said. 'You've reminded us, given us something positive to work on.'

'We just have to pray that the mother did notice this mark,' Tom said.

If he thought his remark would burst her bubble Mel had already done that herself. She was off on a new anxiety trail. Far from being the answer to all their worries, if they found the child's mother, and against all the odds Chloe survived, would she then demand to have her returned?

From the glimpse she'd had of the mother, she'd looked so young and vulnerable. She surely wouldn't be able to care for the child. And she *had* dumped her in a bin bag. She clearly hadn't wanted her child then. Why would she now?

Unless she had family who would support her. Mel realised she was tormenting herself. These were all unknown factors. And yet…

'Oh God, I love Chloe so much. She's the child I longed for. And now, whatever happens, I'm going to lose her.' Mel's anguish was palpable. She looked across to Odile. This must be so hard for her. She knew what it was like to lose a child and Mel's anguish must have opened old wounds.

Nevertheless, she gave her an encouraging smile and said, 'You must try to stay strong, ma cherie.'

Tom looked at Mel in concern. He couldn't really understand how she could be so emotionally connected to someone else's child, but he hated to see her so distressed. 'You don't know that love. You have to give her every chance to get well,' he added with more conviction than he felt. 'That's what you wanted, isn't it? To prove how much you love her.'

'Yes,' Mel replied in a small voice. 'But it's so hard.'

'I know love.'

After a troubled night full of disturbing dreams Mel was anxious to be back at the hospital. Chloe showed no signs of rallying but, while Tom sat silently, Mel persevered with gentle words and even snatches of the little songs Chloe loved. She planted feather-light kisses on the porcelain cheeks and stroked the limp hands that lay tangled in the myriad wires that snaked around the tiny form. But, after a distressing morning trying to get some response, Mel was emotionally and physically exhausted.

Eventually the nurse had suggested they take a break. Now they were sitting on a bench in the grounds sipping a welcome cup of scalding coffee.

In an effort to distract Mel Tom said, 'Would you like to have a look at the Missing Persons website? There may just be some more replies to my message.' He opened his laptop. Mel sat beside him, willing the screen to reveal more positive news. She watched as Tom accessed the site and brought up his emails. There were four more replies. She tried not to get too excited. 'We only need one of them to be genuine,' she said.

'We need to be cautious. Experience has shown me that you can tell by the type of language they use.'

'Do we need to ask them more questions as Odile suggested?'

'Well, my message was pretty basic. Perhaps we could ask them what they know about the baby's birth. I haven't revealed that she was abandoned. Only the mother, or somebody close to her would know that.'

'I haven't given much thought to the father. Suppose he makes a claim?'

'I've thought about him of course. And I came to the conclusion that he wasn't –and isn't – interested in his child. He may not even know she exists.' Tom was matter of fact as usual.

Mel scanned the original message again. *Seriously ill baby, born 15.01.08 in Westerham, Suffolk, urgently needs contact with mother/family.*

'What else could we ask?'

'I don't know. Let's see what they say.'

Together they read each reply, looking for any glimmer of hope.

'This one's out for a start,' Tom said. Look what it says. *I had a baby girl on that date. She weighed 8 pounds and had a lot of blonde hair. I've always regretted giving her up for adoption.*

'It's obviously not Chloe,' Mel conceded.

The next two were no better; one claiming her baby boy was stolen from its buggy, and the other that she'd been told the baby had died at birth, which she'd never believed and 'this proves it'.

But the fourth sounded much more genuine.

'Oh! I'm so sorry,' Tom interjected. 'I completely forgot that woman who phoned told me she sent an email as well. This must be her.

I only learned recently that my daughter had a baby girl on the date and at the place you mention. Sadly, my daughter died soon after. You will understand that this has been a very painful time for me, and I don't want to give any more information by email, but perhaps we could talk. I'll ring you tonight. It was dated for the day she'd called.

Mel looked at Tom aghast. 'Chloe's mother's dead. She can't help her. That's it then.' She could barely take it in, let alone accept what it meant.

'It's a blow,' Tom agreed, 'but it may not be as final as you fear. There may be another family member who's a good match.' Mel knew he was forcing himself to stay buoyant for her, and she loved him for it, but was conscious of the time all this was going to take.

Time they didn't have.

'Is that what you really think?' Mel wanted desperately to hang on to the shred of hope he'd offered.

'There's not a lot to go on,' he answered truthfully, 'and yet somehow I believe in this woman. Do you want me to phone her?'

'Yes, it's our only lead. We have to follow it up I suppose.' Mel's tone was half-hearted.

Tom decided to ignore her despondency. 'Shall I suggest we meet? It's always better to talk face to face. Body language, facial expressions – all that can tell you so much. I'll ring her now. I have her mobile number.' He was happier with something positive to do.

'Why are you so convinced it's a woman?'

'Aren't you?'

'Yes, actually. OK, let's do it.' Mel listened impatiently as the ring tone seemed to go on forever. She felt sick with anticipation.

At last the call was picked up. A wary, but well-modulated voice announced 'Arabella Scott.'

Shock waves surged through Mel's body. Arabella Scott – the famous author whose husband is an MP? Surely that couldn't be right?

Chapter 14

Mel still couldn't believe she was speaking to a famous author. 'Hallo,' she said hesitantly. 'This is Mel Stevens.' It sounded strange using her married name after so long. She struggled on. 'I'm ringing in answer to your email.'

The voice at the other end was wary. 'You'll have to give me a bit more to go on. I send emails all the time.'

'I'm sorry.' Mel was so nervous, having pinned all her hopes on this call. She swallowed hard. 'It's about the sick baby.'

'Ohhh...' The word came out on a sigh, like the release of protracted agony. With an effort she continued, 'I didn't dare hope for a reply. I'm so glad you've rung.'

'Naturally, we will need to ask you some questions. We've had some pretty weird replies and we need to establish that you are genuine and not just seeking material for a new book. You are Arabella Scott, the author?'

'What!' the tone was shocked, accusatory even. There was a pause. 'Of course I am, and suspicion can go both ways you know. 'How do I know you're not just trying to extort money from me?'

This wasn't going well. 'I didn't mean to upset you,' Mel said. 'But it's very important that we find the right person. It may be the only hope we have for the child.' Mel kept talking, anxious that Ms Scott didn't hang up. 'You wanted to meet.' Mel tried to keep her voice calm.

'Yes. Where are you? Can you meet me in London?'

Mel's impatience began to show. 'I'm sorry, no. My child is desperately ill in hospital here in France. She can't be moved and there's no way I would leave her.'

'What do you mean 'your child'? I thought you were looking for the child's mother.'

'Oh dear, I'm afraid that just slipped out. I've been caring for Chloe so long I think of her as mine.'

'You've given her a name? Of course you have, Silly of me. I don't seem able to think rationally.'

For the first time Mel felt compassion for this woman, who was known to so many but whose private life seemed to have been almost as complicated as her own.

'I apologize.' Arabella went on. 'It's a pretty name, and to know it makes her real for me. It was my daughter's middle name you see.'

The coincidence made Mel catch her breath, but Ms Scott would prattle on all day if she didn't stop her.

'Can you tell us a bit more about your daughter?'

'I… I'm sorry, it's difficult and rather painful. Do you mind if we talk about it when we meet?'

Mel was still suspicious, and impatient to know more. 'When will you be able to come to France then?' she snapped. 'If you're sincere in your claim to have a connection with Chloe she really does need your help. I can't tell you how urgent the situation is.'

'I'm still not sure what you want from me. Money, I suppose like I guessed before. But I don't care. I'm sure she's my grandchild and I have to see her. I've longed so much for that.'

'Then come quickly,' Mel pleaded.

'I'll leave tonight. I'll tell my husband I'm going off to research my latest book.'

Mel's bubble burst. 'So I was right all along. You've been wasting our time!'

'No! I should have explained better. It's an excuse I use regularly when I want to be away from home. He won't find it unusual or suspect anything.'

'But won't he want to come with you?'

'Good God no.' Her voice was full of bitterness, and yet heavy with the weight of pain it carried. 'He won't be coming. He's too immersed in politics to notice whether I'm there or not.'

Mel didn't know what to say. She couldn't begin to understand the suffering this woman seemed to have burdened alone. 'I'm so sorry,' she managed at last.

'I may not have been able to help my daughter, but perhaps I'll be in time to help her child. Just tell me where to find you and I'll be there.'

Mel gave her the requested details and put the phone down. She turned to Tom. 'I suppose it's what we wanted, but how involved do you think she'll want to be?'

'She sounded pretty genuine to me. I can understand that she didn't feel comfortable about discussing her daughter over the phone.'

Tom was obviously not concerned about the urgency of their situation and was being far too reasonable for Mel.

Oblivious to Mel's torment Tom continued, 'I guess we'll just have to be patient.'

It was too much for Mel. 'But she's famous. She's got plenty of money and can pay for good lawyers to check us out...'

'Calm down love. It wouldn't do us much good if they dug up our recent history. Think about it.'

He was right and Mel knew it, but she was furious. How could he be so rational when Chloe's life depended on what happened next?

Tom hadn't finished. 'Wait and see what she's got to say. We don't even know if...' He stopped just in time.

'Don't even know what? If Chloe is going to live? Go on, admit it. That's what you were going to say, isn't it Well don't. Chloe must come through this.'

Impatiently, she rose from the bench and made her way back to the ward. Tom had no alternative but to follow.

'How is she?' Mel asked the nurse for the thousandth time.

'She's just finished another dose of chemo. It makes her very tired. She will sleep now, probably for a few hours. Sit with her – and call me if you need me.'

Once again Mel took a tiny hand in hers and stroked it gently, talking softly to her all the time. Her lovely child was barely recognisable. Gone were the rosy cheeks and dark curls. If only Tom could have seen her when she was beautiful and full of life, she thought. She brushed a kiss on the pale forehead, where the veins shone indigo through the almost transparent skin. Holding back her tears, she whispered. 'I like to think she knows I'm here, that I love her so much.'

'I'm sure she does,' Tom answered, putting his arm round her shoulder reassuringly.

Mel was not so easily pacified. 'You don't think we're going to lose her?' she asked tremulously.

'She's a strong little soul, thanks to you. She'll fight it.' He was saying all the right things but Mel had the feeling that it didn't matter so much to him whether Chloe won her battle.

He was trying to be positive Mel knew, but she was still full of doubts. 'What if Arabella Scott wants to adopt her? Chloe's her grandchild after all. Even if she pulls through we may have to give her up.'

'It's a possibility, but don't torture yourself with "What ifs". You'd still want Chloe to get well, wouldn't you?'

'Yes,' Mel replied in a small voice, reluctant to own up to the flash of jealousy; the thought that Chloe would grow up with someone else.

'Well then, we have to concentrate on that. On getting her well. Time then to think of what the future holds.' He sounded almost detached, as if he were talking about someone else's anguish.

Tom's way of dealing with any problem had always been to rely on logic. But it seemed so cold when the poor little soul was lying so ill just a couple of feet away. Perhaps Mel was expecting too much of him. How could he love Chloe as much as she did? He scarcely knew her. He hadn't lived with her, watched her develop and grow into the sunny little character that everyone loved.

And yet she didn't want to distance him, make him feel side-lined. She paced the room restlessly. 'I'm sorry,' she said wearily, 'I can't seem to think straight.'

'It's OK. You're exhausted. Can't you try to get some rest? You didn't sleep much last night.'

'How would you know!' The retort was out before she could stop it. 'You seemed to sleep alright.' The accusation, though unspoken hovered in the air between them.

'I was dog tired.'

'You were tired. Don't you think I was tired?' Honestly, he was pathetic, she thought. Where was the longed-for support on which she had so depended?

'I have to stay here,' she told him flatly, resuming her vigil at Chloe's cot side. 'Get well, little one,' she pleaded over and over again, as if her mantra would work a miracle. Totally unaware of time passing, she sank into a void of waiting.

She failed also, to notice Tom slip from the room. It was his return bearing steaming mugs of coffee that hauled her back from the vacuum she'd been sucked into. She must have dozed off. For how long? Her eyes flew to Chloe's cot. Everything was as before. The machines whirred, the screens flickered and Chloe lay still and barely breathing.

'Here, drink this,' Tom said, handing her a mug of coffee.

Suddenly Mel realised how thirsty and - she hated to admit – hungry she was.

As if reading her mind Tom asked, 'How long is it since you ate something? You certainly didn't touch the toast I brought you.'

'I don't remember,' she replied. Time meant nothing to her, except that it dragged on and on, but didn't deliver what she needed to hear.

'Then it's a good job I've brought you a sandwich. Eat,' he commanded, pulling a beautifully wrapped packet from his pocket. *There he goes again,* Mel thought. *Forever practical.* But this time she was grateful.

She looked at the packet. Why were the French so good at this sort of thing? She thought irrationally. Even a packet of sandwiches had to come in a ribboned box. She studied the label. *Poulet a la Normande avec le salade vert.* It sounded good.

But, hungry as she was, her stomach rebelled against the thought of food. 'I'm not sure I can,' she answered.

'You won't be much good to Chloe if you pass out on her.'

Mel was shocked at his tone. Why did men always have to reduce everything to basics? Where was the love, the compassion he'd shown before? She opened the box and nibbled half-heartedly at the sandwich. God, it was delicious.

Her eyes never left Chloe's face as she tucked in. Surprised, she found the box was soon empty. 'How could I have stuffed myself when she's lying there fighting for her life?' she asked Tom.

'She's not going to get better any quicker if you starve herself, honey,' he replied.

Grudgingly, she had to admit he was right. And she would need all her strength to face Arabella Scott tomorrow.

Chapter 15

'Are you OK?' Tom asked her for the umpteenth time. 'What about money? What have you been living on?'

Mel knew he was only making idle conversation; trying to fill in time with his questions. But they irritated her nonetheless. 'We've been all right up to now,' she answered shortly. 'But I'll need to get a job soon, I suppose. My savings are dwindling. I'd been looking around before Chloe became ill, but I haven't been able to think about it lately.' It suddenly felt good to have someone to confide in.

'At least I can help with something to tide us over.' Tom was resorting to practical issues.

For Mel it was not so easy. Perched, trembling, on the edge of her chair in the apartment on Market Square, her mind was on the news from the hospital. It was not good, and here she was, wasting time waiting for this woman she didn't know from Adam.

'Mumma… Mumma…' in her mind she could hear the thin little voice calling for the mother who wasn't there. Chloe had been restless and asking for her all night, the nurse had said on the phone.

'I couldn't have been thinking straight when I talked to Arabella. Why on earth did I give this address instead of asking her to come straight to the hospital? 'she asked.

The time passed painfully slowly, each minute a lifetime away from the precious daughter who needed her.

She joined Tom at the window again. There was still no sign of the mysterious Arabella Scott. 'She's not coming, is she?' Her voice was as thin and brittle as a sheet of mille feuille pastry. 'She's changed her mind.'

Mel saw that Tom was struggling to keep calm himself, but his tone was quiet. 'Why don't you get off to the hospital? I'll wait for the Scott woman. She'll understand. She's just as keen to see Chloe as you are.'

The glance Mel gave him said it all. 'How can she be,' she snapped. 'She doesn't even know her.'

'That's true of course. But Chloe…'

Mel cut in, not wanting to hear what Tom had to say about Chloe being Arabella's flesh and blood. 'You'll come to the hospital as soon as she arrives?'

'Of course. I don't think I'll be able to stop her.' Mel knew he was trying to stay positive, keep the situation hopeful. 'Don't wait any longer. Chloe needs you.'

Mel hesitated for only a second. She'd so wanted to meet Arabella on neutral ground; to be able to get the measure of her away from the charged atmosphere of the hospital but.... 'You're right. Chloe needs me and that's all that matters.' A lightning flash of pain crossed Tom's face and was gone. 'I didn't mean...'

'It's OK. Just go. I can cope here.'

Pausing only to give Tom a grateful kiss, she shrugged on her coat and went. She tried hard to concentrate on her driving, but her mind was so full of questions. Maybe she should have stayed with him. It was plain that his ego had suffered because he'd found himself playing second fiddle to Chloe, a child who wasn't even related. But she'd make it up to him when Chloe was better, she vowed, refusing to accept the possibility that there could be a different outcome.

She tried vainly to push away the rising tide of doubts, but it only seemed to gather force. So much depended on Arabella Scott keeping her word, on her agreeing to the test that would be needed and, most of all getting there in time. These thoughts pounded in Mel's head in an endless ebb and flow. Mel floundered in the choppy water.

Surprised, she found she was already approaching the hospital. Preoccupied as she had been, she must have driven on autopilot. For the life of her, she could remember nothing of the journey. By then, despite stabs of conscience and the worries over Arabella, she'd sorted her priorities. Arabella wouldn't fail her. Chloe was dangerously ill. She was only a baby. Of course she had to come first.

Tom had seen that surely. And the Gods had been with her; seen her here safely. Would they be with Chloe, too? She scaled the stairs two at a time, urgency and fear giving her the energy she lacked.

Bursting through the door to Chloe's room, she was halted by a crescendo of silence. Unnerved, she hurried to her baby. 'She's not...? She's so quiet, and I can't see her breathing...'

The nurse's smile was reassuring. 'She's sleeping, that's all. She was so restless earlier the little pet tired herself out. The doctor prescribed a sedative.'

'Isn't that too much on top of everything else?'

'Dr Millais knows what he's doing.' She put a comforting arm round Mel's shoulder. 'Chloe needs strength if she's to fight this disease,' she said gently.

'I know. I'm sorry I made such a fuss. I panicked.' It was all Mel could manage through the tears of relief.

'Don't worry about it.'

Recovering, Mel asked, 'What's your name?'

'My name is Vivienne.'

'Vivienne, I think Chloe's Grandmother may be coming to visit her shortly. I hope that's all right. She's travelled a long way.' Even to herself she sounded reluctant, the resentment at the intrusion of this stranger on her closeness to Chloe showing through the thin attempt at concealment.

Vivienne's answer was guarded. It was clear she was puzzled by Mel's tone, and sensed that this was not a normal family relationship. But it was not her business. 'She can see Chloe for a just a little while. It's important not to tire her.'

'I understand. Thank you. And thank you for all you're doing for Chloe.' Mel's thanks were inadequate.

'It's OK,' the nurse replied, it's my job,' she added smiling. 'Now I'll leave you with your child. Talk to her. Sing to her. She will hear and know that you are near. Ring the bell if you need me.'

Mel settled into the stillness in the room, comforting now. She felt her heartbeat synchronize with Chloe's and began to relax. While she softly sang the familiar lullabies, she hungrily studied the well-known contours of the baby's face. Though not so rounded and rosy as it used to be, she was still beautiful. She would always be beautiful to Mel. The tiny butterfly hovered on the child's brow like a benediction, a miniature guardian angel sent to watch over her.

Mel should have found that soothing. Perversely, she shivered with apprehension. The guardian angel had fleetingly turned into the angel of death and made her aware of how much she had to lose. Perhaps Arabella Scott would not be able to help?

Not for the first time Mel considered that she may have been sent as a 'plant' to track down the woman who had stolen a child. And, in all of this, there was still the feared outcome that Chloe could die.

Stroking the translucent skin of her child's once chubby cheek, she pondered again on a future that filled her with dread. Chloe had been making such progress before the illness had struck. Her first birthday already behind her, she had been trying to walk and had spoken a few words. How long it would take her to catch up again didn't bear thinking about.

These macabre thoughts were interrupted by a tentative knock on the door. Looking up from her vigil, Mel watched as Tom entered preceded by a pale woman, elegantly dressed but clearly anxious. Mel guessed her age to be around fifty.

She was clearly nervous as Mel rose to greet her. 'You must be Arabella Scott. It's good of you to come so promptly.' The greeting was polite but formal. She tried, with limited success, to inject a degree of warmth into her voice. There was no point in delaying the inevitable. 'Come and meet...Chloe.' She'd been going to say 'your granddaughter' but her lips refused to form the words.

Without answering Arabella crossed to the cot-side. Mel watched, in a confusion of compassion and anxiety, as tears coursed down the newcomer's face. Every last vestige of colour had leached away, making her look like she'd seen a ghost. Concerned she was going to faint, Mel asked, 'Are you OK?'

'What? Oh, yes.' Mel saw her swallow hard as she tried to compose herself. 'The poor darling,' she managed at last. 'I thought I'd prepared myself for this moment, but she looks so frail, so terribly, frighteningly ill. And I feel helpless.'

'It's been a shock for you I should have given you more of a warning. Here, sit down. Tom will bring us some tea.' She knew that Tom, never comfortable with emotional outbursts, would be only too keen to escape the highly charged atmosphere. The door swung closed behind his retreating figure.

Putting her arm around Arabella, Mel felt the shuddering sobs that shook her slender frame.

'I'm so sorry. I've dreamed so long of this moment, but I didn't want to see her like this. You must have been through hell watching her fading away and not being able to help her.'

'Yes,' Mel replied, for it truly had been a living hell.

They were quiet then, each lost in their shattered dreams, each praying for a miracle.

At the same moment they both became aware that Chloe was awake and regarding them with huge, solemn eyes.

'Oh...' Mel heard Arabella's anguished gasp as, in one movement, they both went to Chloe.

'Mama...?'

'Yes, I'm here darling. And your Granny's here to see you, too. You didn't know about her, did you? But she loves you very much.' The words just slipped out unbidden, but suddenly she knew them to be true.

Puzzled, Chloe studied the new face as if searching for some sort of confirmation. Satisfied at last, she stretched out a hand,' Gan,' she said.

In spite of herself, pure jealousy surged through Mel as she watched Arabella seize the little hand eagerly. With her free hand she began to trace the pale brow where the butterfly fluttered. Looking up, she caught Mel's gaze. 'My daughter... Mandy had...' A recognition hovered between them and then they were in each other's arms. Both were sobbing now.

'Mama...?' It was as if Chloe wanted to remind them she was still there. As they turned, they saw a smile hover on the child's face as she stretched both hands out to them. Their eyes met and they felt the unity of their mutual longing. The longing to hold her close and feel the fragile weight of the precious child. Mel thought it was a feeling that would lodge in their memories for evermore. That feeling of love combined with helplessness.

Chloe was more forgiving. They watched the flicker of a smile play on her face as she drifted back to sleep. Silently they kept their vigil. It was all they could give her.

If asked, neither of them would be able to say how long they'd sat there. Time was meaningless. They didn't feel the stiffening of their limbs or hear the rumbles of protest from empty stomachs.

Suddenly, and without warning Mel, acutely tuned to her child, was punched in the chest by the familiar blow of dread. The silence in the room was deafening. Every last breath of air had been sucked from it by her terror. Unaware of what had spooked her she searched Chloe's face for signs of distress, but she was lying peacefully on her side. Mel looked at Arabella for some sort of shared experience of a world tilted on its axis but found none.

Chloe's sparse lashes brushed her pale cheeks, her baby breaths were inaudible. Mentally, Mel fought the threatening demon, knowing that Chloe needed these deep, restorative sleeps if she was to get well again.

The child slumbered on, oblivious to her mother's fears. But she was so still, so very

still.

Chapter 16

'Nurse! Nurse!' Mel screamed. She didn't think to use the bell as instructed but ran to the door and yelled again. 'Nurse!' The newly learned name was forgotten in her panic.

Vivienne was already hurrying towards her. 'What's happened?' she asked. She crossed to Chloe's cot. The child still looked peaceful, but Mel saw the worried look that passed across her face before she slid the calm mask on again. 'I'll get Dr Millais,' she said.

That was all she said but, with a mother's intuition, Mel knew that things must be bad. She needed Tom *now!* Surely it didn't take this long to get the tea he'd offered them?

*****

Tom sat in the hospital cafeteria, a cup of strong coffee cooling in front of him. His head was pounding. Bursts of acute shame were chased by attacks of bravado. In saner moments he berated himself for having let Mel down when she'd needed him so badly. Damn the man, he thought.

But it was no good dishing out blame. That poor bloke in the cafe hadn't known Tom had a problem. No, it was his own stupid fault.

Not for the first time he regretted going for that walk. He'd only meant it to be a short stroll to get some air. To sort things out in his head. He'd always found hospitals to be overheated and claustrophobic.

He didn't think Mel and Arabella would miss him. They were too wrapped up in each other and made him feel like a spare part, an outsider. They were so focussed on that blessed child he may as well not exist. He loved Chloe, of course he did. She was a cute child. But, hang it all, he had needs too.

Deep in thought, he'd somehow found himself out of the hospital grounds and walking along a street lined with a variety of shops. The café had been so colourful and inviting. A quick coffee wouldn't hurt, he'd reasoned.

Unable to find a free table, he'd approached a youngish chap sitting alone. 'May I?' he'd asked, indicating a vacant chair.

'*Mais oui. Asseyez vous mon ami.*' Sit down my friend. I'm celebrating. You must join me.'

'But...' Tom should have said, 'Thanks, I'll just have a coffee with you.' Instead, he watched nervously as his new acquaintance poured a generous measure of red wine for him.

'What are we celebrating? I don't even know your name...'

'*Pardon.* My name is Jean-Claude. And yours?'

'Tom.'

'Ah. You are English. I thought so. Well Tom, today I am a father.' There was such pride in his voice. My beautiful wife had a little girl this morning. She is as lovely as her mother.' His smile would have floodlit The Louvre. 'But my wife, she had a hard time and needs to rest. That's why I was celebrating on my own.' His face clouded momentarily. 'But now I have you.'

A hearty clap on the shoulder nearly sent Tom reeling. 'Yes.' He didn't quite know what to say. 'Well done,' he added as an afterthought. Seeing the stranger's happiness had given him an essence of what it must be like to have fathered your own child and, for a split second, he envied him.

He was taken unawares by Jean-Claude's next question. 'Do you have children?' he asked.

'The child is very ill in the hospital here. It's touch and go whether she will live.'

'*C'est terrible*! But why do you say 'the' child? Why do you not say, 'my son' or my little daughter?'

'It's complicated.' Tom wasn't ready to discuss the subject with this inquisitive Frenchman.

But Jean-Claude hadn't finished. 'You are not the father?'

Reluctantly, Tom was forced to answer. 'No. But I love Chloe. I want her to get well.' He tried to make it sound convincing.

'And you are happy to bring up another man's child? You are a good man.'

Tom knew Jean-Claude meant well, but he was becoming increasingly uncomfortable with the conversation. It had made him question his real feelings; to admit that he was insanely jealous of Mel's preoccupation with the baby.

What had happened to their previous closeness? He loved her so much and wanted her to be happy. But he also longed for his life to go back to how it was: just the two of them. They were enough for each other then. Now he didn't seem to matter to her.

He watched Jean-Claude refill his glass again and again and didn't protest.

No, he was not a good man.

Not a good man at all.

*****

Mel was so wrapped up in her own worry that she'd almost forgotten Arabella. Now she felt guilty as, for the first time she noticed the fear Arabella's eyes betrayed. Mel wished she could offer the comfort her new friend so obviously craved. All they could do was cling to each other as they resumed their vigil at Chloe's side.

Taking the child's hand in her own, Mel felt the icy cold. Desperately, she tried to warm it, brushing a snowfall of kisses on the baby's face as she did so, in the vain hope that Chloe would somehow know she was there and respond with a smile, a look, anything… 'Hold on sweetheart,' she pleaded, 'the doctor's coming.'

On cue, Dr Millais strode into the room. He took one look at the child and Mel saw in his eyes what she already knew. Numb with shock, she watched as he searched for a pulse, for even a tiny flicker of life. There was a long, agonising pause before he turned to the two women. 'I'm so sorry,' he said, 'so very sorry.'

Unable to let go of the last frayed edge of hope Mel whispered, 'What do you mean? There must be something. There *has* to be something you can do.'

'I'm very sorry,' he repeated, 'but I can do nothing more for her.' His sadness was palpable.

'Oh Chloe, not now. Please not when we have a real chance of getting you well.' She was sobbing, knowing full well her pleas were useless.

'Can I hold her?' a small voice, choked with tears, asked.

Mel resented the request bitterly. She could admit that to learn the whereabouts of her granddaughter, to meet her at last, and then, before she'd had the chance to get to know her, to have her snatched away was cruel. Oh yes. She could see that.

But Mel needed time alone with Chloe. She couldn't be expected to share her with a virtual stranger. She may be Chloe's grandmother, but *she* hadn't spent over a year caring for Chloe, loving her. She wanted to wind back the clock, eliminate Arabella from the equation.

The question still hung in the air. Mel looked at the doctor for guidance. Almost imperceptibly he nodded and began to disentangle Chloe from the apparatus around her. Gently, her lifted the child and placed her in Mel's arms. 'I'll be in my office when you're ready,' he said. 'Take as long as you need.'

Mel held Chloe close, shocked by how light the once chubby child had become. She had no more substance than a summer breeze but was still more precious than the most priceless jewel.

She searched every contour of the baby's face, imprinting it on her memory to take out and linger over whenever she needed to. What she saw was not the pale skin stretched thinly over its bony framework, a vision of the old woman she would never become. In her mind was the healthy, glowing plumpness she remembered, would always remember. She brushed a lingering kiss on the marble brow.

At last she turned to Arabella, who had collapsed into a chair. The once tall, elegant woman seemed to have shrunk with the sudden weight of grief. Filled with compassion, Mel went to her and placed the child in her arms.

Through her tears the older woman whispered. 'Goodbye little one. I may not have known you, but I always loved you.' She clasped Chloe's lifeless body to her as if she could never bear to let her go, rocking and crooning: filling these precious minutes with all the pent-up feelings of the last few years.

Mel watched Arabella as she too began to study the child and saw her pale suddenly when she gently touched the butterfly birthmark again.

'What is it?' Mel asked.

'I was remembering.' Arabella went on to explain how the years had rolled back and the child in her arms became for an instant her beloved only child. The child she'd lost. The first thing she'd noticed when they first placed this baby girl in her arms was the butterfly imprint on her brow. The connection broke her heart.

Neither of the women had noticed Tom enter the room. He stood silently watching the scene, swaying slightly, the tray he carried awash with the tea that had spilt as he'd carried from the café in the foyer. Mel ran to him in tears, but recoiled from the smell of liquor on his breath.

'Oh no,' she said. 'Not now Tom.' She was emotionally drained and had longed for his comfort. This was like a slap on the face. Distraught, she punched angrily at him. 'My baby is dead! And all you can do is…' Disgusted, she turned away, still unable to believe that, just when she needed him most, he'd preferred to spend his time with his friend the bottle.

'What have I done now?'

'You don't know? Look at yourself. You're about as much use as empty money box.' She knew it was a stupid, childish analogy, but in her anger and disappointment could think of nothing better.

I've been a fool, she thought. Kidding myself. Ignoring what I knew to be true. Now she had to admit she'd heard the evidence all too often; the slurred words, the excuses, the pleading. If only she'd realised the extent of his problem. 'How could you?' she asked. 'You're pathetic.'

She had no idea what to do. A host of emotions were fighting a battle in her head. She was heartbroken, furious, lonely. And she needed him to be strong for her. But all she could do was watch him make for the door. 'Where do you think you're going? Don't you care at all?'

'Sorry. Need the loo.'

'Go then, and don't come back in a hurry,' she almost screamed after him, unable to believe that he could go.

Defeated, she turned back to Arabella, who was still cradling Chloe.

'Are you OK?' Arabella asked, shooting her a look of sympathy and understanding.

'No, but he's not important at the moment.'

Saying goodbye to Chloe was proving impossibly painful for both of them. They took turns to hold her, stroke her, kiss her pale, pale face, each resenting the relinquishing of the child to the other, but recognising each other's need. At last, exhausted with weeping, they reluctantly placed her back in the cot.

'We should go and see Dr Millais,' Mel said wearily. 'Find out what to do next. Then I'll take you to see my friend Odile.'

'What about your husband?' Arabella asked tentatively, still embarrassed by the earlier scene.

'I don't know where he's gone. He'll have to find his own way back. He's obviously not worried about us at the moment.'

Arabella was not fooled by the retort. She heard the ill-disguised pain in Mel's voice.

Chapter 17

Mel saw the concern on Dr Millais' face as he welcomed the two women into his office and expressed his condolences once more. They were exhausted and she knew it must be written on their faces. But it was her turn to feel concerned when she saw his look become grave. Now he seemed to be studying them, as if weighing something in his mind. At last he spoke.

'This will be hard for you I know, but I'm afraid I have to tell you that there will have to be a post mortem,' he said quietly.

She couldn't believe what she was hearing. 'But why?' she asked. Chloe was very ill. You know that, you were in charge of her care. You said it was touch and go whether she pulled through.' The words died in her throat as an appalling thought struck her. 'You surely don't think we had anything to do with Chloe's death?'

'Of course not.' His reply was swift. 'I'm very sorry, but it's the law. Because no member of medical staff was with your child when she... lost her battle.'

'She died. Why can't you say it? Is it guilt? Should you have done more?' Mel's way of dealing with his implied accusation was to turn it back on him, her face hot with anger. But she saw that he was unperturbed by her outburst.

'I understand your anger. It's been a terrible shock for you. But let me reassure you we did all we could.'

'I know, I know. I'm sorry. It's just so hard to think of her being...' Words were so difficult. The images in her mind too painful to articulate. She looked across at her new friend for support. But Arabella was sitting quietly, hugging herself as if in physical pain, her face wet with silent tears.

Mel could only watch her despair. She had offered Arabella a lifeline, the chance to get to know her granddaughter, only to have it broken by a cruel twist of fate. Now Mel had to watch her drowning, sorrow dragging her down to unfathomable depths that she knew too well herself.

'Arabella, are you alright?' Mel bent over her in concern and saw her reluctance to struggle back to the surface.

'No, not really. I...' She was searching for words. Mel knew she couldn't even begin to describe how she felt, because she understood. She was feeling this conflict of emotions, too.

Mel also knew it had been talk of a post mortem that had caught them both unawares, sent them reeling. Surely, they had suffered enough without prolonging the agony? She forced herself to ask Dr Millais the all-important question. 'How long will it take? Can we set a date for the funeral?'

'We'll try to get it a priority,' her replied apologetically, 'but it's really out of our hands now. The coroner's office will notify you when the body is ready for release.' Mel wished it could have been said more kindly. In all his years of practice he must have had situations like this. Maybe you never got used to it. She knew it must be so much worse when it involved a child, a young child like hers. She briefly, very briefly, wanted to feel sorry for him in that moment, but she was too submerged in her own grief.

The two women rose to leave, still in a state of shock.

'Thank you,' Mel said out of habit as she closed the door behind them.

*****

Coaxed by Mel, Arabella called her husband.

'Is that you Bella?' he asked, in reply to her tentative hello. 'Where the hell are you?'

'I'm in France.'

'What in God's name are you doing there? I'm rushed off my feet. I need you here. Have you forgotten the election is only next week? We have canvassing to do, people to meet.' His voice was raised in anger and Mel could hear every word.

'Oh God, I'm sorry. I'd forgotten it was so near. But I have to stay here for a while,' Bella replied.

'What? What's so bloody important that you can't be here to support me? This is no time to be playing about with your hobby. Your silly books are nothing compared with my political career. Can't you see that?'

Now only the odd word drifted across to where Mel sat, but she saw Bella's face redden with anger.

'No I can't actually.' Bella no longer felt guilty for abandoning him. He'd always belittled her writing. Even now she'd become an award-winning and respected author he still implied she was wasting her time. 'I'm sorry you feel that way. Support counts both ways you know. But as it happens, my being in France has nothing to do with a book Richard. I'm here because your grandchild has just died.' She couldn't be bothered to dress it up for him.

There was silence at the other end. Simmering rage quivered on the line. 'I don't have a grandchild,' he shouted. It was like a slap on the face. 'You've disobeyed me. You've left me in the lurch to go charging off after Amanda's child?'

Shaking now, Arabella stood her ground. 'I never agreed to write off our daughter. That was your decision.'

Once again his raised voice meant that Mel could hear every word. Shocked by the way the phone call was obviously going, and totally embarrassed by being privy to such a private conversation, Mel made to leave the room.

Arabella waved her back. 'It's OK,' she mouthed.

'I never had a child. You couldn't give me one, remember? I always knew taking on someone else's brat would mean trouble, but you couldn't see it.'

Mel watched as her friend's face creased with pain and she had to clutch at the chair, as if she'd been struck. Fighting for composure, she said quietly,

'I needed to see Amanda's child. To hold her and love her - I'd hoped for many years.'

'What utter tosh! I've never heard such romantic twaddle. Do you think you're writing one of your stories?' 'Amanda made her choices,' he continued, 'and they didn't include us. We gave her everything, but she preferred drugs and living in squalor.'

His voice was getting louder and louder.

'We shouldn't have given up on her. It broke my heart.' If Arabella had expected sympathy she was to be disappointed.

'She was no good Bella. And it was obvious that any child of hers would be useless, too.'

Mel was horrified at how callous he was being, and Arabella seemed to have nothing left to say.

'Are you still there? Then stop this nonsense and come back,' he coaxed. 'There's nothing you can do there. Your place is here with me.'

His little-boy-lost act didn't work. 'I'm sorry to disappoint you but I *am* needed here. The girl who's been caring for baby Chloe all this time is distraught. We both are.'

'Don't be ridiculous. You can't be. You didn't know the child.'

'That's a tragedy I have to live with. But there are formalities to sort out. I shall be staying here until after the funeral. I'm sorry, but there it…'

Her apology was cut short. Mel heard him slam the phone down.

Arabella visibly shrank into the chair. She seemed diminished, exhausted.

'He was angry. He'll think differently when he has time to take in what you had to say,' Mel soothed.

'He won't change his mind. He's a politician first and foremost. Nothing is allowed to get in the way. I pretended that things were OK between us but, clearly, they're not and never will be.'

'You can't say that.'

'I can. If you had heard the venom in his voice…'

'I did.' Mel was apologetic.

'How could he be so cruel? He's not the man I married. To think I loved him once. Loved him with all my heart. He's a stranger now.'

Mel watched her eyes fill with tears, but Arabella still needed to talk.

'I was prepared to put our differences to one side and wish him well in the election; tell him we would talk later. But it was clear he doesn't need my good wishes, and he doesn't need *me.*'

'You don't know that.'

'Ruthless men like him, men for whom life is one big performance, will always succeed, no matter who they hurt along the way.'

'You need time to think things through,' Mel suggested, gently.

'I don't,' Arabella said sadly. 'Sad though it is to admit that our marriage has come to an end, the sense of release is palpable. I can never live with him again.' If there had been any doubt in her mind at all, it was erased once and for all by an item in the press a couple of weeks later. Answering a question put to him about females in high ranking positions in politics he replied, 'It's not even worth considering. Women are fickle, they can't be trusted. My own wife has taken herself off to France for no reason that she'll own up to, but it's bound to be another man. She's always had an eye for them.'

'Isn't that a bit harsh?'

'No, it is not. Why else would she leave a good life in London? Leave me? It's not normal behaviour. The woman's mental.'

'You don't mean that.'

'Yes I bloody do. And you can print it.'

Bella should have been shocked, but the overwhelming feeling was regret that she had made such a huge mistake in marrying him.

'Are you really sure?' Mel interjected.

Bella tore the depressing thoughts from her mind and through them in the metaphorical fire.

'Yes I'm more sure of this than of any other decision in my life. And the sense of freedom is elating.'

'But…?'

'No buts. I'm free at last to be my own woman; make my own decisions; live *my* life.'

Chapter 18

Somewhere in the hidden recesses of her mind Mel had stored Chloe's image away, to visit and revisit while she was waiting. Yes, she had been with her darling baby when she'd lost her battle with life. She'd held the precious, almost weightless child in her arms. Yet still her mind refused to acknowledge that the inevitable had happened.

The mind plays strange tricks, for Mel had convinced herself that Chloe was still in the hospital and would soon be restored to her well and happy. Every night she dreamed of their reunion. It gave her hope, got her through those first, dark days that stretched imperceptibly into weeks. Her empty arms ached to hold Chloe again and the dreams let her feel the joyous, substantial weight of her well child, to hear her ready giggle and her first 'mama'.

She knew the police had requested a Post Mortem, but why did it take so long. The waiting was interminable, but not long enough for, when the report came, it stole her dreams. There it was in stark black letters, imprinting themselves in her brain, yet surely referring to some other child? Ugly words. DEATH… CHILDHOOD LEUKAEMIA… BODY CAN NOW BE RELEASED…

They must have sent the report to the wrong person, Mel thought desperately. But gradually she had to admit that her dreams had turned into a nightmare. Chloe was dead. Mel would never again smell that delicious, baby smell, feel her drowsy warmth or sing her the well-practised lullabies. She heard the wild howl of pain, so raw it tore her apart, and realised with a shock it was her own.

It was as if Chloe had died all over again and Mel's pain was even more unbearable the second time around. She thought she would never recover from her grief.

The weeks scuffed along unwillingly, but she was hardly aware of their passing. Though sedated, she could neither eat nor sleep. She lost interest in her appearance. After all, she wasn't going anywhere: she didn't want to see anyone.

Odile did her best to comfort her, but Mel's sorrow had dragged her down to depths so deep that she couldn't be reached. Tom reluctantly took over making arrangements for the funeral, initially concerned about Mel's state of mind. After all, she had already been a bit unhinged when she made herself believe the child was hers, was meant for her even. But he convinced himself that she only needed some time out to come to terms with what had happened and would soon pull round. She was strong.

Mel was grateful to have it taken out of her hands. She couldn't seem to focus on anything other than her loss.

At first, it was an unaccustomed novelty for Tom to be at the hilt again, having people take notice of him as he orchestrated a simple service suitable for such a young child. When Mel showed no signs of improving, he began to lose patience, spending more and more time at the local café, where the company was cheerful and the wine flowed.

Meanwhile, Arabella was trying to cope with her own loss, made worse by the tragedy of never having had the chance to really know her granddaughter before she was cruelly snatched away. It had happened too soon, much too soon. But she acknowledged that, whenever it had happened, it would have been too soon.

She visited Mel often; desperate to learn more about her granddaughter; to feel she'd known her, to have some happy memories, even if they were someone else's. She'd hoped the grief she shared with Mel would unite them and give them strength. But Mel seemed reluctant to part with precious memories and Arabella got very little response to her tentative overtures, always leaving bitterly disappointed.

Eventually, the date of the funeral was set, and it seemed to jolt Mel out of her despondency. When at last the day arrived, she dressed carefully and applied some make up for the first time in weeks.

She clung on to Tom's hand on one side and Arabella's on the other, as the tiny white coffin, so light it needed only one bearer, was carried into the little country church. A single bunch of wild flowers rested on it, pure and innocent like the short life of the much-loved child who had been taken from them.

Time enough for recriminations and accusations, triggered by queries about the required official documentation. She was unsurprised that the papers supplied by the treacherous Sophie Piquet, including the Birth Certificate, had proved useless and berated herself for being so gullible. It was a small comfort that Mme Piquet had been unmasked and would be punished. But she couldn't think about any of that now.

In the picturesque country church, the cold, grey stone ached with emptiness. Only a handful of people were there to say goodbye to Chloe. Mel glanced around. Behind her Odile was sobbing quietly into her lace hankie. Mel felt a flash of guilt at the way she'd neglected her friend and had brushed aside her attempts to offer comfort. Their eyes met and Mel sent her a plea for understanding. A small smile tried to find its way to Odile's lips as she nodded her forgiveness.

Vivienne was there, too. It was kind of her to attend, but Mel was startled to see that Dr Millais had accompanied her.

All these things were noted, but it was as if Mel were someone else, observing, but not part of the scene. She was blessedly numb, incapable of feeling anything anymore. The worst had already happened.

At this moment she didn't even care if they sent her to prison. It would be worth it for the joy Chloe had given her, for at last knowing what it was like to be a mother. Perhaps the officials would understand how desperate she'd been. And they must know that the baby would surely have died long ago, if Mel hadn't rescued her.

The short service was coming to an end. The vicar had given a thoughtful and compassionate eulogy for Chloe, considering neither she nor her family were known to him. Mel had requested that they sing All Things Bright and Beautiful, a hymn not really known in France, but Mel thought it summed up Chloe's short life and the happiness she'd spread around her.

Tom and Arabella were attempting to sing the words and Mel tried to join in, but suddenly it was all too much. Her voice broke as her legs crumpled and she collapsed onto the pew. She wanted to cry out in anguish as the hot tears streamed down her face. She'd thought she'd cried herself dry, but the music had somehow plumbed a hidden well.

She had to escape, to get some air before she fainted. Fighting her way along the pew, she stumbled for the door, uncaring that the mask of control she had slipped in place this morning had fallen badly askew. Vaguely, she registered Tom's look of concern – or was it embarrassment?

She increased her pace. Bursting through the door, she ran for the welcoming shade of the trees that bordered the churchyard. She'd wanted to be strong, thought she could do it. She used to be strong. Once upon a time she could handle anything that was thrown at her. She didn't recognise the emotional wreck she'd become.

On reaching the trees she turned, expecting, needing Tom to have followed her. She wanted to feel the strength of his arms around her, but the churchyard echoed with silence, broken only by her renewed sobs.

In the church Tom was at a loss. He hated these public shows of grief. At Beauchamp, where the male line of the Stevens family had been educated for a hundred years, they had been taught how to handle themselves. The all-important three Cs. Courtesy, Credibility, Composure. These were given equal status with scholarly qualifications.

He'd quickly learned to don the armour of composure when he'd been dumped unceremoniously at the school aged seven. Bewildered, he'd cried himself to sleep for the first week but, finding it got him nowhere, he'd adopted the stiff upper lip that was expected of him. This strategy had served him well in the police force as well. It was only in his private life that the armour refused to fit, leaving him exposed and sometimes vulnerable.

He wondered if that was how Mel was feeling now. He glanced at Arabella for help.

'Go after her,' she mouthed between the words of the hymn.

Feeling conspicuous, Tom strode out of the church. He saw Mel immediately, crouching under a large chestnut tree, her body shaking. He brushed aside the sudden flash of resentment at the intrusion this child had caused in their lives. He barely knew the person his wife had become. Where was the capable girl he'd married?

Of course he didn't like to see her sad. He loved her and wanted to take her in his arms and kiss her pain away. He wanted to wind the clock back to how things used to be.

He was beside her in an instant. Taking her in his arms, he held her close and breathed in the scent of her. Slowly her sobs eased.

Knowing he should say something soothing, he searched for the right words, words that seemed to be hiding themselves in the whisper of the grass around their feet and the rustle of leaves above.

'Perhaps it's for the best,' he said at last. 'She would never have been strong. What chance did she have with a mother addicted to drink and drugs? I've seen it all before.'

Mel recoiled as if stung. Pushing away from his embrace, she looked at him in horror.

Tom was non-plussed. What had he said?

Red hot anger was instantly replaced by a look of utter defeat as Mel spoke. 'If that's what you really feel there's no hope for us,' she said flatly. 'You think you love me, but you don't know me at all.'

'What do you mean?'

'I was desperate to have your child, but it didn't happen and my body was wrecked with trying. You knew I still longed for a child but you refused to consider other options.'

'I…' Tom didn't know what to say.

'You'll never understand the love I had for Chloe, or how it feels to have lost her. I loved her just as much as any child we might have had.'

'How can you say that?'

'Because it's true.'

'But I've tried to understand. I've really tried.' Tom said.

Maybe he really thought he had, Mel thought, but obviously not hard enough. It didn't change anything. 'Well it hasn't worked, has it?' she said sadly, forced to acknowledge the truth, painful though it was. 'Bringing up someone else's child was always going to be too much for your stupid ego. I see that now. You saw it as some sort of slight on your virility. Admit it.'

It was Tom's turn to be shocked. If he were really honest he had to admit she was right.

It was Mel he wanted, without the baggage.

Just him and Mel. Together. 'You've changed,' he said finally.

'We both have,' Mel replied. 'But at last we've been forced to acknowledge how we really feel.'

'What do you mean?'

'I mean that all these years I've cherished the hope that it would all work out for us. Now I know it never will.' Her voice was thick with tears.

'You're upset. You don't know what you're saying. We *can* still make this work.' He was a drowning man clinging to the driftwood of their marriage.

'It's no good Tom. Face it. It's time to say goodbye.' She turned away to hide her tears. The pain was unbearable. She was alone, just when she needed him most. But she couldn't crumble now.

'I can't cope with this. I need a drink,' Tom muttered, before storming away from her.

Mel watched him go. That was it then, she thought, nothing had changed. He'd offered no regrets, no expression of love, no attempt to get her to change her mind. His pretence at caring for her had all been a façade, a ploy to get her back.

It all came back to **him**. His needs. Life on his terms. His addiction.

A drink was all he wanted.

It was his answer to everything.

Chapter 19

In her city days, when life had meant the constant pressure of marketing, sales and deadlines, Mel had longed for a more leisurely life. Never had she thought that the alternative life she craved then could be so cruel. She'd lost the precious child she'd fought so hard to keep, and now she'd lost Tom. Once more, she couldn't eat or sleep, and lost interest in what the future might hold. Her life couldn't get much worse.

But in this she was wrong. The day had come all too soon when Odile had answered the door to find a gendarme standing there. His sidekick stood behind him.

'Madame Dubois, elle habitez ici? Je dois lui parle, s'il vous plait.'

'Oui. Entrer.'

Odile had no choice but to take them to Mel, though she hated seeing her recoil in shock. She longed to stay and give Mel her support, but it was made plain that he wanted to speak to Mel on her own.

He didn't stay long but requested that Mel accompany him to the Gendarmerie where she was charged with wilfully obtaining false documents. Terror-struck, she'd pleaded to be allowed to put her case, but was abruptly silenced and told she would be hearing from them in due course. Meanwhile, she should make the most of her freedom. This last statement was not offered as a gift. The sneer on his face said what he really thought.

In a daze she drifted around the apartment, not caring about her appearance and not answering the door or phone when Odile was out.

She was aware that Odile and Arabella were worried about her, and had flashes of guilt about that but, for the time being she needed to be on her own; to come to terms with what had happened and to mourn.

Post, such as it was, she tossed aside unopened, until she was forced out of her apathy by the official-looking envelope that announced its arrival with a heavy thud. Shaking, she drew out the letter. Her French was good, but the staccato phrases of officialdom didn't make for easy reading. She grabbed the letter and ran downstairs and knocked on Odile's door.

When the door opened she blurted out, 'Odile, this letter just came. I think I'm in trouble. Can you tell me exactly what it says, please?'

'Come in my dear,' Odile said, as she took the proffered letter. She led the way into the salon where Mel was surprised to find Arabella.

At once she jumped up and threw her arms around Mel. 'It's great to see you.'

It felt so good to be in someone's arms, to feel the warmth and to know that someone cared. Mel momentarily forgot about Odile and the fateful letter.

Odile's tactful cough brought her back to reality.

'I'm so sorry,' Mel said, hugging her friend. 'You'd better tell me the worst.'

'It's not good news. The letter invites you to a meeting with the – how you say – the magistrate.'

'Why?'

'It says you are charged with child abduction and obtaining false documents. It is a serious offence.'

'Oh...' The colour blanched from Mel's face as she collapsed into the nearest chair. 'I guessed it would come to this but, in the three months it's taken them to get around to it I pushed it to the back of my mind; even managed to convince myself that perhaps it wasn't going to happen.' Suddenly it was real and Mel's eyes betrayed her fear. 'When do I have to go?'

'Le quatorze Septembre.'

'More delay. Why?' Mel was anxious to get it over with.

'To give you time to find someone to speak for you, to put your case. And you'll need people who know you – friends, a previous employer peut-etre. They'll want to know what kind of person you are.'

'Would you be prepared to speak up for me in court Odile? I probably haven't the right to ask...'

'But of course. I would be honoured. You are a good person, ma cherie and now I know that you trust me. Don't worry, I'll make them believe me.'

'Thank you. I don't deserve it after the way I treated you.'

'Forget it. I have.'

'Will you need anyone else?' a small voice asked.

Mel turned to see Arabella looking uncertainly at her. 'You're offering to do it, too? Can you stay in France that long?'

'If you need me. But I haven't known you long. Will that matter?'

'Arabella, time doesn't matter at all. You know more about me than most. You share my pain. You understand what drove me to it all. I'm humbled that you want to help.'

'I'll do it on one condition.'

Mel's heart sank. 'And that is?' she asked anxiously.

'That you call me Bella. All my friends do.' She smiled as she continued; 'Arabella is only for my agent. He thought it made more of a statement for the book covers.'

Mel knew more than a bit about the pretentiousness of the publishing world, and they shared the wry humour. It certainly relieved the tension. 'Bella. That's sweet of you, thank you,' she said as she turned back to Odile. 'You say I'll need a notaire. Do you know anyone?'

'Mai oui. My brother is a very good lawyer. He will do it.'

'Hadn't you better ask him?'

'Don't worry. It will be OK, as you people say. And when all this is over, we'll have a big party. Then I have a proposition to put to you both.'

'Can't you tell us about it now?'

'It can wait. It will be better for you to have a clear head before making such decisions.'

Mel was intrigued but Odile would not be drawn.

'When you are free we will talk again. I just wanted you to have something positive to focus on.'

'What happens if they lock me up?' Mel had tried not to think about that but perhaps it had to be faced.

Odile was affronted. 'With Roger Matthieu on your side? They wouldn't dare! Do not worry. It will be une pièce de gateau.' She laughed heartily at her joke, and it was infectious, as she'd known it would be.

The lighter atmosphere certainly made Mel feel more optimistic about her future.

*****

The time since that conversation had stretched like an over taut elastic band. All too suddenly it had snapped and Mel didn't feel so light-hearted as she stood in the unfamiliar surroundings of the Magistrate's office.

The Magistrate, Pierre Novin, adapted a serious expression as he outlined the charges. 'Do you realise that your situation is not good?' he asked in fluent English.

'Yes,' replied Mel. There was little else she could say.

'I would like to ask for your leniency,' Roger Matthieu intervened, before continuing. Madame Dubois was under a lot of stress and her health was not good.'

Despite Monsieur Matthieu trying various tactics, the Notaire was still not persuaded.

'I'm afraid that none of this is sufficient reason for breaking the law.' His tone was dismissive, impatient. He turned to Mel. 'Were you aware that you were doing wrong Madame?'

'Well… I suspected Sophie Piquet was not entirely honest – but I was desperate. My child was very ill. Please…'

'I am sorry for you and your child of course. I have studied your case. But I am unable to ignore the fact that you have broken the law. I have no choice but to transfer this charge to the court.'

'Oh, please no. Is there nothing we can do?'

'I'm afraid not. I'm very sorry. You will receive a date for the hearing in due course. Good afternoon.'

*****

Following the meeting with Pierre Novin, Mel had had several meetings with Odile's brother, Roger Matthieu, and had liked his approach. He exuded confidence and, although the case didn't look too good on paper, he wasn't daunted.

'We have a strong case,' he stated firmly. 'I've found some good people willing to vouch for you, including Dr Millais. He volunteered, insisted, in fact.'

There was no time to speak further. Mel should have been reassured by the lawyer's positive attitude but, as she gazed round the court, she was sick with nerves. It didn't help to see Tom lurking by the door.

What's he doing here? She wondered, before acknowledging that of course he would have been called. He was her husband as far as they were concerned.

Now she recalled the day she'd phoned to ask about her share of the house. She'd been determined to be as amicable as possible because she needed the money. Funds were running low and it had been impossible to get a job once rumours of the court case were circulated.

But Tom had known he had the upper hand. He'd hurled obscenities at her until he'd become incoherent and she'd put the phone down in disgust. She'd just have to try again after the court hearing.

Now here he was. Once his presence would have sent her pulses racing. Now she was surprised and saddened that she felt nothing for the dishevelled specimen he'd become. She just hoped he was sober and not out to make trouble.

'All stand.'

Mel's nausea threatened to overcome her as she waited for the judge to make his appearance. Thinking she must be seeing double, she experienced a moment's dizziness as she watched not one, but two imposing men in resplendent robes enter.

Alarmed, she looked questioningly at Roger Matthieu.

'It's OK,' he mouthed back, and Mel tried to stay calm.

The judge who'd led the way rose to his feet to address the court. 'This is an unusual case. The plaintiff is accused of two crimes. The first took place in England and the second here in France. Because the accusations are related, I have invited my counterpart from England, Christopher Darnley to be in the court. I am also grateful for the help of the British Police.'

A buzz of interest went around the room at this announcement.

'Silence. We are ready to begin.'

The rest of the morning went by in a daze for Mel. It was as if she were watching an old movie with someone else in the lead part. She heard herself answer the questions, as truthfully as she could, and yet her voice sounded strangely unfamiliar. She was conscious of brushing away tears as she was forced to remember the day she'd found the pathetic little scrap in the bin-bag. How the newly born infant had been blue with the cold, unclothed and close to death. How she'd caught a glimpse of a thin young woman, little more than a girl, she took to be the baby's mother, but she'd managed to simply disappear. So Mel had warmed the child against her own body, had taken her home, had fed and clothed her and called her Chloe.

'You must have known you were doing wrong.'

'No. If I hadn't cared for her, she would have died. I truly thought I was doing the right thing for the child.'

'But it was someone else's child, wasn't it. You knew that, didn't you?'

'Yes, but she clearly didn't want her and I did. I was desperate for a child. We'd been trying for years. It felt like this child had been given to me. It was my last chance to be a mother.'

There was silence in the court as the counsel consulted his notes. The questions then took a different tack.

'Was anyone with you when you found the infant?'

'No, my husband was away on business. When he phoned that evening I told him all about it. I was so excited. I expected him to be as happy as I was.'

'And was he?'

'No. He was appalled.'

'And why was that?'

'He was a senior policeman and wanted to do what he saw as right. To take the baby to the local hospital.'

'And you disagreed.'

'Yes. I was afraid they would take her away from me. I couldn't bear to let that happen. She was meant to be mine. I loved her from the start, you see.'

'But your husband didn't share your feelings.'

'No.'

'So what did you decide to do?'

Mel was quiet. She knew that, as she'd related her actions on that day they'd sounded slightly irrational. How could she make them understand how badly she needed to keep the baby? She had to try.

'I admit I was torn,' she began. I loved my husband, but he refused to understand. I knew he was due home the following evening so I had to make a prompt decision. I packed up a few things and brought Chloe to France.'

'On the spur of the moment?'

'I was pushed into it,' she replied defensively.

The questioning went on relentlessly, until Mel was dropping with fatigue.

'There will be a two-hour recess. We will resume at 2.00pm. All rise.'

Mel swayed slightly as she struggled to her feet to watch the two judges leave the court.

Chapter 20

Roger Matthieu was waiting for her down in the holding cell. He was furious – or was he anxious? Mel couldn't tell.

'How do you think it's going?' she felt obliged to ask.

His answer was short. 'The break came just in time.'

'What do you mean?'

'I mean, my dear, that you were in danger of incriminating yourself.' The term of endearment was condescending, as if he were talking to a small child.

'I only spoke the truth.'

His voice grew kinder as he said, 'They don't need to know *everything*. What you said didn't do us any favours.'

Mel sighed deeply, still confused as to what she'd done wrong. The legal system was a minefield and she needed a lie down.

But Roger Matthieu hadn't finished. 'You'll be alright if you remember these two things. 1. Don't volunteer anything and 2. Answer their questions as briefly as possible.'

'I'll try,' she replied, because she knew that was what he wanted to hear.

He smiled and left her in peace.

Someone planted a bowl of soup and a hunk of baguette on the table in front of her but, too tired to eat, she pushed it aside, leaned forward and rested her head on her folded arms. She must have slept, because suddenly she was being helped to her feet and led back to court to continue her ordeal.

With a shudder of dread, she heard Tom's name being called. *Please let him be sober,* she prayed.

He was smartly dressed, but something about him made Mel suspect that all was not well. He seemed barely in control. His movements were jerky and irritable and his eyes didn't focus for long. Uneasily, she waited for the questioning to begin.

After the formalities of name address and status, the counsel for the prosecution came straight to the point. 'Mr Stevens, do you love your wife?' he began in French.

Tom was struggling with the language and had to concentrate hard. 'What sort of question is that? Of course I do, always have.' He was immediately belligerent, not a good sign.

'But is it not true that you have been living apart until recently? Why was that?'

'I didn't get that. What did he say?' This was addressed impatiently to the interpreter nearby. The question was quickly translated.

'It was not my choice. She took off and I had no idea where she was,' Tom answered.

'Why would she do that?'

'It's clear she didn't need me. What she wanted was a child – anybody's child.' The words came out in a spurt of venom.

They poured over Mel in shockwaves. Her eyes were full of questions as they met his. She couldn't understand why he had chosen not to mention their years of trying for a child together, making her seem hard and calculating. There was no hint of the love they'd once shared in his cold stare. Why had she got it so wrong? Where was the loving man she'd thought she'd known?

Ignoring Tom's outburst, and with a warning look to him, the questioning continued. 'Did it have to be this way? Couldn't you have a child together?'

This was Tom's opportunity to put the record straight, but he pretended not to understand the question. As it was patiently explained Mel saw Tom's face darken. He was seething with anger and ready to erupt. 'My private life is my affair,' he hissed.

'You will withdraw the last question,' the judge intervened.

The counsel nodded his submission. Turning to Tom he said, 'I'm only trying to establish why your wife was driven to steal another woman's child.'

'I've told you; she was obsessed.'

Mel's own anger was ignited at his tone. She was incensed that he was painting such a ruthless picture of her and unable to understand why he hated her so much. He needed to look at his self-portrait. He would see that it was no masterpiece. This must be the drink talking, turning him into a stranger and making him act like a spoilt child.

Realising that this line of questioning plainly wasn't working, the prosecutor changed tack. 'You say you are a senior policeman.'

'Yes. Well I was.'

'Can you explain for the court?'

'I was suspended from the Force because of all this,' he replied bitterly.

'But you *were* a dedicated policeman.'

'I was a D.C.I. I'd worked bloody hard to get where I was. And for what?'

'It's understandable you're angry, but you must try to control yourself.'

'Control myself! Bloody cheek! You don't know the half of it. She's ruined…'

The prosecutor interrupted, admitting defeat. 'Thank you, Mr Stevens, that will be all,' he said.

Counsel for the defence rose to his feet. 'Mr Stevens, in the early years of your marriage you must have felt close to your wife. You loved each other, yes?'

'I've already said that I love her.' His anger still simmered.

'Then you would have liked to have a child with her?'

'If it had happened. But it didn't. Seven times I got her pregnant. It wasn't my fault that she lost them.'

Mel choked on a sob that was clearly audible in the hushed courtroom. His emotional battering was more painful than the most severe of physical blows.

Defence Counsel looked at her, concerned and questioning.

She nodded for him to continue.

He turned to Tom again. 'You must have been very upset at the loss of all those babies.'

'I dealt with it. She didn't. She moped around the place crying all the time, especially after the last one.'

'But you did your best to comfort her?'

'I paid out thousands of pounds for IVF treatment. But that didn't work either. Her body wasn't up to it, I suppose, must be defective.'

Mel couldn't believe his cruelty. Was that what he'd really felt at the time? It was all too much. She felt the colour drain from her face, and she would have crumbled to the floor but for the strong arm of support she was offered.

'What happened then?'

'I tried to get her to move on, but she was having none of it. I told her she'd feel better if she went back to work. She had a good job at the publishers.'

'And did she consider going back?'

'No. She didn't want to do anything. She just sat and brooded.'

'Isn't it possible she was grieving?' Counsel asked gently.

'How can you grieve for something you've never had?'

'Isn't that the whole point here?' Surely she needed your support and understanding at such a sad time.'

'Well I couldn't stand it. I hated going home. The place was a mess. **She** was a mess. So I just got stuck into my work.'

'You felt you had some status there that you didn't have at home?'

'I deserved some respect.'

'Is it true that you were away from home a great deal?'

'I suppose so. I enjoyed it.'

'You didn't think that your wife might feel neglected?'

'She wouldn't have had time to if she'd gone back to work as I'd suggested. She needed to get out and mix with people again.'

'Thank you, Mr Stevens. I have no further questions.' It was plain that Counsel had heard more than enough.

Relieved, Mel watched Tom walk unsteadily from the court.

The rest of the afternoon went by in a blur. After the emotional tightrope of earlier, Mel was humbled by the glowing testimonials from her friends Odile and Bella.

When asked, Odile had described their meeting, and how easily Mel and Chloe had settled into their new life.

'Is it true to say that you became very close?'

'She was the daughter I never had,' Odile replied simply. 'And little Chloe was a beautiful child. A real credit to her. It was obvious that Amelie – I mean Madame Stevens – loved her very much. Everyone did.'

In turn Bella spoke equally warmly of her new friend.

'You haven't known each other very long and yet your friendship seems very strong. Is there a reason for that?'

Counsel was leading the witness but this time it was waived.'

'We met under very sad circumstances. But I will always be indebted to Mel, Mrs Stevens, for enabling me to know my little granddaughter, even if for far too short a time.'

'How long was that?'

'Sadly, only a few hours, but I was able to hold her and tell her I loved her.' Her voice became husky as she relived the scene. Recovering herself she carried on, 'It was our shared grief that cemented out friendship. We have supported each other through this awful time.'

'But what do you *know* of Mrs Stevens?'

'I know she was a dedicated mother. That Chloe wanted for nothing. And that Mrs Stevens was generous enough to share her sick child with me.' She spoke with emotion and conviction and it seemed to strike a chord of sympathy in the courtroom.

Mel was grateful for these testimonies but saddened when they had both been asked about Tom. Odile described how she had been taken in by his charm initially, but that he'd soon begun to show his true colours.

Bella could only tell of his unforgivable behaviour at the hospital, both to Mel and to the staff.

This was endorsed when the nurse, Vivienne Partout, took the stand. She described Mel as a loving and competent mother who was constantly by her sick child's side, but her husband offered no support and seemed to be at the hospital unwillingly.

Mel was totally amazed when, following the Nurse's testimony, she heard Dr Millais' name called. When questioned he answered clearly and convincingly.

'Were you in charge of the child's care?'

'Yes.'

'Did you know from the start that the baby was very sick and may not survive?'

'Yes. Sadly, she was very weak, but I still wanted to try to get her well. When it was confirmed that it was Leukaemia we were dealing with, I started her on a course of chemotherapy immediately, but she was so young and very ill. However, I still hoped for a miracle.'

'But it didn't happen.'

'No. It was a time of great distress for everyone.'

'How did Mrs Stevens cope?'

'Of course she was very upset. There were plenty of tears, but throughout she had been a devoted mother and, at the end she behaved with dignity. She even remembered to thank me for caring for her child. That meant a lot.' His eyes sought hers when he said this, and Mel felt humbled and rather overwhelmed.

But she was being called to the stand again. The interrogation was never-ending and exhausting, her tension added to by her fear of saying the wrong thing again. The questioning led her back to her brief time with Chloe and caused her to relive the harrowing time of her precious baby's subsequent death.

The disintegration of her marriage following so soon afterwards had been almost too much to bear and, as she was forced to recount these events, she was frequently in tears. Several times the questioning was paused to allow her to regain her composure, resulting in the time being fragmented into short sections that she could cope with.

At the end of it all she still didn't know how it had gone for her. She hoped with all her heart that they'd been able to catch a glimpse of the strong and capable woman underneath the emotional wreck she'd become. Her fear was that in reality they'd only seen her as weak and pathetic – and guilty as charged.

Chapter 21

Exhausted from her day in court, Mel slept surprisingly well. Waking suddenly, thoughts of the day's ordeal leapt into her mind. The charge of obtaining false documents had not yet been addressed and that was the part of the proceedings that especially interested the French court. A wave of nausea swept over her at the possible outcome. She closed her eyes and waited for it to pass, but the panic seemed to have taken up residence. Her whole body was rigid with fear.

She knew there was no way round her stupidity, no excuse. She racked her brain for a way to mitigate her error, but drew a horrible, yawning blank. The hopelessness of it all was like a barren plain stretching into an indeterminate distance and, the more she tried to cross it, the longer her journey became.

It didn't look good. There was no getting away from the fact that she'd stolen a child though, at the time, she'd thought she was doing the best for the child - and herself if she were honest. But then she'd compounded her crime by paying an unscrupulous woman a substantial sum for false papers. Whatever had possessed her to think she could get away with it?

She'd very soon be acquainted with her fate, for now she stood in court once again. It had taken all her willpower to get herself there. She was visibly shaking as she waited for the questioning to begin.

'Mrs Stevens would you tell the court who put you in touch with Sophie Piquet?'

It couldn't have been more direct and Mel was momentarily thrown by the counsel's bluntness and shocked that he should think anyone else was implicated. 'No one,' she replied emphatically.

'You were a stranger in France and you just happened to find someone who could supply you with what you needed?' The level of sarcasm was apparent, but the rapid French was difficult to follow. Her cover of masquerading as a French woman totally thrown by now, she looked to the interpreter for confirmation.

Turning to the prosecuting counsel again, she looked him steadily in the eyes and stated, 'I had no need to involve anyone else.

Madame Piquet came to my apartment. Originally, she said she was looking for a previous tenant, Paul Guillaume, who was in trouble with the police. I've no idea how she knew of my arrival in Mortagne, or that I had a very young baby with me, but she subsequently turned up again and seemed to know all about me.'

'You seriously expect the court to believe that?' It was obvious that he'd made up his own mind about what *he* thought.

'It's true. She appeared very friendly at first. I was lonely and needed all the friends I could get. She said she wanted to help me and that she could get me all the correct papers I would need for myself and Chloe.'

'You weren't suspicious?'

'I had no reason to be. She told me she worked at the Town Hall. She made it seem as though it was part of her job to see that newcomers had the appropriate paperwork.'

'So she got the papers for you?'

'Eventually, but she wanted payment first.' Mel shifted uncomfortably. Told like this it made her look like a gullible fool.

'How much money?'

Mel hesitated. She really didn't want to admit what she'd ended up paying. Reluctantly, she decided that she would have to tell the truth. 'Two thousand Euros in all.' The leech of shame clung to her as if it would never let go.

'The lawyer stared at her in disbelief. 'Where did you get such a large amount?'

'I'd had a good job in England. I had savings,' she replied defiantly.

'And you were happy to give it all to such a woman?'

'I realise it looks ridiculous now. I agree I should have known she was a crook. But at the time I was desperate. I needed the right documents to be able to stay in France.'

'Really.' His expression and derisory tone said it all.

It was obvious that Mel had been lulled into a false sense of hope by the sensitive questioning of her defence counsel the previous day. His emphasis had been on the criminal activities of Sophie Piquet, thus – it had seemed at the time - relieving Mel of a substantial share of the blame. She thought now of the way Mme Piquet had insinuated herself into their lives. It had been a superb piece of acting Mel had to concede. Her offer of friendship had seemed completely genuine. Of course she should have suspected the motive when money was mentioned but Mel was in too far by then.

Mentally, she replayed the scene and saw Sophie's smirk of satisfaction as the cash – she'd insisted on cash – was handed over. If she were honest, she'd felt the first niggles of suspicion then but had brushed them away and prayed that it was a one-off payment, and all would be well. Now she berated herself, although it was all too easy to be wise in hindsight.

It was this awful man chipping away at her fragile hope that had caused her to revisit the time when things had started to go wrong and left her at rock bottom once again. And what had it all been for anyway? She'd lost everything. Chloe, her cherished baby, had been taken from her. There were times when she still felt the weight of the warm little body in her arms and heard the delicious chuckle that resonated of better times. But the sense of loss was always worse afterwards. Her eyes filled with tears as fresh sadness swept over her.

Life had collapsed around her and now she was forced to consider that she would not survive this present torment without a prison sentence. Panic caused bile to rise in her throat and she swallowed hard. She made herself think about an alternative outcome. Of Odile's promised business opportunity and what the venture might be.

'Mrs Stevens, you may sit down.' The voice was loud, as if it were not the first time it had been directed. Like an automaton she obeyed and, as if watching a movie, saw a British Police Officer take the stand.

Only half conscious of the voices that droned on and on in a never-ending loop, she suddenly became aware that a new line of questioning had begun.

'Superintendent Manley, when did you begin to suspect Detective Inspector Stevens had problems?'

'It became obvious that he had developed a curious detachment from his work, most unlike him. I was not the only one to notice the change in his performance.'

'In what way was this noticeable?'

'He'd always had a meticulous, almost obsessional, attention to the details of his job. That's how he'd risen up the ranks at such a young age. But gradually severe errors of judgment were being made.'

'In your opinion what was the cause of this change?'

'I thought he must have something on his mind.'

'I'm told you got on well. Did he never confide in you as to what was troubling him?'

The Inspector looked puzzled. 'I'm sorry…'

'Do you not understand the question?' Without waiting for an answer the Interpreter, who had been kept busy throughout the case, was instructed to translate once again.

'My apologies. No, he did not.'

'Didn't you ask him?'

'On several occasions. He was adamant nothing was wrong.'

'But you weren't convinced.'

'Objection. The witness is being led.'

'Objection over-ruled. Continue.'

'I asked his Sergeant if he knew of anything. At first, he was reluctant to say but, when I probed further, he reluctantly admitted that DCI Stevens had paid him to carry out some private investigations.'

'Please tell the court the nature of these investigations.'

'He was required to make several trips to discover the whereabouts of Stevens' wife and child. This information rang alarm bells.'

'Pardon?' Counsel turned to the interpreter. After a short consultation he was ready to continue.

'You didn't know he was married?'

'Oh yes, I knew that. But I was unaware that he had a child and wondered why he hadn't mentioned it. Most men are only too anxious to show off their offspring.'

This last remark was ignored. 'Surely he must have mentioned that his wife was…away?'

'No, that's the strange thing. He hadn't and they'd always seemed so close.' The officer paused uncertainly.

'That must have puzzled you.'

'Well, I'd known him for a number of years, both as a colleague and socially. It seemed odd that he hadn't mentioned the child. I knew they'd been trying to have one for some time.'

'Did you talk to him about it?'

The Superintendent looked uncomfortable. 'Not immediately,' he admitted.

'Why was that?'

'As his senior officer, but also as a friend, I still hoped he'd come to me for help.'

'What made you change your mind?'

'His health began to deteriorate.'

'In what way?'

'He deteriorated and I didn't think he was fit for duty.'

'Let's not waste the court's time. He had a drink problem, didn't he?'

Manley was still searching for excuses for his colleague but, put so bluntly, he couldn't hedge any longer. 'Yes,' he admitted grudgingly. 'But I thought when he'd resolved his personal difficulties, he'd get over it,'

'But he didn't, did he. So what happened then?'

'He got worse and I had to suspend him. I thought that might bring him to his senses.'

'And did it?'

'No. He was eventually dismissed the Force. Bloody shame. He was a damned good officer. '

'In your opinion, could there have been a different outcome for DCI Stevens?'

'Almost certainly, if he had confided his predicament.'

'What stopped him then?'

'When the whole story finally came out, he made out that this whole sorry business of his wife acquiring a child had been down to her. Not only that but it was a threat to his masculinity, his status as a man, and as an officer even.'

'In what way?'

'The fact that he'd been so successful in his career but couldn't give his wife the child she craved,' Manley explained.

'Did his wife know he felt like that?'

'He made it quite obvious; he said he bitterly resented the "vast sum of money" - his words – he'd spent on failed IVF treatments and said he'd always told her it must be her fault that they couldn't have kids. This matter was discussed in my hearing. It was most awkward.'

The counsel again went into a huddle with the interpreter. In a low voice Mel heard him ask him for a full explanation of what the Inspector had said.

She was glad of the pause. She'd been jolted out of her semi-stupor by the remark about Tom's accusation and asked herself why she hadn't challenged him at the time. The thought that their childlessness may have been Tom's fault after all clamoured in her head. How could he have let her believe otherwise – even insisted on it?

But the interrogation had been steered skilfully back on course.

'Please tell the court what might have happened if Inspector Stevens had opened up to you, or another senior officer, earlier.'

'He would have been given help, both with his addiction – which I strongly believe only got hold of him because of the stressful situation he found himself in - and with his family situation.'

The court was totally unprepared for what came next.

'It's perhaps a little-known fact,' Manley continued, 'that there are precedents where, depending on the circumstances, families have been allowed to keep an abducted child.'

This announcement produced a hum of amazement from the court.

'Order!' barked the Clerk.

The lawyer, whose eyebrows had raised in disbelief at the revelation now recovered himself enough to ask, 'How so?'

'For instance, if, despite our best efforts, no trace of the mother – or any other relative - is found, it has been deemed less of a burden on the state to allow the foundling to remain in the finder's care. With supervision of course,' he added hurriedly.

As the courtroom was cleared for the day, the counsel beamed, inwardly congratulating himself on the expert way he had led up to this denouement, and the desired effect it had had on the court.

Chapter 22

The following day, Mel stumbled into court, neither seeing nor hearing what was going on around her. She was in turmoil but, though her body felt numb, her head pounded with conflicting emotions, brought on by the previous day in court. Throughout the night she'd lain awake tossing and turning on the narrow bed. She went over and over the day in court and was still uncertain of her fate. Hope flashed a bright, momentary flag, only to be felled by despair.

Through this whole traumatic period it had been the dreams of getting back with Tom; of him accepting Chloe when he saw what a lovely child she'd become, that had sustained her. She'd had a vision of the three of them as a happy family unit.

But now she knew she had been deluding herself. Even her dreams had been snatched from her. Now she had nothing. No Chloe, no Tom, just an empty, aching void.

She began to question whether she'd ever really known Tom. He'd certainly never sought the real person she was. Not the woman he fantasised about, but a real woman whose love for him had spilled over to embrace the wider world.

It seemed he didn't know the meaning of the word love. How had she ever imagined that she loved him and he her? The lead in her heart was the result of the sickening realization that the pressure he put on her to report the finding of the baby to the local hospital was not because it was the right thing to do, but because it was his way of getting rid of the problem that threatened to undermine his burgeoning career.

She had to accept that he could never have loved a child that was not his own, especially one of whose background he knew absolutely nothing. Yes, he'd gone through the motions of trying to find Chloe's relatives, but Mel was pretty sure now that he hadn't expected much response.

Looking back through all those years when they'd been trying for a child of their own, he'd appeared to be happy. But he'd been cruelly intolerant of her grief after the repeated miscarriages. With hindsight, he'd seemed almost relieved, brushing her misery aside and telling her to move on.

At last she'd learned the painful truth. He hadn't really wanted the responsibility of fatherhood at all. He didn't want the intrusion in their comfortable lives. What he wanted was the sole right to his wife. And it was the thought of having to share her love with a child that had caused the blinding fury that engulfed him when she'd dared to leave him. It had driven him to the bottle and, powerless to rectify the situation, he wallowed in self-pity.

Mel knew she should be seething with anger at his deceit – and that would surely come – but for now she was overwhelmed with sadness for the love she'd never had.

*****

The courtroom was hushed as those present waited for the verdict. They had listened patiently while the judge had summed up the complicated case.

After a sleepless night Mel had been shocked at the bleached face and hollow eyes that stared back at her from her reflection in the window of the holding cell that morning. Now she stood, trembling with fatigue and anxiety, to hear her fate.

'How do you find the defendant on the charge of obtaining false documents? Guilty or not guilty?' The French judge was addressing the Jury spokesman.

His reply was brief. 'Guilty.'

Mel had resigned herself to that. She knew there was nowhere else it could go. She held her breath as she waited for her sentence.

The judge turned to her. 'You have heard the verdict. It is my duty to see that you are punished.'

Mel nodded, then stood with head bowed, dreading what would come next.

'Because of the immense suffering you have already endured, I want to be lenient. You will spend the minimum term of twenty-eight days in custody.'

A gasp went round the courtroom.

Suddenly losing all feeling in her legs, Mel almost collapsed and had to be supported by the officer who had brought her into court. She knew she should have expected this outcome but had inwardly prayed that somehow there would be an alternative.

All this time the British Judge had sat in silence. Now he nodded to his counterpart, who continued, 'You will return to England to answer the charge of abducting the baby. You know that, don't you?'

Coming straight on top of the previous ultimatum it seemed cruel beyond endurance.

Mel was appalled. She hadn't thought further than getting through the French sentence

'Will I have to serve another prison sentence?' she whispered.

'It's not for me to say. That case will be handled by the British court.'

The judge looked over his spectacles. His expression was grave, but his words were unexpectedly soft after the harshness of what had gone before. 'You must be aware that abducting a child is an extremely serious offence.'

'Yes.' The shadow of her voice seemed to belong to someone else.

'Are you alright Mrs Stevens?'

'Yes. Thank you.'

'Then, with regret, I must tell you that you will soon be contacted by letter, telling you the date that has been set for your hearing.' It seemed so callous to warn her of another possible sentence, when she hadn't yet started this one. But he had no choice. It was his job. In the midst of Mel's anguish she saw his discomfort and sympathy. It gave her strength.

*****

The cell door clanged shut with a hollow finality and the sound wove itself through Mel's body, chilling her very soul. Climbing onto the narrow bed, she curled herself into a foetal arc, clasping her knees to her chest. Silent tears soaked the unforgiving mattress as again and again she asked herself the question *how did it come to this?*

She was unaware how long she'd lain there, face to the wall and gently rocking; vainly seeking some shred of comfort. The metallic grind of the opening door made Mel turn to see a figure in the cell.

'Diner,' a voice snapped. In fractured English the gruff French voice continued, 'Don't get used to room service. Tomorrow you will eat with the others.'

Mel recoiled from the solid woman who stood there, looking as severe as her prison warder's uniform. 'Th...thank you,' she stuttered, because some acknowledgement seemed expected.

The warder gave her a dismissive glance and left.

Mel looked at the food and felt her stomach rebel. She had obviously been an afterthought and the no doubt once acceptable meal was now a congealing mess on the plate, looking like it had been already digested. Some sort of anaemic meat oozed its grease towards a heap of lumpy wallpaper paste and khaki, unrecognisable greens. Heaving, she turned her head away. She wasn't hungry anyway.

But her throat was still dry. She'd been so thirsty that she gulped down half of what she'd mistaken for tea, but turned out to be pathetically weak coffee, before realising how disgusting it was.

Drinking the coffee, particularly on an empty stomach, had been a bad idea. She was now desperate for the loo. She had no idea where the toilets were, or if there were any communal ones. And anyway, she wasn't ready to face the other inmates. Frantically, she looked round the small cell. In one corner she saw a bucket with a makeshift lid. It was obviously what she was meant to use.

Turning her back to the door for a modicum of privacy, she squatted over the bucket. Too late she heard the warder enter the room.

'What's going on here? Toilet block not good enough for you madam?'

'I needed to go urgently and nobody had told me where the toilets were.'

'You could have asked. That thing's only for nights. Now you'll have to go and empty it.' There was a malicious grin on her face. 'Follow me,' she ordered.

Mel felt the hot flush stain her cheeks as she picked up the bucket and carried it through the throng of jeering inmates. Things couldn't get any worse. She'd just have to get through it somehow. But she wouldn't be making that mistake again. She'd keep out of their way.

Chapter 23

She guessed the other inmates found her incommunicative, because she preferred her own company. They continually jostled her, called her coarse names and were only too ready to pick a fight. There was nothing better for some of them than a good brawl. It relieved the monotony, she supposed, and provided some short-lived kudos if they won.

One day she was goaded into losing her temper and answered back. She was taken off guard by the ferocity of the attack that followed.

'Merde! You little shit! You think you're so much better than the rest of us,' the girl yelled as she punched and kicked. Her nickname, Marteau (*hammer),* said it all and she'd built a notorious reputation on the strength of it.

They were forced apart by two warders and, mopping her bloody nose, Mel was marched back to her cell.

'We don't tolerate such behaviour. You will learn,' one of them threatened as the door clanged behind them.

In private she massaged her sore head where a clump of hair had been torn out by the roots, furious that she was being punished for something she hadn't started and was only trying to protect herself.

But the attacks were frequent and shockingly, she became hardened to these outbursts and learned to give as good as she got, earning the grudging respect of a couple of the girls.

She sometimes managed to chat with them when they exercised twice a day, and occasionally in the TV room.

'What's your name?' the one Mel knew as Yvette asked.

'Amelie.'

'You don't mix with the others much, do you. Why are you here?'

'For obtaining false papers for my baby.'

C'est tout? But why did you need these papers?'

'I needed them, that's all.'

Yvette was puzzled. 'I don't understand.'

'It's a long story.' She refused to say more. Friendly as the girl seemed, Mel wasn't naïve. She knew very well that anything she told Yvette would be circulating round the prison before she could blink.

Next day, although Mel knew her French was good, as they all watched TV together, she wondered if they knew, or suspected, she was English and would connect her with the abduction of the English baby they'd heard about.

It was something she dreaded, knowing full well how violent they could be towards those convicted of crimes against children. However, she found the French language reasonably easy to follow and didn't think she'd made any slips that would cause them to connect her with the case.

No sooner had she convinced herself of this than she saw Yvette approaching and prepared herself for more questions.

But not the one she got.

'You're getting out soon, aren't you?

This seemed relatively safe ground, and Mel replied, 'I've got another couple of weeks to do and then it's over. I can't wait.'

'Lucky you. At least you can see the light at the end of the tunnel. I've still got ages to do.' She paused, her eyes on Mel as if summing her up. 'Amelie,' she said tentatively, 'would you do something for me when you get out?'

Mel was wary. 'Depends what it is,' she told Yvette.

'It's my friend's birthday soon. Would you take a little gift to her, please?' Mel hesitated.

'Please. She won't be expecting anything from me as I'm stuck in here. It will be a nice surprise.'

Yvette sounded very convincing, but Mel eyed the small package and, immediately suspicious, stopped herself just in time. Too used to taking people at face value, she'd been on the verge of agreeing to the request. But prison had taught her to be cautious and she wasn't born yesterday. 'Sorry, she said. 'I can't do that.'

'But why? It's not too much to ask.'

'I think it's better if I don't get involved.'

'What do you mean "involved". It's only a present. The girls are right, you're a snob.'

Mel watched her stalk off. Once again, she'd been gullible, greedily accepting Yvette's apparent friendship. But it was now all too obvious that she'd just been grooming her. Her mood plummeted. Yvette had seemed genuine, her only guide through this minefield. Mel clearly had a lot to learn.

She'd had plenty of time to think while she'd been in jail. Time to consider at length what she'd done, and to admit that, from any other person's point of view, her actions had been bizarre. In fact, looked at objectively, even to herself, they had a touch of madness.

It was impossible to explain how, at the time that she'd found Chloe and taken her home, her whole being, body and mind, had been crying out to nurture a child. She hadn't seen it as stealing another woman's baby, more like doing the mother a favour by relieving her of the responsibility of caring for a child she clearly didn't want and was anxious to be rid of. Why else would she have left her in such a place on that bitter March morning?

But Mel had been there and had seized the chance to fill her empty arms. Arms that had ached for so long with the weight of the baby she couldn't have. She still found it hard to shake off the feeling that it had been meant.

And yet…

She was tormented by questions. It sometimes crossed her mind that the mother might have regretted abandoning her child: had longed to hold her, love her? Perhaps Mel, in her own delirious happiness, had robbed her of that chance.

At these times she comforted herself that her spontaneous reaction to Chloe's need – and her own if she were honest – had given the child what she might otherwise have lacked. Her short life had been filled with so much love.

She thought, too, of how Bella would have loved to know her granddaughter. But her daughter had been determined to keep the child a secret. Because of Mel, Bella had at least been able to see Chloe, to hold her close and feel a grandmother's love, albeit far too briefly.

Mel had no way of knowing whether things could have turned out better for Bella. All she knew was that Bella had been remarkably forgiving, grateful even for Mel's intervention. And, against all the odds, they'd become firm friends, tied as they were by a common bond.

And Odile, who had done so much for her had been rewarded so badly: with lies and deceptions, and finally, with the awful realization that she'd harboured and befriended a criminal.

But she, too, had known the pain of losing a child and amazingly had been understanding and forgiving. It made Mel feel ashamed to think of how she'd treated her.

A picture of Tom flashed unbidden into her mind. She felt again how passionately she'd loved him. Once he was her world, and she mourned anew the loss of the love she'd thought she had. She'd had such dreams of their life together. Of a house filled with love – and children, lots of them.

But it had all gone dreadfully wrong. And she still wondered if he'd ever really loved her. She'd desperately hoped he would try to make contact with her here. She knew that some inmates were allowed the occasional visit. But the days dragged by in a monotonous chain with no word from him.

It was still hard to believe that all he'd wanted was a high-flying, reasonably good-looking woman on his arm: an asset to his advancement in the Force, a partner for official occasions. It seemed those heady days she remembered had meant nothing to him.

Mel recalled only too well the conversation they'd had.

'Tom, I'm so sorry I've been unable to give you children,' she'd begun tentatively.

'It doesn't matter,' he'd replied, preoccupied with some report he was reading.

'Well it matters to me. You don't talk about it much. Aren't you sad that we can't have a family?'

'Not specially.'

Mel couldn't tell whether he was playing it down out of deference to her feelings or if he really wasn't concerned. She had to know.

When he'd finally admitted baldly that he'd gone through the repeated tries for children, including the insult of IVF, because if it had given him his own child it might have been bearable. But, other than the wasted expense, it didn't bother him that they hadn't succeeded. 'Kids would hamper our lifestyle anyway,' he'd stated with no regard for Mel's feelings. The shock had hit Mel like a physical blow, and she had wept for the wasted years.

If he could deceive her about something so fundamental there was surely no future for them, she thought, and yet couldn't accept that the love between them had died.

She'd poured all that love on Chloe. And now she was gone, too. What was left? The future was grim.

Some good had to come out of this tragedy. She must make plans for the future. She'd applied a deal of thought to what she could do. Somehow the publishing world had lost its appeal. She was tired of the back-scratching, endless fight for supremacy. She longed to do something more worthwhile and a few days ago she'd come up with an idea that excited her.

Inspired by Chloe's mother, her plan was to set up a home for women who felt they had nowhere to turn when they found they were expecting a child they wouldn't be able to care for. Women who, for a host of different reasons, had been discarded by the baby's father.

She saw it as a refuge. A place where they would not be judged but would feel safe and have support when the time came to make decisions about their lives.

Perhaps it was something Odile would be interested in doing, too. She'd intimated that she would like them to work together in the future. And Bella? Perhaps it was something she could get involved in with them. That is, if she'd still have time to wright her novels.

The more she thought about the plan the more excited about it she became. She couldn't wait to discuss it with her friends. It didn't even cross her mind that, because of her history, she may not be able to work with babies.

Each remaining day in prison was a lifetime. Had her sentence been any longer she thought she'd have gone mad. As it was, there was nothing she could do but will herself to remain calm, stay out of trouble, and mentally count off the remaining days as they limped past.

The food had improved, now that she queued up with the others. At least it was recognisable - hot and not congealed on the plate. Nevertheless, she knew she'd lost a lot of weight and looked forward to one of Odile's nourishing and oh-so-tasty casseroles.

The highlight of Mel's days was that she had access to the prison library. Reading definitely helped to pass the time. It was the regimentation she found most difficult. Each day had a rigid timetable, which only served to accentuate the time to the next ringing of the bell.

Often, she looked back to her first days at the prison. They'd been the worst. She'd inwardly rebelled against being locked up with thieves and murderers but dared not let it show. When allowed, she'd sought solace in her cell; a space that had a tenuous link in her mind with her room at University where she'd initially felt safe.

Here in the prison she'd been unable to eat or sleep. And communal washing had taken a lot of getting used to. But gradually, she'd resigned herself to the situation, learning to tolerate the lack of privacy and at least some of the food. She kept reminding herself that, for her, it was only temporary. She must look forward now, not back.

Never had time gone so slowly but now there were only four days to go, then three…two…one. At last Mel collected her meagre belongings and was escorted to the gate. Warily, she edged through, not knowing quite what to expect.

Maybe it was just the bright sunshine that sent the tears streaming down her face. For a long moment she stood, her face raised to its warmth, eyes closed. When she opened them her two friends were rushing to greet her. The release of tension was like shrugging off a heavy load. Enveloped in warm hugs, she relished this breathing space, an oasis in the unknown desert she had still to cross.

Chapter 24

Taking hold of an arm each, Odile and Bella led Mel away. Bella's car was nearby and soon they were at Odile's house. Mel was ushered into the salon. There she was stopped in her tracks by what she saw. 'Bienvenue – Welcome' proclaimed the bilingual banner straddling the chimneybreast. There were streamers and flowers everywhere, and the table groaned with edible treats of all kinds. Mel was quite overcome.

After the austerity of the prison she found all this abundance hard to take in. Forcing back tears of gratitude, she stuttered, 'I...' She was unable to carry on, to articulate all she was feeling, so she hugged each one of them instead.

'You don't need to say anything. It's just so good to have you home.'

How Mel wished this homecoming was going to be more permanent. She just wanted to sink into the nearest armchair and absorb the familiar, safe feeling of her surroundings. Odile had a gift for making her home warm and inviting. The furnishings were bright and fresh and flowers scented the air.

Mel closed her eyes, wanting to go to sleep and wake up when the hovering ordeal was over. She tried hard to enjoy the spread, and the joy of being back with friends, but was too aware of the impending hearing in England.

With a supreme effort, she pushed that thought to the back of her mind, deciding to make the most of these precious few weeks. After all that had happened, she considered herself lucky to still have her two generous friends.

'You really shouldn't have gone to so much trouble,' she said inadequately.

'Pah! That stuff they give you in prison! Now you must taste real food again.' This was Odile in her element. She liked nothing more than seeing friends enjoy the food she'd prepared.

Mel had thought she would never be hungry again after the monotonous and bland prison food. But she couldn't resist the tasty morsels arranged in front of her. Odile had done them proud.

Little golden pastries glistened with melting cheese and local mushrooms. The crusty bread still had its freshly baked aroma. Platters displayed an assortment of cured meats, and circles of toast spread with tomato and garlic - or home-made pate - they all tempted even the most jaded of palates.

As if all that wasn't enough, there were desserts in abundance. Ruby red jellies made with local wine were set with blueberries, strawberries, and apricots from Odile's store of preserves nestled into crumbly discs of pate sucre, and crisp meringues sat begging to be anointed with a selection of fruits and freshly-whipped cream. Mel's taste buds were working overtime.

*****

That happy day seemed a lifetime ago now, and the intervening weeks had flown. She'd hardly recovered from her time in the French court, and the shock of the sentence, when she'd had to make the journey to England. Now, here she was, enduring the same ordeal all over again in Guildford. It was no easier, except for the slight advantage that she understood the language better.

All the evidence from the French Court had been heard again and Mel, hardened by her spell in the French prison, grew angry at this picture of the pathetic creature that was painted.

It wasn't like that! she wanted to shout but knew she must bite her tongue and wait silently for the verdict.

Judge Christopher Darnley, misinterpreting her flushed face and continued restlessness, looked at her with concern. 'Do you need a break Mrs Stevens?'

'No, I'm alright, thank you.'

'Then I'll continue. Having listened to all the evidence put before this court, it is my belief that you had been weakened both mentally and physically by what had gone before, and consequently were not thinking clearly at the time of the offence.'

Mel was wary. Surely they weren't going to accuse her of being insane? But maybe she had been naïve to think there was any way they would find her not guilty.

Darnley was still speaking. 'I feel that there are extenuating circumstances in this case and that it would not help you to be given another lengthy prison sentence.'

What was he saying? No prison sentence? Mel's heart soared for a microsecond. But he hadn't finished. 'Instead, you will receive treatment in the Patterson Clinic in Marsham Green, not far from here. A place has been booked for you. Do you understand?'

'Yes.' Her head was reeling and she didn't know what to think. She wanted to ask questions. What type of treatment, for example? But she sensed that now wasn't the time. She'd find out soon enough.

There was one question she could ask though. 'How long will I have to be there?'

'Initially for six weeks. Then your case will be re-assessed. It's possible you may need further treatment.'

Each mental blow that was delivered winded Mel, making her double up with pain. Her punishment was far worse than she'd expected and, not for the first time, she wondered what the psychiatrist's report had said about her. Her mood couldn't have been lower, but she had to ask again, 'When will I have to go to this clinic?'

'The sooner the better. You will start treatment next week. Report at the Clinic at 10.00am on Monday.'

The usher rose to dismiss the court, but there was one more question that Mel had to ask.

'Will I be able to return to France afterwards?' she asked quietly.

'As I have said, that is not my decision to make. Your case will have to be reassessed. But I feel you have learned from this experience. My feeling is there should not be a problem.' He was offering her a thread of hope and she was unbelievably grateful.

Her eyes sought out Bella, and Odile, who'd insisted in coming to England for the hearing. They smiled back encouragingly.

Then her eyes flicked to the back of the court, from where a fleeting sound had filtered through the court. Her hand flew to her mouth. Now she was seeing things. The man all eyes turned to was François Millais.

She vaguely recalled giving her permission for him to write a paper on her case. But she had been numb with shock at the time and had promptly forgotten about it. Now she felt absurdly heartened to see him there, even though she knew he was probably only seeing through his study of her case to its conclusion. She resolved to think about the positives. To centre on the time when this whole dreadful ordeal would be over and she could return to her friends and resume normal life.

But first she had to work through the tedious weeks at the Clinic and she had no idea what to expect.

*****

She was soon to find out. She waited nervously in the lounge of the Rehabilitation Clinic in Surrey. It was furnished attractively enough, with its muted colours and comfortable sofas. Everywhere was light and bright, but she had yet to meet the other patients.

On arrival she had been introduced to the four members of staff and told to think of them as friends as well as counsellors. Never one to air her problems with complete strangers, Mel wasn't looking forward to the one-to-one sessions that were intimated. Even less, she dreaded the group therapy sessions that were held each afternoon.

The patients were asked to call the members of staff by their first names, a pseudo friendliness that Mel abhorred.

Jez, a member of the staff she had met on her first day, and an experienced counsellor, had an additional remit to devise joint fitness programmes for the patients' morning sessions. The theory was that, if they felt fitter they would be able to cope better with whatever life had thrown at them. The others: Sarah, Maggie and Ben, took the afternoon group sessions and were on hand for individual advice if requested.

Mel considered that she was in the clinic only to fulfil that part of her sentence. They already knew what had gone on in her life. There was nothing more to add, and she found the group discussions crucifying. She had accepted that what she'd done sounded slightly

138

unhinged, and had long ago come to terms with the fact that, tormented by grief after all the miscarriages and IVF failures, she'd acted irrationally back then.

In spite of all that had happened since; the cruel blows of Chloe's death and Tom's abandonment - from which at the time she'd thought she'd never recover - she felt that, at last, she'd come out a stronger person. She failed to see how they could improve on that here.

Feeling that it wasn't helping her to keep going over old ground in the daily sessions, she asked for a private consultation. To her consternation she was assigned Ben. In retrospect Mel could have kicked herself for not having requested one of the women, who would surely be more sympathetic.

What would a man know about female hormones, the deep longing for a child and the fulfilment of what she'd been created for? After all, the man she loved, and who professed to love her, had failed to understand.

The session began badly. Mel resented Ben's probing and was abrasive and uncommunicative. But slowly and gently Ben drew it all out of her.

'Tell me,' he said, 'if you were faced with the same situation would you do the same again?'

'I'd be tempted,' she replied honestly and without thinking how it might sound. She had vowed to be rational and was annoyed that she'd allowed that to slip out. She should have taken a second or two before answering.

Ben was not perturbed. In fact, he smiled. 'I appreciate your frankness. It would have been so easy to deny it.'

Mel was caught off balance and tried to explain. 'After all, the mother didn't want her and I was desperate. At the time, I honestly thought I was doing her – and everyone else – a favour.' Now she was making things worse, but it was the truth.

'I can understand that,' he said quietly, as his eyes searched her face.

'But I think I'd handle it differently now,' she volunteered. 'With hindsight, I think I'd go through the proper channels. I might still have been allowed to keep the baby if they were unable to find the mother.' She was aware that she was showing vulnerability but felt compelled to speak the truth. 'It's a chance I would have to take. I realise that now.'

Unnerved, she looked away. 'I suppose I've scuppered my chances of getting out of here sometime soon, she stated, defeated.

'I wouldn't say that', Ben answered. 'Your honesty does you credit. We can always tell when patients tell us what they think we want to hear.'

He changed tack. 'Do you have any hope of getting back with your husband?'

'No,' she replied sadly. 'It was never going to work. I thought he loved me, but he loved his work more.'

'Do you still long for a child of your own?'

'Of course, I'd still love to be a mum. But I know what that's like now. I've had Chloe, albeit for far too short a time. Now I've accepted that it's probably never going to happen for me and I have to move on.'

'I believe you worked in Publishing before all this. I have an excellent character reference from your boss. He's happy to have you back. Is that what you want to return to?'

'No, that life has lost its appeal. I have this dream of setting up a home for distressed mothers-to-be. I don't care what their circumstances are. I just want them to know that someone cares.' She paused for breath.

When Ben remained silent she ploughed on. 'And I would love to run an adoption agency along with it. So that those mothers who, for whatever reasons, are unable to keep their babies will know that, not only are they giving their children a better life, but they will come to realise that there are women out there with arms aching with longing for a child to love and they could give them hope.'

It was a long speech and Mel broke off in confusion. She'd got carried away and now she blushed under his scrutiny.

'How do you plan to finance such a scheme, and where?'

'I've thought it through. I would love it to be in France. I still have some savings, and I have good friends there who would put in capital and work with me.'

Ben seemed to be reflecting on something she'd just said. He scribbled something on the pad in front of him.

Mel seized the opportunity to ask the question that was uppermost in her mind. 'Do you think, with my record, I would still have a chance of doing that?' she asked bluntly. She realised that she'd never faced the possibility of being refused permission before and was desperate for his answer.

Ben seemed taken by surprise. It was obvious she wasn't acting on a whim. She'd given the project a great deal of thought. This was not the pie-in-the-sky idea of an unbalanced mind and he had to admire her spirit.

Mistaking Ben's silence as a reluctance to tell her the truth, Mel continued. 'But I definitely don't want to go back to the rat race of inflated egos and deadlines.'

It didn't come out quite as she'd intended. Perhaps she'd gone too far.

'I imagine lots of people come up with impossible ideas,' she said, suddenly deflated, 'but I really mean it. Will you help me?' Oh God, now she was pleading with him. This wasn't going well.

He smiled encouragingly. 'Don't worry. I think you're eminently suitable for what you're suggesting. But it's not my decision. You should prepare yourself for the possibility that the authorities may see things differently.'

Mel knew he was being realistic, but it was like a slap in the face. This dream had given her something to cling to, but it seemed that, though she'd accepted that she wouldn't have children of her own, now she might not even be able to care for other peoples. She knew she wasn't a threat to them. The problem was proving that. A long dispirited sigh escaped her as she asked, 'How long will I have to stay here?'

'You will have to complete the full six weeks, I'm afraid. That's the term of the placement.'

'Oh.'

'What is it that you dislike so much? Don't you get on with your room-mate?'

'Vicky, she's OK, I quite like her.'

'Then what?'

'It's the group sessions. I don't want to go over and over all the awful stuff that's happened. That's all like a bad dream now. What I want is to make a new start.'

'We could find you something else to do in the afternoons. Perhaps you'd like to work in the library? You could continue to see one of us on a one to one basis. How does that sound?'

Mel was so relieved it was hard to find the right words. Her future was still uncertain but at least Ben was prepared to listen. His offer was a start and she was grateful. She would just have to prove she meant business by getting through her term at the clinic as stoically as she could.

'Great,' she managed, smiling for the first time that afternoon.

Chapter 25

Working in the library reminded Mel of how much she loved books: the smell, the feel of the pages rippling through her fingers, the sense of promise each one carried. She became so engrossed in arranging eye-catching displays; re-categorising and re-labelling, she almost forget where she was. Time stopped dragging its feet and eased into a jog.

She began to resent the intrusion of her enjoyment by the afternoon sessions with Ben, but she had to admit that he was a good listener.

'Are you still set on the ideas you had for when you leave here?' he dropped into their conversation one afternoon.

Mel was surprised that he remembered. It had only been part of an informal chat. But she had to admit that she'd thought about little else. 'Oh yes,' she replied. 'It gave me great hope that you thought there would be nothing against me setting up the home and associated adoption agency.'

'I didn't say exactly that. Yes, I agreed that you would do very well with such an idea, but I also said it wasn't down to me and you would have to wait for the authorities' decision.'

A huge stone plummeted to the bottom of Mel's stomach. Ben seemed to be retracting his former statement and was unable to meet her eyes. 'Are you saying now that there might be a problem?' She made herself ask the question.

'You'll have to cross that bridge when the time comes,' he said non-committedly, 'but remember, I did warn you that things may not work out as you wanted.'

Mel was incensed. 'You said no such thing,' she accused him 'You led me to believe it would be OK.' If she were honest, it was all coming back to her, his repeated statement that it wasn't his decision to make. But in her desperate need for her plan to succeed, she had blocked any negatives from her mind. Hugely deflated and near to tears, she made a concentrated study of the pattern on her skirt until she felt able to look at him again. 'Can you tell me why you've changed your opinion?' she asked him. She knew she hadn't been mistaken but, as her anger began to abate, she thought it fair to give him the chance to explain.

'I haven't changed my opinion, but perhaps I was a tad hasty. In my defence, I wanted to give you something positive to latch on to.'

'That wasn't a lot of help if I was likely to get disappointed later, was it,' she replied.

'No. I apologise.'

Mel wasn't about to let him off the hook so easily. 'Call yourself a counsellor and you can't get the basics right. You've left me not knowing what to believe. I have to say I expected more.' With that parting shot she made for the door.

'Wait!' he called after her. But anything further he had to say was lost in the resounding slam of the door.

Out in the corridor Mel paused for breath. She was confused. 'Men!' she shouted as she took off again at some speed, only to cannon into Jez as she rounded the corner.

'Whoa! Where's the fire?' he said, steadying her.

Angrily, she shook herself free.

'Let me make a guess. Not an altogether successful session with Ben?'

The insufferable man was grinning from ear to ear. It was more than Mel could take. What was it with men? Could nothing bruise their over-inflated egos? The hardest frost could not have been more withering than the look she gave Jez as she stalked off.

Back in her room, Mel began to calm down. She tried to work out Ben's real motive in giving her the answer she wanted rather than get her to face reality, and questioned whether she'd over-reacted.

Then she remembered a conversation she'd had with Jez soon after coming to the clinic.

'I believe Ben's been assigned as your therapist. I'd be interested to know how you get on,' he'd said.

He'd smiled as they'd parted, so why was Mel left smarting with indignation? Because everyone seems to want to pry into my business, that's why, she told herself. And now, several weeks after that conversation, she felt like a deflated balloon. Just when she'd thought she was making progress, when the rapport with Ben had boosted her confidence and made her feel that sometimes even dreams were possible, he'd turned out to be a sham.

She pondered on what she was doing here anyway. She longed to be back with Odile, in the bright and airy apartment where her life had centred around Chloe. For a moment she felt the warm weight of the child in her arms, before the ache of her loss settled grey and heavy on her heart once more.

The conversation at dinner that evening passed her by. She was unable to shake off the feeling of hopelessness and ate virtually nothing. Not feeling up to the after-dinner banter, she pleaded a headache and went to her room.

Next day, when she reported for her afternoon session, it was no surprise that Ben had opted out. Instead Jez was waiting for her. It was not a good start.

'If I've got to start all over again with someone new, I'd rather have one of the women,' Mel stated, somewhat peeved.

'They're not free so I'm afraid you're stuck with me.' He smiled, apparently unfazed by her less than encouraging greeting.

'Let's get to work then, shall we?' she interjected, not quite knowing why she felt wrong-footed. 'There's one thing I need to clarify,' she ploughed on, in an effort to cover her confusion. 'Ben has changed the goal posts on his answers to this one, so I want you to be honest.' She hesitated, sensing that she was about to hear bad news. Taking a deep breath she asked, 'What chance do I really have of setting up this home for unmarried mothers and their babies?'

'I was hoping you wouldn't ask me that one. At least not straight away. I have to say it...'

Mel cut in. 'There's a gap that needs to be filled. After all that's gone on, I'd love to feel that I could make a difference to the lives of these women.'

Jez looked at her, his face serious. 'I don't want to be the one telling you this,' he began, 'but, with your history, the chances are slim. It wouldn't be helpful to tell you otherwise, and it's better you know now. I'm sorry.'

'But Ben said...'

Jez shrugged, his look saying the words he couldn't, or wouldn't, articulate. He seemed to be searching for something constructive to say. 'There are other things you're good at,' he offered, knowing that whatever he suggested at this moment would fall far short of the mark. He ploughed on. 'You love books. That much is obvious. I know you've told us you don't want to go back into publishing. It's in your notes. But there must be something else in that line that would interest you. You know the field better than I do.'

Mel was grateful for the lifeline Jez had thrown her, but she wasn't yet ready to consider other options. First, she had to let go of her dream. But, as they continued to talk about the possibilities in the field of books, a glimmer of interest struggled bravely to take hold.

After the initial shock he'd delivered, she had to admire him for the courage he'd shown in getting her to acknowledge the unpalatable truth. It couldn't have been easy, knowing that the news would not endear him to her.

However, this first meeting had been constructive, too, because he hadn't left her in limbo after crushing her dreams. He'd come up with an alternative project for her to think about. He'd obviously done his homework. Maybe at last here was a man she could trust.

Reluctantly, she found herself warming to this quiet man who was so different from the brash persona he projected in the gym. Now, having planted the seed, he let Mel do most of the talking.

He sat quietly, letting Mel process the mixture of thoughts that bombarded her.

Her mind had received the jolt it needed. With a pang, she watched her mental picture of a house full of mothers and babies slide out of focus. She wondered how she would find the strength to give up on her lifelong dream of caring for children, her own or, as it had turned out, other people's.

But she had to try. Now, as the dream faded, she superimposed reality. She had to do something. She had loved working in the clinic's library it's true. So working with books again was a distinct possibility. Perhaps she could set up a specialist library, or open a shop with an added service of sourcing out of print books on request? Her brain buzzed with opportunities that were there for the taking.

Moreover, this was a field that Bella might well be interested in. As an author, she might welcome the chance to be part owner of a bookshop. She would not need to work full time, leaving her free to write.

But what about Odile? Mel had totally forgotten Odile's original proposition. She hadn't even asked her what it entailed. She'd been so taken up with her own ambitions she'd taken for granted Odile's readiness to share them instead of pursuing her own plan. Just like Mel, she'd set her heart on a future with all those babies she'd never had. She may see this alternative as a poor substitute. In any case Mel owed it to her to at least talk about what she'd originally had in mind.

And, if Mel still decided to go ahead with the bookshop idea there were so many decisions to be made. Like where to set up the venture. France or England?

Odile had been so good to her. How could Mel expect her to leave her home? And yet she'd hate to lose touch with her. Oh dear, so many questions to be addressed.

But Mel was well and truly fired up. The seed had been planted and she couldn't wait to discuss the project with her friends and hear what they had to say. She hoped and prayed they would still be on her side. If only she was free to discuss it all with them straight away. If only she wasn't stuck in this god-awful place.

She had three more weeks to endure.

Only three weeks.

A lifetime.

Chapter 26

Time dragged and Mel had too much time to think. It was all too easy to berate herself for her gullibility. Once upon a time she'd been able to sum people up within a few moments of meeting them, but life had dealt her too many hard knocks for them not to have chipped away at her confidence. She didn't seem able to trust her own judgement anymore.

However, she had to start somewhere. She couldn't spend the rest of her life looking back; wondering what might have been. She wouldn't let Tom have that satisfaction. She must move on.

Having made the decision, she was filled with a new strength. Shrugging off her previous despondency, she seized the moment to use her allocated phone call to speak to Odile.

'Amelie!' her friend exclaimed, still clinging to the French name Mel had adopted when she had first come to France. 'It's good to hear your voice. 'How are you, ma petite?'

Mel was so moved by Odile's warmth that she found it hard to continue. 'I'm well, merci,' she managed at last.

'When will you be coming home?'

'I still have a few weeks to go, but I have something to tell you. Something for you to be thinking about.'

'Is it about all those petits enfants? 'Ave you found a nice big house for us?

'Odile, I…' How could she tell her without erasing all her friend's hopes? She'd just have to tell her the truth. 'Odile, I'm so sorry. I've really messed up. Because of what's happened, it seems I won't be able to get permission for the mother and baby home.'

'Oh…'Odile's sigh held all she couldn't say.

Mel felt the weight of her friend's sadness settle in her own chest.

'Ma pauvre, you must be so sad. But what will you do?'

Humbled that Odile had pushed aside her own disappointment in concern for her, Mel had to force her next words round the lump in her throat. 'Someone here has suggested that I might like to work with books again. Not in publishing, but in a more specialised way. Maybe a bookshop? I would love it if you and Bella were still able to join me.' She went on to describe some of the options Jez had mentioned.

There was silence at the other end.

Mel was worried that her news may have been too much for Odile to take in. 'Odile, are you ok? Is Bella there with you?'

'She will be here this evening. She had to go to England for a few days. Be calm, we will talk.'

'Thank you. Now I have to go. I'll ring again at the weekend. I wish so much I could be with you.'

Replacing the receiver hurriedly, she returned to her room and sank onto the bed, head in hands. This was all her own fault and she was appalled at the blow she'd had to deliver to Odile. She wished she could have handled it more sensitively. She'd just have to hope that her friends were still on her side. She'd find out at the weekend.

She had no time to dwell on things; she was due to do her stint in the library. Engrossed in cataloguing some of the books, she was startled when Vicky, her room-mate, collared her.

'I've been given my own room,' she announced excitedly. 'I told Jez you'd been a bit upset lately and he seems to think you need to have some time on your own. I'm going to move my stuff out now.'

Though grateful for her newfound privacy, Mel was puzzled by Vicky's motives. Why had she decided to tell Jez that Mel was upset? She hadn't been acting any differently. And, after all, the reason they were all there was because they'd suffered some trauma in their lives. This sudden change of events was bizarre and Mel couldn't shake off the feeling that something didn't add up.

Increasingly, she sought refuge in her room. But even there she didn't feel safe, constantly sensing an unwanted presence watching her every move. And when she went to the drawer for clean clothes, she had the uncomfortable feeling that someone had been there before her.

The clothes were neatly arranged as usual, and yet there was something not quite right. With a jolt she realised that all the clothes had been colour coded. Bile rose in her throat as she thought of someone going through her clothes, and particularly her underwear; handling it, sorting it and then stowing it back in the drawer.

Surely Vicky couldn't be responsible? What on earth could she be trying to prove? She shuddered at the thought. You're getting paranoid, she chided herself.

In any case, she couldn't do anything about it. Because of what had happened when she'd kidnapped Chloe, they thought she was unhinged already. All she really had to go on was a feeling, a hunch. The only piece of concrete evidence – at least to her – was the perpetrator's obsession with colour. If she mentioned that they really would think she was barmy and would probably say that she had subconsciously arranged things that way herself.

She decided to say nothing and hope it was a one-off incident. Days went by and Mel began to relax. A disco had been arranged at the weekend and they were all looking forward to it. Mel had chosen her favourite top to wear. Its zingy colour always boosted her morale.

As soon as she returned to her room to change for the disco, she noticed a prominent space on the wall facing her. With a shock, she realised that the photo of her graduation was missing. She'd hung it there to remind her that, once upon a time, she'd been capable of great things and it made her think she would be again. But what interest would it be to anyone else?

In a flash, all her old suspicions returned. Feeling nauseous, she sank, shaking, onto the bed. The disco had lost its appeal. She knew she had to confide in someone. Mentally, she questioned whom she could trust enough to take her seriously.

After lunch the next day, she was talking to Karen, another patient who, she'd confided in Mel, had gone to pieces when her husband had run off with her best friend. Mel's words had come tumbling out. 'Karen, have you ever noticed anything missing from your room?' she began, feeling somewhat foolish.

Karen's eyes filled with alarm. 'That doesn't happen here surely?'

'I'm pretty sure something of mine had disappeared recently and, before I go accusing someone, I thought I'd check if anyone else has missed anything.'

'I don't think I've lost anything, but then I've had no reason to check.'

Karen still looked shaken and Mel regretted mentioning the incident. 'Don't worry about it,' she said. 'I expect it's me forgetting where I've put things.' She was relieved to see the anxious look leave Karen's face, but the conversation had got Mel nowhere.

Was someone targeting her after all? She couldn't begin to imagine who would do such a thing, or for what reason. They'd have to be pretty sick.

Perhaps, if she were brave enough, she would mention it to Jez at their next session. As long as he didn't think she'd gone completely mad.

She needn't have worried. Jez put the whole matter in perspective when she told him about it. Some of the people here are very insecure. I makes them act very strangely sometimes. Seeing you making such good progress may have made them envious. Perhaps they 'borrowed' your picture to remind them that they, too, could be successful.

Put like that, it didn't seem threatening at all. But there was still something bothering Mel. 'How did they get the key to my room? I thought our rooms were meant to be private, except for staff. Oh my God!'

'Come on. You're not suspecting a member of staff now. You have more sense than that. There'll be a simple solution, you'll see.'

Although Mel's question hadn't really been addressed, somehow Jez had the knack of making her relax and making her worries seem trivial. 'You're probably right,' she acknowledged, determined not to waste any more time on the recent incidents.

In this new positive mood, Mel began to feel she was getting somewhere in her sessions with Jez. She trusted him and, when he suggested she join some of the others in the gym, she decided to give it a go.

She particularly enjoyed her time in the pool, and her naturally slim physique began to feel more toned. Both physically and mentally she felt better than she had in a long time and was no longer embarrassed by the admiring glances from some of the guys on the course but found herself relaxing and enjoying their company.

Laughter played a big part in her life now. Jez had a wicked sense of humour and was an incorrigible mimic. He had developed this to a fine art, and she was never sure who she was going to find when she reported for her sessions. 'Good morning,' he'd greeted her at today's session.

The high-pitched voice and the affected flick of his hair was the Senior Psychiatrist to a T and had Mel in stitches. It certainly made for a relaxing start. 'You're priceless,' she told him. 'How did you acquire such a gift for the absurd?'

Becoming serious for a second, he replied, 'It's something I cultivated to see me through the more difficult side of life. You should try it, it's good therapy.' His customary infectious grin was back on his face in an instant.

Mel was in a good mood when she made her weekly phone call to Odile.

'How are you?' Mel began.

'Good, thank you. But how are you? I worry about you.'

'I'm OK. Much better in fact. It's all going well here.' She wasn't about to add to Odile's concern by telling her of the strange things that had occurred. And anyway, they seemed insignificant now.

Mel tried to restrain herself while they chatted about what had been going on in the French market town where Odile lived, but she could wait no longer to voice the question that had been on her mind all week. 'Odile, did you get a chance to speak to Bella about the bookshop idea? What did she think? Is she up for it?'

'Slow down ma cherie.' Odile sounded subdued. 'She thinks it's excellent,' she said at last.

'I hoped it would appeal to her. But what about you Odile? You don't seem too happy. It won't be the same without you on board. Are you still on my side?'

'I'll always be on your side; you must know that but...'

'What is it?'

'Bella thinks your new 'venture', as she calls it, should be somewhere like London or Paris. But she only said that about Paris to please me. I'm sure of it.'

'It could easily be run from Paris. I speak the language fluently, and Bella can write anywhere.'

'But she has her contacts in London already: her agent, her publisher. She knows people there. It would be better.'

Mel could almost see the shrug of her friend's shoulders as she conceded defeat.

'You could still come with us Odile.'

'It is kind of you, but I have never left France. It's my home. I can't leave now I'm getting une vielle – an old woman.'

'I can understand your doubts, but it makes me sad to think you won't be with us after all we've been through. Won't you think it over?'

'No. I'm sad also, but I won't change my mind.' Her voice took on a lighter note. 'But of course we won't lose touch. You will still visit.'

Mel was unsure whether this last was a statement or a question. She was quick to reassure her friend. 'Of course I'll visit. You mean such a lot to me and I'll never forget your kindness. Even when you knew I'd deceived you. And you were there to dry my tears when...' She couldn't go on.

'When your dear little one left us,' Odile finished for her. 'That was a sad time for all of us.'

Mel blessed her for that 'your'. She'd loved Chloe as her own and it was a comfort that Odile had seen that. 'Yes,' she admitted.

'You were the family I never had and I knew you were hurting. Bella and I were, too. But you were the one who had cared for her and risked everything to have her with you. You needed your friends and we were glad to be there'.

'I couldn't have got through it all without you, but now...' Mel gave herself a mental shake. 'Now I must try to move on.'

'You will want to talk to Bella, yes?'

'I'll write to her. I'm afraid my allotted phone call time is up. Goodbye Odile. We'll speak again soon.'

There was so much to think about. Deciding to clear her head with a swim before dinner, Mel was deep in thought as she made her way back to her room to collect her swimming things. Opening the door, she stopped dead, as if she'd seen a ghost.

Chapter 27

The swim was forgotten as she stared in disbelief at the chaos. It was a battlefield. The contents of every drawer had been upended on the floor. Torn photos peered through shards of glass left clinging to shattered frames and the bed had been stripped, the sheets torn into ready-made bandages.

In the bathroom, she tiptoed through the spirals of shampoo, talc and nail polish that patterned the floor. One lipsticked word glared back at her from the mirror.

BITCH.

A vivid picture of the aftermath of one of Tom's alcoholic rages flashed into her mind. In a matter of seconds the new found confidence she'd thought she had, crumbled to dust. She swallowed hard on the bile that rose in her throat. Surely Tom hadn't followed her here? But she couldn't think who else would have done this. And yet, out there, was someone who must hate her so much. Why?

What she'd done to trigger such venom she hadn't a clue. A stiff, black coffee might clear her head. She picked her way to the kitchen and waded through the broken china and scattered tea bags wallowing in a lake of milk. Finding a mug that was still almost intact, she made the coffee with shaking hands and contemplated what to do.

She was so angry she wanted to rail against the world but, in a flash of inspiration, she suddenly realised that the best thing to do was… nothing. She would call this unhinged person's bluff, reasoning that, if the one responsible received no reaction from her, perhaps they'd lose interest.

She still thought it was the right decision, even though only days later it seemed to have had the opposite effect. Something had very definitely rattled this psycho's cage. When she switched on her kettle, a massive shock sent her arm into temporary, and very painful spasm. Even getting into bed meant dodging a minefield of drawing pins. The earlier episodes had been just a foretaste of what the perpetrator had in store.

The onslaught didn't let up either. Days later, seizing her towel after a swim, she'd already wrapped it around her, before she realised it was full of tiny pieces of glass that sprinkled the floor like sparkling fragments of confetti. The stunts got more and more bizarre. This sad person was clearly deranged, she thought as she endeavoured to mop up the shards of glass.

Mel patched up the small cuts as best she could. She'd have to hide them under high necks and long sleeves for a few days. She was not about to let someone gloat over the visible signs of what they'd done.

Her nerves were shot, but she still held back from telling anyone what had been happening, fearing that, with her past record, *she* would be the one they thought was mad. So still, in public, she managed to project a sunny disposition, laughing just as hard at Jez's awful jokes and ever helpful and smiling in her tasks in the library.

But it was a terrible strain to stay cheerful. All the time she scanned the faces of those with whom she came in contact, for signs that things may not be as they seemed. Always the tenacious voice of suspicion nagged at the back of her mind and everyone's motives were questioned.

Sometimes she wished that Vicky was still sharing with her. They'd got on so well and maybe Mel would have plucked up courage to talk to her about it all in the privacy of their room. But, since she'd moved out, they seemed to have grown apart, each involved in their separate interests.

Now Karen was the only one she felt she could possibly confide in, but still she held back. It was true their friendship had grown since Mel had taken Karen under her wing, when she'd first arrived at the clinic lonely and bewildered. To some extent this friendship had become a bolster, a safety valve against the unrelenting campaign against her. But, judging by Mel's previous attempt to enlist her help, it was too much for Karen to cope with.

It was so hard not to let these events dominate her life. She was near to breaking point and was afraid to sleep. But still she told herself that, if she could just hang on for one more week, she'd be out of here and they couldn't hurt her.

But she hadn't reckoned on the pent-up fury of that one unbalanced inmate who, for a reason Mel couldn't fathom, decided to take things a step too far.

After going through her accustomed ritual of checking her room and bed for booby traps, Mel had sunk into an exhausted sleep. Only minutes later, it seemed, she awoke gasping for breath. The room was full of smoke and there was an eerie glow all about her. As Mel watched, a ball of flame erupted and carried burning debris to the ceiling. Still fighting for air, Mel crawled to the window and struggled to open it. 'Fire!' she shouted, before running to the kitchen for water to douse the flames.

She couldn't believe that this was another vicious attack on her personally, but she didn't smoke and had no use for matches. There must have been an electrical fault. She looked around for possible sites where the fire might have started.

Horrified, she noticed for the first time that the waste-basket had been pushed against the element of the electric fire Water would be no good.

All rational thought fled. It terrified Mel to think that someone hated her so much they wanted to endanger her life. She felt suffocated, physically and mentally. She had to get out. Cannoning out of the door, she plunged straight into the stone wall of Vicky's solid frame.

'Oh Vicky,' she sobbed, relieved to see her friend.

'Whatever's up?'

'Someone's set fire to my room. Why would they do that?'

Too late, Vicky erased the satisfied smirk from her face. 'Calm down. You're imagining things.'

Stunned by what she'd seen and heard, Mel pulled away. All she'd wanted was a bit of comfort and reassurance. Surely, she must have misinterpreted her ex room-mate's reaction. She decided to give her the benefit of the doubt. Linking arms with her again, she pleaded with her, 'Would you fetch someone for me, please. I called for help, but nothing seems to be happening. I can't deal with the fire on my own.'

'I suppose you'd like me to get Jez,' Vicky sneered. Well, you can fetch him yourself. You think you own him, don't you? Never mind that he was mine before you came.'

'What?' Mel couldn't believe what she was hearing. This new Vicky was a stranger and it sickened her to think she had been taken in by her pretence of friendship. Fury gave Mel new strength as she pummelled Vicky aside. She saw it all now. No wonder Vicky had wanted her own room. How she'd managed to conceal her hatred so well up till now, Mel had no idea, but conceded that she herself had been vulnerable and needy. Vicky had traded on this.

'You need help,' Mel shouted as she turned to make her escape.

Vicky's sick, echoing laugh of victory bombarded her, mingled with the sirens of approaching fire engines.

'She certainly does,' agreed Jez, who'd witnessed the whole scene. Putting his arm around her he added, 'I'll get someone to come and look after you.' I've been concerned for some time that she was unstable and have tried to keep an eye on her. But it's difficult to keep track of patients. I do have other commitments. And I never thought she would go this far.'

'It's not your fault,' Mel whispered. 'Within his comforting arms everything seemed more bearable. Please don't go.'

He looked at her with regret. 'I must,' he said quietly. 'I have to sort this young lady out. I promise someone will be along to help you.' Letting go of Mel, he took a firm hold of Vicky's arm and marched her off to his office.

'You taking me somewhere private?' Vicky smirked. 'I knew it was me you really wanted.'

'I was just doing my job. I was only ever doing my job.'

'You led me on.'

'I was just trying to be friendly.'

'Oh yeah? Well, that bitch won't get away with this!' This last hurled in Mel's direction. 'She's the one that's sick.'

'You've got it all wrong. It was never…' The voices faded as they reached Jez's office and were cocooned inside.

Mel was surprised at the wave of jealousy that swept through her. Until now she'd only ever thought of Jez as a friend. Now she realised that she needed not only his comfort but a whole lot more besides. The only safe place was in his arms. 'Heaven help him if he's in that woman's clutches,' she breathed.

She felt completely drained by these latest developments. She'd come here for help. Instead, she'd been thrown into a madhouse of inflated egos and warped personalities. She came to the conclusion she was the only sane one there.

Chapter 28

The shriek of the fire engine's siren was now deafening. Mel clapped her hands over her ears and screwed her eyes shut, trying to blot out not only the noise that threatened to rent her head in two, but also the awfulness of the whole campaign against her. But the terrible wailing only increased, invading her whole body. With a shock, she realised the dreadful noise, like that of a tortured animal, was coming from within her.

The eggshell veneer of her sanity was too fragile to withstand this latest onslaught and had split apart, exposing the quivering wreck she'd tried so hard to conceal.

She slid down the wall and sat in a crumpled heap on the floor. 'Mum, mum, why aren't you here when I need you?' Never had she missed her mother so much. She would never be able to forgive the reckless driver who had robbed her of her parents. Life would have been so different.

Huge, wracking sobs tore from her with a raw, physical pain. She curled into a ball and rocked her shaking body, trying to ease the tremors that seized her. But it was no good. A crescendo of anguish erupted in a primeval scream before a huge pall of blackness enveloped her.

She awoke in a quiet room whose unrelieved whiteness hurt her eyes. She squinted round the unfamiliar space. Someone was approaching. It looked like a nurse.

'Welcome,' she said. 'You've had a nice sleep dear.'

'My head aches.'

'You've had a nasty experience, and we've kept you sedated for several days to give you some rest. We'll look after you now and soon you'll feel a lot better. Would you like a drink?'

'Drink?' Her brain wouldn't function. 'No…Thank you', she added, because it seemed to be expected. She was neither thirsty nor hungry. She wasn't anything, could feel nothing.

'Mr Matthews will be in to see you after the doctor's been. He wanted to be told when you woke up.'

'Mr Matthews?'

'I think he said his name was Jez. He said to tell you he'd be in.'

'Oh.' The effort of conversation was too much She closed her eyes on the tears that slid silently from under her eyelids. Turning away, she felt their dampness on the pillow under her cheek.

So they'd put her in hospital. But it didn't matter. Nothing did anymore. Inside she was in a far worse place. Worse than being betrayed by the love of her life. Worse than losing her precious baby. Worse, even, than the terrible French prison she'd endured, for now she was in a prison from which she felt she could never escape.

Mel was unable to recognise the person that now inhabited her body. Violent, uncontrollable tremors shook her. A rising panic took hold, filling every space, every fold of her body. This couldn't be her. She was someone who coped.

'Escape,' an internal voice demanded. 'You must escape.'

She slid out of bed and tried to run on legs that would not obey her. She collapsed crying with exhaustion. She felt a sharp prick in her arm and someone leading her gently back to bed.

'You'll sleep now dear. It's what you nee…'

The sentence trailed off as oblivion rescued her.

This was to be the pattern of her days. Mel supposed there were days. Days and nights were the same, grey and endless. Food didn't interest her and she was unable to sleep unless drugged. Her heart raced, her stomach thought it was on a rough sea and she was cold, so cold.

They said her friends came to visit, but she had no recollection of it and didn't want to see anyone anyway. She'd had enough. She just wanted it all to be over and the sooner the better. It would be a kindness to let her die.

A succession of doctors came. They asked the same questions. Questions that she couldn't be bothered to answer.

'Just give me some pills,' she pleaded. 'Put me out of this misery.'

'You're having a bad time,' they said, as if she didn't know. 'But it won't last forever. You have to believe that.'

She didn't, but she let them carry on, too tired to object.

'Your mind can get sick just like the rest of your body,' they said. 'Trauma can cause an imbalance of the chemicals that usually keep your brain stable. It just needs help to recover.'

No matter what they said, however they tried to wrap it up, she couldn't accept their reasoning. There was only one phrase that threw her a lifebelt and she clung on with the last of her strength.

'I promise you; you will get better.'

She repeated it to herself several times a day, trying to convince herself that there was a grain of truth in it. Until one day when she woke, she felt hungry. It was an unfamiliar feeling and she hoped it was a good sign. So, when she saw a nurse approaching, she called out, 'Could I have a piece of toast please?'

'Of course you can. Would you like a cup of tea as well?'

'Yes please.' Her answer surprised her.

As she sat eating and drinking, savouring every mouthful, a familiar face appeared at the door of the ward.

'May I come in?'

Jez. Considering she hadn't been interested in seeing anyone since she'd been in the hospital, Mel was ridiculously pleased to see him. She was suddenly tongue-tied. She'd forgotten how to make conversation and was embarrassed by what she must look like. 'Yes,' she managed.

'It's good to see you tucking into some food at last. Keep this up and they'll be able to take the drip out.'

'How long have I been here?'

'A few weeks.'

'Is that all. It seems like a lifetime.'

'Never mind. Let's concentrate on getting you better now you're back with us.'

'Have you been before?'

'Only every day. I knew you'd pull round given time and I wanted to be here.'

'I wish I had your confidence.'

'You've been ill. I'm surprised it hadn't happened before with all you've been through. But you're strong. That's why you managed to fend off all the blows life threw at you.'

'I don't feel strong.'

'You will. The fire was one thing too many, that's all, and the shock of it released all the pain you'd suppressed for years.'

'It felt like a dam bursting,' Mel admitted self-consciously.

'That's a good analogy. And it was bound to happen sometime. But now you need to get some more rest.'

There was so much she wanted to ask him but couldn't summon the energy. 'I do feel a bit tired,' she conceded. 'Will you come again tomorrow?'

'You bet!'

Chapter 29

Mel leaned back on her pillows and closed her eyes, feeling more relaxed than she had for... how long? Now she realised she'd been tense all her life. Orphaned at twelve, she had been left bewildered. All she'd wanted was to be loved.

He life was littered with the mistakes she'd made, and recent history only lengthened that list.

When she'd met Tom she thought she'd found the someone special she'd been searching for. She'd loved him with her whole being, but he'd been an imposter, just playing at being her lover, husband and soul mate. He hadn't meant any of it and had left her life in shreds.

He'd become more interested in his work and less in her. When she had been unable to conceive it had brought all the old anxieties to the fore again. The fact that Tom couldn't understand her pain had compounded her isolation.

Finding Chloe had been her salvation. At last she had someone to love and to love her unconditionally. But Fate continued his vicious vendetta, and this latest torment was one from which she thought she'd never recover.

When Chloe became sick, she'd turned to Tom for love and support. Instead, he'd brought his own problems. His reliance on the bottle had turned him into someone unrecognisable. It was during one of his drunken rages that his true feelings came out, revealing his resentment at Chloe's intrusion in his life and his relief at her death.

Already grieving, Mel felt an almost physical blow as Tom threatened her self-control with his alcohol-fuelled revelations, leaving her questioning her judgement in falling for such a monster.

She thought fleetingly of the other child she had had briefly, the result of yet another love affair gone wrong. But it hadn't mattered that Julie had been a mistake. Mel had loved her unconditionally. But even that love had been taken from her when her cold-hearted aunt had forced her to give the child up. She'd been more interested in shielding herself from the shame of housing an unmarried mother than Mel's desperate pleas to keep the child.

But then there was Jez. He knew everything about her, had seen her at her worst and still stuck around, making her think that he was the one man in a million who was a genuine friend. She was looking forward to his next visit.

Meanwhile, her thoughts turned to Odile and Bella. Through the haze of sedation, it hadn't registered that Odile was in England. She was humbled to know that Odile had left her home – a rare occurrence - and made the long journey just for her. She assumed she was staying with Bella but knew Odile wouldn't want to be away too long.

How good it felt to have these two friends. She felt so bad that she'd refused to see them and prayed that they would understand that it was the nature of her illness, and not any change in their friendship, that was the cause. Now she worried that she'd taken so long to come to her senses that Odile would have returned home before she could thank her. This was no way to treat the woman who had given her a home and forgiven her deceit. It took a true friend to do that.

And Bella had put aside the writing of her latest book to support her, ignoring deadlines just to be there for her. Mel pulled the comforting blanket of these warm friendships close. She smiled as she thought of the good times they'd shared. Yes, there had been some painful ones, and her empty arms ached with the weight of her broken dreams. But it would do her no good to dwell on those. She must try to be positive and look to the future.

Already, she longed to be back with her friends and yet, whenever she thought of leaving the safety of the hospital, the leeches of all her old fears latched on and began to suck away all her brave resolve, leaving her shivering and helpless once again. She was obviously not as mentally strong as she thought, and was frightened by doubts that she ever would be.

It was obvious she was trying to push herself too hard too soon. She must learn to be patient and give herself time to recover. She would take it slowly and attempt a little more each day.

As her appetite improved and she began to regain strength, she began to take short walks around the wards. She handed out drinks and meals and forced herself to chat to the other patients, most of whom were in a considerably worse state than she. How she longed to be free of these walls. She would find the courage from somewhere.

To her joy, Odile and Bella visited regularly. After an initial awkwardness, the conversation flew.

'How are you ma Cherie?' Odile wanted to know.

'I'm getting there at last,' Mel replied. After scrambling up the steep sides of the darkest, bottomless pit, Mel certainly wasn't going to dwell on it now. But Odile was looking puzzled.

'Where is it you are getting? They are moving you to somewhere else?'

Bella and Mel laughed.

'She means she's getting better,' Bella explained.

The frown left Odile's forehead. 'Ah bon. So when are you going to be with us?'

'I'm still not sure. But soon, I hope you can stay on a little longer. I'd love us to spend a few days together before you have to return to France.'

'Bella has said I can stay as long as I like, and I'm beginning to like London. Mon Dieu! I didn't think I would ever be saying that!' She smiled mischievously, knowing full well Bella thought of London as the centre of the universe.

But Bella wouldn't be drawn. Turning to Mel she said, 'It's so good to see you looking brighter. Just keep concentrating on getting better. We'll be waiting.'

Mel waved as they left the room, feeling greatly cheered by their support. Closing her eyes she relaxed, really relaxed, for the first time in months and allowed her mind to drift.

She was smiling when Jez put his head round the door. 'I saw your friends leaving. I hope they didn't tire you too much.'

'I'm fine. Come in.'

Mel lost all sense of time as they chatted about this and that. Jez always had some funny anecdotes about life at the clinic. Today he'd been practising his impression of the principal, Nigel Harrington. She watched as he smoothed back his hair, adopted the customary furrowed brow, straightened his imaginary tie and strutted about the ward, head forward, hands behind his back like a worried hen.

'This morning,' he began, in an uncannily recognisable, slightly quavering voice, 'I've called you together to discuss the difficult problem of how to proceed with Scooter Bailey's programme of treatment. 'Stupid name,' he muttered, still in character. 'Whatever we try to do for him, he refuses to respond. I want to hear your comments.'

'I've got one Nigel.' Jez had adopted Ben's voice now. 'He's winding you up, like he always does. You must have been aware of that. Underneath his façade he's a good bloke. I've had some insightful conversations with him.'

'Come on Ben. As counsellors, we see more of the inmates than Nigel does. We can see that's what Scooter's doing. Obviously, Nigel can't.' At first sounding sincere, there was a distinct echo of Ben's sentiment lodged in Jez's words.

In Nigel Harrington mode, the weight on the pseudo principal's shoulders increased visibly. 'I will not be made a fool of,' he retorted. Once again, the hair smoothing, the tie adjusting, the clearing of throat. 'I… Apparently lost for words, as Nigel frequently was, he stalked through the door and slammed it behind him.

Mel couldn't help laughing at Jez's skill in such a perfect impersonation, but her face clouded as she was reminded of the place that seemed to have done her more harm than good.

'Is something troubling you?' Jez asked.

'Will I have to go back there when I leave here? It has such unhappy memories I feel nervous just thinking about it.'

'I can understand that. However, your case came up at the last meeting. They respected my opinion that it would be contrary to your recovery to return there. Because of that, we will arrange for you to have an assessment before you leave here.'

'What then?'

'I'm hopeful that you will be released.'

'It certainly feels like I've been in prison,' Mel replied.

'Sorry, bad choice of words. Just the terminology you get used to in this line of work. What I mean is, providing you have someone living with you when you leave, you should be able to return home.'

'Home? I don't know where that is any more.' Without warning his words had snatched the oars from her hands and left her adrift on a vast, empty ocean.

'Oh God. I'm making things worse and I'm supposed to be delivering good news here. You don't need to worry about leaving here. Your friends said they will look after you for as long as you need them. They're good people.'

'I know. I owe them a lot.'

'There's a couple of other things.'

Mel looked at him in alarm.

'When I arrived you were sleeping. I didn't want to disturb you, so I just sat by your bed. You seemed to be dreaming and kept calling for Julie. Who's Julie? You haven't mentioned her before.'

'Oh... ' Mel felt a guilty flush warm her face and travel to every corner of her body. 'I...' She didn't know where to start. This was something she'd buried deep in her subconscious for years. She'd never talked about it to anyone. Now the raw wound had been slashed open once more. Her eyes filled with tears.'

'What is it?' Jez was clearly uncomfortable. 'I didn't mean to upset you.'

'It's something that happened a long time ago. I've tried not to think about it.'

'Might it make you feel better to tell me about it?'

Mel nodded, suddenly needing to tell someone. 'When I was a teenager I had a baby. I thought the father loved me, but he refused to admit that the child was his. The aunt I was living with made me give my little girl up for adoption.'

'That's cruel.'

As if Jez hadn't spoken, Mel carried on, 'I was heartbroken, but I was forbidden to tell anyone. The worst thing is, I never knew what happened to her.'

'That's a dreadful thing to do and explains a lot.'

'I've learnt to live with it.'

'You shouldn't have to. It's a huge burden to carry.'

'I do feel better for talking about it.'

'Good, because I have another thing to ask you.'

Mel was wary.' What's that?'

'Calm down. I only wanted to say that, when all this is over, I hope we can still be friends?'

She tried to read his expression. Was friendship all he wanted? She wasn't ready for another relationship and didn't want any further complications. But she needed all the friends she could get, so she'd have to take the chance. 'I'd like that,' she replied.

Chapter 30

Now that she was regaining her strength, Mel felt like a captured bird, flapping her wings against the confines of her enforced environment. Only the continued visits from her friends relieved the boredom of hospital routine.

In between she read snatches of a book Bella had brought in. Her concentration wasn't great, but gradually The Summer Book, a story set on a small island off Finland, wove a kind of magic that kept her reading on. The developing relationship between grandmother and granddaughter made her yearn for such closeness. Yet the story, punctuated by touches of gentle humour, was so simply told and their surroundings so beautifully described, it brought the kind of peace she needed.

It was good to hold a book in her hands again. She missed that aspect of her job in the clinic's library and before that in her job at the publishing company. She breathed in the unique scent of print and paper and began mentally forming a business plan for her new venture. There would be the inevitable cost involved in setting up the proposed bookshop, and she acknowledged that she would have difficulty getting a loan from the bank in view of her recent history.

Yes, she'd had the money from the sale of the house. The house she'd shared with Tom and he had sold without even consulting her, so that all her memories had been erased, all the reminders of Chloe's very early life wiped out. But never forgotten.

In her depressed state she'd even wondered if she would see her share and, although it seemed a large amount, the money wouldn't last long. She couldn't invest all of it in the business. Her recent experiences had told her she needed money to live on.

Bella had told her money would not be a problem, and Odile had promised a contribution from her savings. But Mel's pride wouldn't let her accept their help without being able to donate a substantial sum herself. In the past couple of years, while she hadn't been working, her bank balance had been severely eroded. And her eventual share from the house sale had rescued her just in time.

She needed to start earning some money. With the bolstered confidence that life in the hospital had inspired, it was all too easy to think she could move mountains if necessary. But she was also aware that she shouldn't push herself too hard and undo all the work they had done with her. However, there must be some kind of temporary work she could do until the new venture got going.

As the day of her assessment drew near, she confessed to Jez that she was more than a little worried. 'My mouth seems to have a life of its own – you know that,' she said ruefully. 'I'm so afraid of saying the wrong thing and I don't want to jeopardise my chances of getting out of here.'

'Just relax,' he countered. 'Be truthful and natural, that's all they want. You'll be fine.'

'I wish I could believe you.'

'Tell you what,' Jez replied with a grin. 'When you get the all clear, we'll celebrate with a pub lunch – my treat.'

The idea of being able to enjoy something so simple, something that most people took for granted, suddenly brought tears to Mel's eyes. She'd forgotten what normal life was like and couldn't wait to be part of it again. She was so grateful for Jez's faith in the outcome of her assessment. It gave her hope.

His words echoed in her head as she sat waiting two days later. *'You'll be fine, you'll be fine, you'll be fine.'* They were like an echo of Mother Julian of Norwich: *'All will be well, and all will be well, and all manner of things will be well.'* She repeated Jez's words, over and over in a silent mantra, willing them to be true. Her eyes closed in concentration so that she failed to see the door to the interview room open.

'Come in,' the voice from the smartly suited guy was gentle, trained. She'd expected brusqueness, or even a forced jovialness. But gentle? Somehow it seemed false to Mel, but she still struggled to make her legs obey her as she followed him into the sunny room.

'Take a seat. I'm Dr Selberg.' The woman seated behind the desk smiled, 'This is my colleague Peter Tennyson,' she volunteered. That she was a female had surprised Mel, but immediately made the situation more bearable somehow. There was a trace of an accent in Dr Selberg's words. Austrian? Scandinavian? Mel couldn't quite place it but, wherever it was from, for Mel it had an instantly soothing effect. She guessed it had been cultivated over a number of years, she assumed somewhat cynically. But she still found it easier than she'd expected to answer her questions. It was like talking to a trusted friend.

Mel instantly got the impression that Peter Tennyson wasn't too happy being second in command to a female and was determined to take the lead in the conversation.

'What makes you think you're ready to leave here?' His sudden interjection was jarring, and his forthright question momentarily threw Mel.

'Well I...' She clung grimly to the threads of composure that threatened to snap at any moment. She began again. 'I think I should have sought help some time ago,' she admitted frankly. 'Looking back, I think I'd been heading for some sort of breakdown for a while and it had to happen.' She paused for breath. 'But I've learned that there's a limit to how much bad stuff you can submerge, and I know now I needed help to deal with it.' *Oh God,* she thought, *I've well and truly blown it.*

Tennyson seemed unperturbed and gave a self-satisfied smile. 'So, tell me what you've gained from being here?'

Mel had no idea what they wanted her to say. She decided to give an honest answer. 'I've received appropriate medication and been able to rest in a safe environment. I feel so much stronger as a result.'

The two professionals exchanged glances.

Mel persevered. 'There have been no pressures and I've been able to talk through my all my issues with people who understand.'

'And where does Jez Matthews fit in? He seems to have visited you rather a lot while you have been here.'

Mel bristled at the directness of Tennyson's question. She eyed him warily. 'He's been a good friend.'

'But surely he's your counsellor?'

'Yes.' She didn't like his tone. Perhaps it was odd that Jez and she had become friends. But was there a law against it? It's true her record with men wasn't brilliant, but she knew Jez was genuine. He'd stuck by her all through this frightening time and it couldn't have been easy. 'I've needed a friend and he's been here for me. And he's promised to keep in touch when I leave here.'

Dr Selberg intervened at this point, as if she sensed that the atmosphere needed diffusing. 'And do you think you're ready to face the world again? she asked.

'Oh yes. I feel more energised than for a long time. And very enthusiastic about a new project.'

In the midst of elaborating on the book researching idea, she was again interrupted by Peter Tennyson. 'Have you somewhere to go if you leave here?

Not 'when', Mel noticed, just 'if'. She wondered if there was some significance in this but wasn't going to rise to his bait. 'I shall be living with the friends who've supported me while I've been here. They've been very good to me.'

'I think we've heard enough,' Dr Selberg said quietly. 'Thank you for being so frank with us. We will let you know our decision in a day or two.' Rising, she shook Mel's hand warmly. Tennyson followed her as she left.

The interview was over. There was so much Mel had wanted to say, things that she'd rehearsed for days. She just hoped she'd said enough to convince them of the progress she'd made.

As she returned to her room, she reviewed the meeting, worried that she had ruined her chances by being too frank. Too late to ponder on that now. The agony of waiting for the outcome was enough to contend with. The prospect of having to spend more time here was something she couldn't, wouldn't contemplate.

Bella and Odile were waiting for her.

'How did it go?' Bella wanted to know.

'Difficult to say. I have to wait for their decision. I just hope I said the right things.'

'Mon Dieu! A man whose eyes cannot see would know you are well again. It will be good, you'll see.' Odile clasped Mel to her in an impulsive gesture of confirmation.

The subject was dismissed, and they talked of other things. Their visits always boosted Mel's mood. Odile was such a character, with her flamboyant clothes and spontaneity of actions. And Bella, though more serious, usually had some tale to tell about the latest battle with her publisher. Deadlines meant nothing to her and, truth to say, she had built up such a following for her historical novels the punters would wait. The publishers were on to a good thing and they knew it.

Just as Mel's friends were leaving, a nurse arrived with a message for her. 'Your young man, I mean therapist, called. He's sorry he couldn't wait to hear how things went, but he left these for you. From behind her back she produced a bunch of gaudy, but ridiculously cheerful, anemones. Mel couldn't help smiling as she accepted the flowers. 'Thank you,' she said, deciding to ignore the reference to her 'young man'.

She was disappointed she had missed his visit. It was thoughtful of him to leave the flowers, though sometimes she worried that he expected more than friendship from her. She must make sure he understood that she wasn't ready yet for another relationship. In fact she wondered if she would ever be able to trust a man again and the thought saddened her.

But Jez's flowers had made her smile, and her smile was mirrored now in the nurse's face.

'He said to tell you he will come tomorrow,' she relayed to Mel with a wink.

Still Mel ignored her innuendo. 'Thanks for the message,' she replied brightly.

That night she was restless. When at last she fell asleep, fragments of sadness and fear tormented her. She was a child again, crying for the mother she could barely remember.

Then she was a mother herself, but not for long, her aunt had seen to that. And later, after being torn apart by the loss of all those babies, finding Chloe had felt like balm, a healing, but then she was callously taken away, too. Mel had sought comfort in Tom's arms, needing him to smother her with kisses to wipe away her tears.

But Tom turned away from her, leaving her weeping for the loss of his love, the love that she'd believed was hers forever. She was seized by fear. Her body shook, her heart pounded and her mouth dried.

She woke with a start. Tom was here and he wanted to kill her!

It was tempting to call the nurse, but she must be strong. Instead, she switched on the light at her bedside. There was no one there. It was a bad dream, that's all. The interview must have brought it all to the surface again. Shakily, she poured a glass of water just as a nurse popped her head round the door.

'I saw your light on. You all right?'

'Yes thanks. I was thirsty,' she lied.

Chapter 31

Mel thrust the bad dream to the back of her mind, determined to be positive about the outcome of the interview. If only they would let her know one way or the other. She hated living on the edge of a precipice, her heart dropping like a stone and her stomach contents like boiling lava every time she thought about the possibility of a negative outcome.

She needed to leave the protective confines of the hospital and get on with her life. But she worried that Dr Selberg and her objectionable colleague may have decided that she was not ready and send her back to the clinic again. Surely they wouldn't be so cruel as to place her back in an environment where she'd suffered such trauma? Not knowing was torture.

Only two days had passed since the interview, but it seemed like a lifetime. Reason told her it was too soon to expect an answer, but how was she supposed to occupy herself while she waited?

Jez continued to visit, and she looked forward to seeing him. He lightened the atmosphere with his latest tales from the clinic. She honestly thought he'd missed his vocation and should have been an impressionist. His astute study of people meant that he had them off to a tee.

The day after his last visit, Mel had settled down for an after lunch read. She must have dosed off, because she thought she heard someone softly calling her name. Opening her eyes, she was astonished to find François Millais seated at her bedside.

Her initial reaction was one of irritation. Not only had he caught her off-guard, she wanted to know why he was here anyway. She was grateful for his sympathetic treatment during Chloe's illness, but why did he have to keep turning up unannounced everywhere? She didn't need reminding of the worst moments of her life.

She'd noticed him at Chloe's funeral, and was mortified that he'd witnessed the unpleasant scene with Tom. Then he'd been in court at her trial and, Jez had told her, he'd turned up at the clinic while she was still sedated, claiming to be doing some research into the effects of the loss of a young child and how mothers coped subsequently.

Personally, Mel didn't believe this and it really annoyed her that he wouldn't leave her alone. She hated being seen at her most vulnerable. She'd been a strong woman once, with a responsible job and respect from her colleagues. She aimed to be that way again, but it wasn't going to happen if people kept harassing her like this.

However, Dr Millais was apologetic. 'I'm so sorry I disturbed you,' he said. 'I'd heard that you may be leaving here soon and...' He broke off, momentarily disconcerted.

Perhaps he wasn't encouraged by Mel's obvious antagonism. 'And what?' she asked defiantly.

'I was hoping you might tell me some of your thoughts about the prospect of going back out into the world. For my book,' he added.

He looked so uncomfortable that Mel relented a smidge. 'I would rather people stopped trying to analyse me,' she replied. 'But, since you've made the journey, I suppose I could answer a few questions. Will you back off then?'

He smiled ruefully, 'If I must.'

'What do you want to know?'

'Your history is very complicated,' he began. 'People who've suffered tragedies, and subsequently been treated badly, react in different ways. They either cave in and decide that life is not worth living or find reserves of strength they didn't know they possessed, enabling them to recover and make a good life for themselves.'

'And which kind am I?' Mel wanted to know.

'I think you're an amazing lady,' he replied, a sudden flush of colour creeping to his face. 'I've learned of your early years, and seen you suffer more heartache than anyone should, but I've also seen a glint of tenacity in your eyes.'

His observation shook her. There was admiration in his voice, a glimpse of tenderness even and, despite herself, it touched a chord. Embarrassed, she felt the sting of tears.

Pulling herself together, she said, 'I have good friends who've given me their support'. But, in the end, it comes down to me to decide what I make of the rest of my life. I'm tired of being a victim, so I have to be strong from now on. I have already made a few plans.'

'You should be proud of yourself,' he said, and gave her hand a squeeze.

It was no more than an encouraging few words from doctor to patient, but the electric shock that surged through Mel at his touch took her by surprise. Confused, she didn't know what to say, but acknowledged, reluctantly, that her confidence had received a welcome boost from his appreciation of the stand she'd taken.

'Thank you,' she said and tried out a tentative smile.

'I'll leave you in peace now. May I visit again tomorrow?'

She paused, still unsure of whether she really wanted his continued intrusion. But she found herself nodding, unable to trust herself to speak. Her emotions were all over the place.

This new turn of events had taken her by surprise. Like the prick of a thorn, she felt again the familiar irritation when she relived waking and finding François observing her. And yet her hand still tingled from his touch. She'd deliberately kept Jez at arm's length, believing she was not ready for another relationship, and uncertain whether she ever would be.

Could it be that, with one touch, François Millais had ignited the flame that she'd thought was doused forever? She convinced herself that she was reading too much into his gesture. It was probably meant as an expression of encouragement, nothing more. Perversely, her mood plummeted at the thought.

It was a beautiful day and she decided to go for a walk in the hospital grounds to clear her head. As she left the nurses' desk having registered her intention, Robert, another recovering patient, caught her up.

'Do you mind if I join you? he asked. 'I fancy stretching my legs. When you're in here you tend to forget there's a world outside.'

Mel nodded in agreement.

'How are you getting on?' he continued. 'I heard you may be leaving us soon.'

'Oh God, I hope so. I'm waiting for the result of my assessment, but I'm not too sure of the impression I gave. I was a tad outspoken.'

'Don't worry, they probably like a bit of spark in a patient. It shows that the treatment you've received here has worked I would have thought. When do you expect to hear?'

'Any day now.'

'Best of luck then.'

Entering the grounds, they walked in companionable silence, each deep in their own thoughts. Mel, busy with her current turmoil, let the minutes tick by until, coming to a bench that looked over a fantastic display of tulips, she indicated that they should sit for a while.

Feeling that she should make some effort with conversation Mel asked, 'Do you mind my asking what brought you here?'

'Not at all. We're here. There's no point in being coy about it. I had a nervous breakdown.'

'Do you know what caused it?'

'Stress at work, the break-up of a long-term relationship. You know the kind of thing. It had been coming on for some time I reckon.'

Because of her own history, Mel wanted to know, 'What finally triggered the breakdown then? I hope you don't think I'm being too nosy. It's just that, having been in that state myself, I'm interested in other people's experiences.'

'It's OK. I don't mind. I was in a car accident. It was my fault entirely. I was already on medication, a sedative, and shouldn't have been driving that day. I just didn't see the other car.'

'How awful.'

Robert didn't speak for a few moments, as if reliving the trauma of the crash. When he finally continued, his face was ashen and he was shaking. 'When they cut me out of the car I was a screaming wreck. I'd completely lost it. They brought me straight here.'

'I'm so sorry. I shouldn't have asked you all those questions. It's upset you, and I know how tiresome it can get when people keep making you go over the awful events that sent you over the edge.'

'It's alright,' he offered, although plainly it wasn't.

'For what it's worth, we're strong now. The worst has happened, and things can only get better from now on.'

'That's a great sentiment to give anyone. You should be a counsellor.' He had recovered and was even attempting a touch of humour. Always a good sign.

They rose and continued their stroll. The bright sunshine shone on the new leaves of the oaks and coaxed vibrant colours from the spring flowers, lifting their spirits still further.

They were laughing over some silly joke when they returned to the ward, feeling better for the fresh air and shared conversation.

'We should do this again,' Robert said, smiling.

'We should,' Mel agreed.

She pulled her book from the locker and settled herself in the chair beside her bed. For some time she hadn't been able to concentrate on reading more than a paragraph or two. That she had automatically reached for her new book, made her aware for the first time that she really was getting better and she was soon involved in the story of the author's travels in Kerala.

The walk in the fresh air had certainly improved her appetite. It was good that it was nearly lunchtime. A nurse approached and Mel put down her book in readiness to move to the area where recovering patients ate together.

But it wasn't a call to lunch that brought the nurse to her bed. 'I have news,' she announced. 'Dr Selberg has asked to see you at 2.00pm in her office. Good luck!'

Suddenly, Mel's appetite had vanished, to be replaced by a turbulence akin to seasickness. She couldn't eat a thing until she knew her fate. Never did time pass so slowly.

At last she knocked on the door to Dr Selberg's office, hoping the doctor wouldn't be accompanied by the obnoxious Peter Tennyson again.

'Come in.' The doctor's voice sounded cheery and encouraging.

Chapter 32

Mel opened the door, relieved to find Dr Selberg on her own.

'Come in my dear,' she said. 'There's no need to be nervous.'

'Thank you.'

'Sit down and make yourself comfortable. Would you like some tea?'

'No thank you, but perhaps a glass of water.' It would give her something to do with her hands rather than sit on them to hide their shaking.

'Help yourself.' She indicated the water cooler in the corner of the room.

Mel filled her glass and managed to make it back to her chair without spilling any. 'It's been a long few days,' she admitted, to fill the silence.

The doctor lifted her head and smiled. Mel's honesty was one of the things she'd liked about her. 'Yes, I apologise. It was a difficult decision. There was some dissention between my colleague and myself. In the end, I won.' She chuckled, and the smile that lit her face made her seem almost human and not the terrifying person Mel had mentally ^made her out to be.

Mel immediately relaxed. Whatever decision she'd come to, she trusted her to do the best for her. If she thought she should stay a while longer she'd just have to endure it. But maybe it was possible she could hope for a better outcome. She tried to hide her impatience while Dr Selberg appeared to consult her notes.

When she finally spoke, her voice was grave, and Mel prepared herself for the worst. But the words she uttered were not the ones Mel had feared. They came gift-wrapped. She opened the package slowly cherishing the jewel contained therein.

'You gave a very good performance at your assessment,' Dr Selberg began. 'You were completely frank with us and I liked that. It showed a maturity, a trust in your capabilities and in your future.'

Mel could hardly contain the flare of hope.

'Therefore, I have decided you can be discharged from the hospital tomorrow.'

The words reverberated round the room. They lit every corner, gathering the sunshine streaming in the window and reflecting it back at her. But she knew she must ask the one question she dreaded more than any other.

'Will I have to return to the Clinic?'

'I think it has served its purpose. There would be no advantage obtained from sending you back there. In fact, it may undo some of the work that has been done here. You are free to go to the friends who've offered you a home.' She beamed like a benevolent fairy. Mel could almost feel the touch of her wand.

She couldn't have received a better gift. This was the ultimate and she felt like kissing the doctor. 'Thank you,' she said. 'Thank you so much.'

'You may go now, and I wish you a fulfilling future.'

Crossing to the door, she turned to give one more smile to the woman who'd granted her a new life.

Waiting was torture now, and soon she was on the phone to Odile and Bella. 'It's good news. I can leave here tomorrow.' No preamble, no dressing it up, the words burst from her, unable to be contained any longer. There was whooping and laughter on the end of the phone. Arrangements were made to collect her from the hospital. Mel could almost feel the warm hugs of congratulation she knew she would undoubtedly receive.

She was on a high when she went to find Robert to give him her news and tell him that she wouldn't be able to walk in the grounds with him again after all.

He tried to smile. 'I'm really pleased for you,' he said. But his voice was flat, and Mel was sorry she hadn't broken the news more gently.'

'I really enjoyed our time in the garden yesterday you know. I just wish we had made friends before. It was good to have someone to talk to who understood the horrors of a breakdown.' Mel tried to soften the blow.

'It's OK. It's just that I enjoyed it, too, and was looking forward to doing it again. But I sincerely wish you all the best. I expect my turn will come soon.' He smiled bravely as she left to return to the ward.

Jez phoned soon after. 'I gather congratulations are in order,' he began. I had been going to offer to collect you tomorrow, perhaps take you out to lunch, but I understand your friends have got in first.'

'Yes, but thanks for the thought. You're a good friend and I don't know what I'd have done without you in the past few months.'

'It's nothing. I would suggest coming over, but I don't suppose you want a visitor now.'

'Of course I do. But I'm just going for lunch. I couldn't eat until I'd heard the result. But it would be great to see you after that.' She hoped she wasn't giving him the wrong impression, being too effusive. The fact was she intended to use the opportunity to make sure he understood that, while she valued his friendship, that's all it was. She'd like to keep in touch with him on those terms, but she'd have to leave that decision to him.

It must have been a coincidence that her late lunch tasted especially good. There seemed to be no problem with her appetite now she knew she must get fit and strong to give herself the best chance of succeeding with her plans.

When she returned to the ward she was mildly irritated to find Jez already there waiting. She had been hoping for a few minutes to savour the good news she'd received.

She plastered a smile to her face as Jez sprang up and clasped her in a fierce embrace. 'Hey, let me breathe,' she gasped as she fought free.

To her horror, Jez seized her again and began smothering her with kisses. Suddenly, his mouth was on hers, his tongue urgent and probing, and once more she gasped for air. This was too much.

'Jez….,' she began, pushing him away.

'Oh Mel, it's such great news. I've been waiting and hoping for this for so long.'

Mel had wanted to break things to him gently, but now she knew she would have to be firm. 'Jez, I don't know what you were expecting of me, but it's quite obvious that it was more than I can give. I'm really sorry if I've given you the wrong impression.' The words were out before she could stop them. She saw his face pale.

'But I thought we had something good going on.'

'We have. I shall always treasure your friendship, but I'm afraid that's all it is.'

'But you encouraged me.' He thumped his fist on the table.

'As I said, I'm truly sorry if I gave you that impression. I honestly thought you were just being friendly.'

'I was at first, but you're a very attractive woman. It was bound to happen.'

'I'm sorry Jez. I don't feel ready for anything more yet. I have to come to terms with all that's happened, restore some of the trust that's been eroded, before I can let someone get close to me again. I thought you understood that.'

It was as though she hadn't spoken. 'I was all set to look after you,' he said miserably.

This was the final straw. 'I don't need looking after now Jez. It's important to me that I stay strong, without relying on others.' She'd tried to say it kindly, but he looked so dejected Mel felt truly sorry for him. She even wished things could be different. But they weren't, and there was nothing she could do about that. 'You hadn't said anything,' she added lamely.

'I wanted to surprise you. I'd intended to ask you to marry me.'

It was getting worse. Mel didn't know what to say. 'I'm really sorry. We can still be friends though, can't we?' she asked.

'It's not enough. I need time to think,' he said and turned to leave the ward.

'Jez, don't leave like...,' Mel began but he was gone.

The incident had shaken her. Perhaps she should have expected Jez would react like this. She wished she could have been kinder. But at least he knew how things were and she mustn't let his reaction spoil her plans.

She must start preparations for her discharge from hospital. She could hardly believe that all the traumas of the previous year were over. She intended to start living as never before.

Chapter 33

After a near sleepless night, and too excited to eat breakfast, Mel was running on adrenalin alone. She busied herself collecting together the last remnants of the possessions she'd gained while at the hospital.

Her discharge papers signed, the first nightmare weeks had faded into insubstantial snatches of memory, akin to the wisps of mist that clung to the low-lying Normandy fields in autumn. These thoughts brought Odile to mind, and how much her friendship meant to her. She would never forget the warm welcome she and Chloe had received when they first arrived in the bustling market town of Mortagne, weary and confused. Without her, Mel's life would have been so much harder.

Bella, too, had been generous, despite the painful reason for their meeting and the fact that they hadn't known each other long. She couldn't wait to be back with her friends. Now her future was bright. She felt strong and bursting with ideas.

'Madam Dubois. Mel.'

Lost in her thoughts, the gentle male voice startled her. She spun round, expecting to find Jez, and irritated that he was spoiling her happy mood with a threat of another scene. It was the last thing she wanted right then.

But it was not Jez that stood there. Instead, an apologetic François Millais hovered uncertainly at the door to the ward. 'I'm sorry to disturb you. May I come in?'

'I suppose so.' Privately Mel wondered why they couldn't just leave her alone and knew her answer was less than gracious.

'You don't like me using your first name?' he asked. 'We've known each other a long time now. I would like us to be friends. I'm in England for a while, working at the children's hospital in Birmingham.'

His words were simple and honest but, to Mel, they were loaded with more meaning than he probably intended.

Oh God, she thought. Here we go again. 'You're my doctor, or were,' she stated somewhat obviously.

He smiled; an uncertain, rather attractive smile, Mel acknowledged grudgingly. 'But you're well now. I just wanted to see you before you leave. To perhaps close your case history for my book, although, with your permission, I should like to stay in touch.' He handed her his card.

Mel took it and said, but we'll be living and working in Harrow. Birmingham is not exactly nearby.' She smiled, hoping to lessen the harshness that had found its way out of her mouth, and which she now regretted. She put the card in her pocket. 'Thank you. For the card and for your care. You've been very kind.'

'But?'

'You will understand that I'm not sure yet what the future will hold, and I need time to adjust.'

It was only too plain that it was not what he'd wanted to hear. 'Yes, of course,' he replied in a steam-rollered voice.

Mel was saved any further embarrassment by the arrival of Bella and Odile. They were like a breath of fresh air wafting through the room. 'Oh sorry,' Bella stopped short, clearly uncomfortable. 'They didn't say you had a visitor. We'll wait outside.'

'No need for that. I think we'd finished.' She glanced at François Millais questioningly.

He nodded. 'Au revoir,' he said. 'A bientôt.' Till we meet again. He wasn't giving up then.

Bella seized her by the arm and began marching her from the ward. 'Let's go,' she said cheerfully. Odile picked up Mel's bags and the three of them practically danced out of the room. Mel tossed a happy smile over her shoulder. 'Au revoir,' she called to the disconsolate Millais.

Now she was free. Free from the horrors of the last year, and free from the unwelcoming pestering of the male sex. Time to move on.

She had expected that Odile would have been busy preparing for her homecoming, but the lavishness of the welcome took her breath away. Flowers, wine and so much food filled the room she felt like the Prodigal son. Only the fatted calf was missing. Unable to speak through the rock in her throat, she stood smiling like an idiot, though tears of gratitude washed her cheeks.

'Do not cry, ma petite. Be happy! You have a new start, a whole new life. And you have friends.'

'I know, I know. These are happy tears. I can't begin to thank you. Where would I start?' At last Mel had found her voice.

'It's so good to have you out of that place. Now we can really make plans.' This from the ever-practical Bella. 'But first eat, drink and enjoy!'

The next few days were filled with finalising plans for the business they would run together. Bella, with her contacts in the literary world, had managed to secure a retail unit in Harrow, North London. Researching antique, out of print and specialised books, would slot into the area well. At least something positive had come out of her time with Tom. She had sufficient funds from the settlement to contribute to the new venture.

The shop was situated in Harrow-on-the-Hill, very close to the prestigious Public School. Mel fell in love with the surroundings from the outset. She loved to see the boys, in their formal dress and boaters, filling the narrow streets. The residents were intellectual and well-heeled and lived in substantial houses, many with staff to look after them. She hoped with all her heart that these wealthy people also loved books.

Bella had done her homework well. She'd even found a good-sized apartment nearby. She would be able to leave the clamour and grime of the city behind and live in the quieter suburbs. And Odile had decided to stay with her friends in England. She would visit the apartment in Normandy regularly and it would always be available. It would be a new start for all of them.

There was a deal of work to be done on the new premises before they were ready to open, but they set to with a will, anxious to get the business up and running.

'We should be able to open in around three weeks,' Bella said, full of enthusiasm.

'Won't you need some time out to write?' Mel questioned her. She was only too conscious that Bella had put in the bulk of her earnings from the sale of her books to get the business started and she felt the shortfall in her own contribution keenly.

'I can put that on hold for the time being. I'm already ahead of schedule.'

There was something else on Mel's mind. 'Bella, I hope you don't mind my asking, but I feel responsible for splitting up your marriage. Because there was no time to lose if we were to save Chloe, I called you away at a difficult time for you. Is there no hope of a reconciliation?'

'No there isn't. It was over long before I met you. I was just afraid to acknowledge it.'

'Are you quite sure?'

'Yes. When he put all that vitriolic stuff in the newspapers it showed what he's really like.' Bella smiled drily. 'His public face is somewhat different,' she added.

'Yes, but...'

'But nothing. You put everything in perspective, and I thank you for that.' Cheerfully, she wielded her paintbrush while Mel continued with the fitting of the substantial shelves that would soon bear their load of precious books.

'I can't wait to get my books out of store and see what I've got.' Mel said.

'Don't you know what sort of books they are?'

'Dad had acquired some rare, and sought-after books, I believe, but I was too young to appreciate them when I inherited them from him. I haven't seen them since.'

'Can you remember what they looked like?'

'Well I was only twelve when he died, but I have a vague memory of hefty, leather bound jobs, tooled in gold. Shelves and shelves of them. Several times I've been going to retrieve them, but Tom didn't want them in the house. He said we didn't have room for dozens of weighty old tomes.'

'Philistine,' Bella muttered under her breath.

Odile looked puzzled. 'What is that?'

'Put simply,' Bella began, 'they are people with no regard for, or who are even opposed to, intellectual or artistic values.'

'That's the simple version?' Odile chuckled.

'Sorry... I'll try to put it better.'

'It's OK. I was only teasing. I think I know what you mean.'

Odile was being such a tonic to the atmosphere. She had given up so much to come to England and be part of their joint project. Mel knew she must miss her beloved France.

Overcome with guilt for being instrumental in uprooting her, Mel asked, 'Don't you ever get homesick, Odile?'

'Homesick? I don't think I know that word. But I think I can guess. You think I regret leaving France, n'est pas? Sometimes it hurts un petit peu – a *very* little.' Nostalgia crossed her face for an instant but, giving herself a shake, she carried on. 'I have made my decision and I am happy here with my friends,' she stated with a smile.

The atmosphere became more like a party then. Spirits were high as they set to with a will; all of them glad to be back together and working on an exciting joint project. Every few hours they had a break, and picnicked on the floor of the shop, spreading a clean dustsheet before laying out the tasty variety of salads or pastries courtesy of Odile. The endless cups of coffee she supplied were welcome, too.

In quiet moments, without warning, Mel was overcome with loss, for the life and love she'd had all too briefly and, at these times she ached to feel Chloe's chubby weight in her arms, and to hear her baby chatter and giggles.

'What's up?' Bella asked one day. 'Having second thoughts about all this?'

'Oh no, not at all. I was just thinking about well... things... you know.' She found it difficult to put it into words as her throat closed round the threatening tears. Determinedly, she pushed away her sadness and looked around her at the progress they had already made. She'd been given the chance to make a new life for herself and she was so grateful.

'I'm so lucky to have found you two,' she blurted. She wanted so badly to let them know how much she appreciated their friendship and loyalty.

'It's for us, too, you know,' Bella replied, slightly embarrassed by Mel's effusive praise.

'Yes, but...'

'No buts. Just get those shelves sorted.' She playfully flicked a few drops of cream paint in Mel's direction to let her know she meant business.

There was to be no more discussion of what Mel saw as the inequality of her contribution to the venture.

Chapter 34

It was now three weeks since the Bookshop had been up and running. The stylish sign above the door spelled out *'TRIO – suppliers of Antiquarian and out of print books'* in gold script on black. Trade had been good from day one. The Harrow boys and their tutors had flocked to the new emporium and hadn't tired of doing so.

Some of the requests had been pretty obscure – almost as if the friends' ability to track them down was being tested. But nothing fazed them and, though they hadn't been successful in every case, they'd had a good try.

The erudite residents of Harrow-on-the-Hill frequented the premises regularly. Maybe it was the lure of the excellent coffee and pastries that drew them. Odile had volunteered to supply the snacks in the sunny area set aside for reading and reflection Whatever the reason, the visitors still made time to peruse the books on display and spend their plentiful cash. Perhaps their chatter was a touch distracting for some of the more learned customers, but they seemed to take it all in good part.

There'd been a few hiccups along the way. On the very day a local journalist came to do a write-up, they were in chaos. One of the shelves decided it was going to rebel at the load of heavy, leather-bound volumes it carried and collapsed in pieces shooting the books in all directions.

Immediately, they called in the chap who had carried out other shop fittings for them.

'The wall's damp,' he announced. 'You must have a leak somewhere. I would have noticed it if it had been like this when I was here. And there was nothing on the surveyor's report. You need to get it checked out before I can do anything.'

Frustratingly, the plumber was unable to come for several days, but at last he tracked down a leak from the bathroom immediately overhead.

'Soon have that fixed,' he said cheerily, as he tucked into one of Odile's pastries. 'But it'll be at least a couple of weeks before you can put books back there.'

The precious books were irreplaceable, being part of Mel's father's collection, and she was concerned that they'd been damaged beyond saving. The books were the only mementos she had of her father. But, although it took a while, after some skilled work by a restorer Bella suggested, they were returned looking just as they were when they'd first put them proudly on the shelf. Now they took pride of place in their original position, the new unit, at Mel's request, having been reinforced to make doubly sure it could carry the weight.

The journalist, glossing over this calamity, still wrote a colourful, and very favourable, report about 'the fantastic new business on The Hill'. Soon there were rave reviews in The Times, The Observer and upmarket literary magazines. The website grew busier day by day.

'We'll maybe have to think about taking on someone to deal with that,' Bella remarked one day. They all agreed, and soon they had increased their staff by three: Cassie, a bookbinder, was kept busy with the new service they now offered, Karl manned the website and, with the confidence of the young, tracked down the titles their clients requested with apparent ease. Richie carefully packed the many mail orders for dispatch. The name TRIO had been well chosen. They seemed to be doing everything in threes – three partners, three extra services and three more staff to man them.

The friends were exhausted, but it was a satisfying kind of exhaustion, born of gratitude for their success.

It was only when they did their usual stock check at close of business one day that Bella spotted that some very valuable, and beautifully engraved, books seemed to have gone missing.

'Have either of you moved the Restoration Manuscripts?' she asked. Mel's heart sank. Not those, she pleaded inwardly.

'I certainly haven't,' she replied. 'And Odile doesn't handle the books a great deal now. She's far too busy cooking.'

Trying not to panic, she sought Odile out to make certain. As she'd expected, Odile put her hands up in horror.

'Mon Dieu! I don't touch those special books if I can help it,' she stated. 'But a man asked me if he could have a look at them earlier.'

'And did you get them for him?'

'Non. My hands were sticky, so I showed him where they were, and he got them down himself.' Odile was pale and on the verge of tears. 'I shouldn't have done that. I'm sorry.'

'It's not your fault. We don't know for certain that they're missing yet. Perhaps he put them back in the wrong place.' Mel wasn't at all convinced of that, but she hated seeing Odile so upset.

After examining all the shelves of books meticulously, there was still no sign. Bella was on the point of contacting the police to report the robbery when she saw the books tucked in a neat pile under the table where the man had sat to study them.

Panic over, they all relaxed, locked up and made for the comfortable apartment where they had time to think about other aspects of their lives.

*****

One night, as Mel collapsed into bed, a brief picture of François Millais flashed unbidden before her. She immediately felt guilty at the brusque way she had treated him on his visit to the hospital. Suddenly, she wanted to talk to him, to make amends, to… what? Was she so short of male company that any man would do? She blushed at this thought, or was it the unashamed admission that she longed for the feel of a man's arms around her, his mouth on hers and…

Her body responded with such longing and regret. Yes, she was happy in the new venture and in the camaraderie of her friends, but now she acknowledged that there was definitely something missing from her life.

She remembered François' kindness to her on the train when she first arrived in Normandy, tired and distraught. She also remembered the frisson of attraction that had passed between them.

Had she been so emotionally battered since then that she was unable to acknowledge her true feelings for the opposite sex, and François in particular. It was possible, she conceded.

She pulled out his card, which she had been using as a bookmark ever since he gave it to her. She fooled herself it was a matter of convenience, but now wondered if she'd deliberately kept it handy. Perhaps she was reading too much into his efforts to keep in touch on the pretext of following up her case for his book. Perhaps that's all it was. She decided to sleep on it. She would find the courage to ring him in the morning.

Eventually she sank into a deep sleep, only to be awakened by the trill of her mobile. 'Yes?' she asked, barely awake.

'Pardon. Did I wake you Madame Dubois?'

'Who is that?'

'It's François Millais.'

'Then what's with the formality?' All Mel's hackles were up at what she perceived as his deliberate misinterpretation of her mood at their last meeting. Perhaps she had been too prickly on that occasion? Tom had destroyed her self-esteem and the truth was she hadn't known how to handle things. But this was not how it was supposed to go at all. She tried to calm down.

François cut in on her thoughts. 'I'm sorry. I seem to have upset you again. I thought you wanted to keep things on a business footing. Did I make a mistake again?'

His question may have been innocent enough, but Mel's confidence was nil and it seemed to her that he was teasing her. Trying to wrong foot her. She was unsure of how to respond.

The silence lengthened.

At last François spoke. 'How is your new business going?'

They were safely on neutral ground and Mel was grateful to him. 'It's going very well, far better than we had expected. We are very busy and have branched out in other associated directions. So excited was she at the bookshop's success that she'd prattled on for some time before François politely interrupted.

'I'm so pleased things are going well for you at last.'

Mel thought she detected a wistful tone creeping into his voice.

'It's hard work,' she conceded, 'but…'

'What's the but?'

She'd been going to say 'but I still have time for friends'. She stopped just in time, not wanting him to think she was being too forward, sending out the wrong signals. 'Oh nothing,' she replied. 'It's not important.'

'I was calling to ask if you were ready to speak to me about how you are coping now? I want to get the manuscript ready for the publishers. I thought it would be good to finish it on a high point.'

'I...' Mel was unsure how to handle his request.

'It's OK. I understand you are very busy.'

'Oh but...' There was no alternative. If she didn't meet him now she may lose him forever. Her heart sank at the prospect. 'I should like to talk to you,' she said.

'That's great, because I'm in London for a conference. Can you suggest a meeting place?'

'Would you like to come here? You could see the shop and how well it's doing. And how happy I am,' she added. Oh dear, that came out wrong again. She'd made it sound as if she was totally fulfilled; in no need of his company. If only she could strike the right balance between genuine warmth and giving him the come on.

But he didn't seem fazed. 'I'd very much like to do that.'

'Can you come tomorrow evening at around seven?'

'Tomorrow would be fine, but I may be a little later than seven. Is that a problem?'

'Not at all. See you when you can get here.' Mel loved listening to his voice, the pitch of it, and the gorgeous French accent which she'd fallen in love with on her first French lesson at her grammar school. She wanted to keep him talking but didn't trust herself to say more. She was shaking, her emotions confused.

'I will bring you a copy of the manuscript so far. We can go through it together. Then we can discuss your part in the closing chapters.'

'That would be good,' she replied. It sounded inadequate somehow.

'Until tomorrow then.'

Chapter 35

It was a little after 8.00pm when François Millais arrived at the flat. Mel had been distracted all day by how she would – or should – react to him. Now she was paralysed by his ring at the doorbell.

Seconds ticked by and still she hesitated.

'That must be Dr Millais. Aren't you going to let him in? You've been wittering on about him all day.'

Mel felt the giveaway flush colour her face. 'Have I?' she stuttered, embarrassed. She still couldn't sort out her feelings. She was eager to read what François had written about her case, but it was more than that. She wanted to see him. And yet... There were still relentless doubts hovering in her mind. Why was he so interested in her case? He must see other similar distraught mothers during the course of his work. After all, he was head of a Paediatric Oncology department. Had he chased them around, too?

Her head was still buzzing with questions as she went to the door. 'Sorry to keep you waiting,' she said to him. 'I was just…'

'It's OK,' he replied. 'I'm sorry to be late.'

'Well you're here now. You'd better come in.' Mel's reply came out all wrong, sounding brusque and unwelcoming, revealing her awkwardness.

'You remember my friends Bella and Odile?' she said as they entered the light and spacious lounge.

'Yes, of course.' He gave a slight bow as he acknowledged each in turn.

He was every woman's idea of a typical sexy Frenchman: tall, dark, incredibly good-looking and utterly charming. Mel watched the others flush with pleasure as he greeted each one, planting a kiss on each cheek in the French fashion. She was a tad irritated that they were getting more attention from him than she was, but reluctantly admitted it was her own fault. She hadn't given him the chance, with her less-than-welcome greeting.

'Have you eaten?' Bella asked him.

'I have, thank you.'

'You'll have a little something though,' Odile interjected. It was more of a statement than a question and you didn't argue with Odile when it came to food.

In a couple of minutes the aroma of fresh coffee filtered in from the kitchen and soon Odile appeared carrying a large tray loaded with her special pastries. Whether your taste was for sweet or savoury, you were spoilt for choice. Odile had surpassed herself once again. Cooking, and the pleasure it gave to others, would seem to be her main pleasure in life. She beamed happily as they tucked in, although they had all eaten well not long before.

'God, these are so good,' Mel exclaimed. You are not good for my figure though Odile.'

For a moment Odile looked guilty.

'I didn't mean to criticise; it's just that your cooking is so irresistible I end up eating more than I should. I'll be getting fat.'

'Poof! You could do with putting on a bit of weight. You're too – how you say – too skinny.' She smiled broadly, obviously pleased with her mastery of the English vernacular.

'How do you find time to write a book as well as head your busy department at the hospital?' Bella asked François. 'I find it so difficult to write while we are so busy at the shop, and my publisher is getting impatient.'

'It's not easy,' he conceded, 'but I love doing both, so it's not a problem for me.'

'It's sad that there are so many children suffering from that terrible disease.' Odile said sadly.

'Yes, it is. But very rewarding that I can help many of them to beat it. They don't all end up ...' He'd been going to say 'dying' but was worried that, sometimes, his handling of the English language made what he said sound insensitive. He looked at Mel, not knowing quite how to continue.

'Don't worry,' she comforted him, 'I know that. Chloe was just unlucky. Too young to fight it, I guess.'

'Yes, but I still wish... It's hard to lose a patient at any age.'

The previously lively conversation seemed to run out of steam and become strained, each of them considering, and being grateful for, the hard job François applied himself to on a daily basis.

Bella did her best to liven the atmosphere. 'You'll want to discuss the manuscript for your book with Mel. I believe that was the object of this visit.' Her eyes shone mischievously as she addressed François, suggesting that the book was not the only reason for his visit.

'Mais oui. But I have to say thank you to La Chef for all this wonderful food.' Ever the charmer, he made Odile glow with his effusive praise.

'Well if you don't make a start on your manuscript you'll be here all night. So we'll leave you to it,' said Bella.

'Your friends are very lively,' François remarked when they had the room to themselves.

'Yes,' Mel replied. She didn't know what else to say.

There was an uncomfortable silence.

François spoke again. 'You don't seem very happy,' he said. 'Have I behaved badly again? I didn't mean to upset you.'

'No, it's not your fault.' Mel was at a loss to explain. After all, she didn't understand her own feelings, so how could she tell him how she felt? 'Let's look at the manuscript,' she said to diffuse the tense atmosphere.

It was his turn to look worried. At this moment he wasn't the confident, expert physician she had once relied on. He had an endearing air of vulnerability. He reached into his briefcase and drew out the manuscript. Handing it to Mel he said, 'I have tried to make your part in it an honest appraisal of your baby's case – and the anguish you suffered as a result. I hope you approve of what I've written and that you think I've been fair.'

Mel nervously began to read the marked section. She could feel his eyes on her as the words blurred in front of her. She was horrified at what she was reading. 'How dare you!' she said, bursting with rage. 'Who is this pathetically weak creature you describe? It certainly isn't me! Is that really how you see me? Then you don't really know me at all. I think you'd better leave.'

'But…'

'No buts. That was a tough time for me. Anyone would have buckled under what life threw at me then. I expected a degree of sympathy. Can't you see I'm a strong woman underneath all that stuff that was going on?

He spoke quietly. 'I'm sure you are. But back then you just had too much to endure. Even the strongest person could not survive it,' he added gently. 'But I'm truly sorry if I've revealed too much of what you suffered.'

'You've betrayed me. You befriended me for your own purposes and I never guessed. It was a painful time and I needed a friend. Your kindness was a comfort. I thought we...' She had been dangerously near giving herself away. Her secret hopes that they had a future together had been shattered in a few minutes. All the sleepless nights, the soul-searching the longing had been in vain.

'Amelie...' he said softly. 'You are wrong about my intentions. Is there no chance we could talk some more about this? I don't want to lose touch with you.'

'You've got a nerve.'

'But you don't understand. I admire you. Your bravery, your strength. I had to show your suffering and subsequent collapse in order that people would know what a strong person you are to have come through it all and become the person you are today. I wanted to give people hope. If...'

'It's no good trying to make excuses.' Mel interjected. 'What's done is done. I think you'd better leave.'

'If that's what you want.' there was resignation in his voice.

Mel recognised it but was powerless to relieve it.

'I hope you will think about what I've said. I'll leave the book with you. Please read it. Maybe you'll see things differently. Whatever you feel, please get in touch. You have my card.' And he was gone.

The empty sound of the door closing behind him echoed in the hollow space inside her. She had expected so much more from this evening. How had it all gone so badly wrong? It seemed she'd never learn. She put her head in her hands and cried as if her heart would break. No amount of sympathy from her friends was enough to help her come to terms with what had happened.

In the exhausted sleep that followed, blocks of words floated past her, blurred and troubling.

The first case history is a complicated one… When I first met this patient… unstable condition… due to a chain of unfortunate events… needed counselling…

Mel woke sweating and mortified. It was as if someone had lit a fire in her chest. Anger and humiliation had rubbed together and ignited an inferno. 'Oh François,' she whispered, 'I trusted you. How could you do this to me just when life is good for me again?' The tears flowed once more and she brushed at them angrily, determined not to be undermined by yet another man in the long line of people who had revealed their true colours in the end.

Stronger now, she snatched up the book to read on.

The baby's death was a tragedy. But she bore it surprisingly well, with the help of good friends. It was the relentless ordeals which followed afterwards that proved too much. Ultimately, she suffered a breakdown. I want to stress that this is in no way a weakness, rather the body's way of reacting to an overload of stress.

There followed a passage of rather technical medical detail that Mel chose to skim over. The case review continued:

After receiving the correct treatment, I am pleased to report that this patient has survived and now helps to run a very successful business. She is to be congratulated for surmounting more traumas than seem apparent here, more than any one person should have to endure. That she has revealed such supreme strength of character is to be admired.

(Full case notes available on request. Dr Millais has agreed to run a series of free lectures on the study of trauma connected to the death of a child. Please apply in person.)

Oh my God! Mel didn't know whether to laugh or cry. It seemed she had totally misjudged François by being too hasty. Though, from choice, she'd relegated those awful times to near extinction, she had to admit that his assessment of her condition when they first met at the hospital was probably pretty accurate. She had long ago admitted that she must have been slightly unhinged to have considered appropriating a baby, let alone making off to a foreign country with it. But to know that it had now been shared with the world needed a bit of getting used to. And yet he'd also recorded for posterity that he admired her. She liked that bit – she liked that a lot.

Chapter 36

'May I speak to François Millais, please?' Mel was through to the London Conference Centre.

'I'm sorry, he's in conference.' The secretary's reply is dismissive.

'Then please give him a message.' Requesting that François call her back when he had time, Mel left her number and hoped she wouldn't have too long to wait.

All day Mel was unable to concentrate. Customers, who normally had her undivided attention, stood perplexed by her lack of understanding of their requests. Several times she snatched the mobile from her pocket thinking she must have missed his call. Still the hours dragged on.

Convinced that she had completely blown it this time, and he wanted nothing more to do with her, she took herself home with the others. They did their best to lift her spirits while they walked.

'He probably **is** really busy,' Bella said.

'He has to look after all those *pauvre enfants,*' Odile reminded her.

Mel knew they were trying to help but their words did nothing to cheer her.

'You will feel better with some food inside you, you've eaten nothing all day.' Food was Odile's answer to everything.

Eyes to the ground, Mel concentrated on putting one foot in front of the other. As they rounded a corner, she felt Bella nudge her.

'Wake up. You look like you're in some sort of a trance. Look who's here.'

Looking up, Mel saw François hurrying towards them.

'Thank goodness,' he said. 'I thought I must have missed you.'

'You can blame Mel for our lateness. She's been mooning about all day.' Bella's eyes crinkled attractively as she teasingly exposed Mel's preoccupation with his hoped-for call.

Hot colour surged to Mel's face and all her carefully rehearsed apologies disappeared. 'I don't know what to say,' she confessed, 'but I'm so glad you came.'

'You don't have to say anything.' He seized her arm and led her away, calling over his shoulder, 'You will excuse us, we have some catching up to do.' The friends laughed as he gave a huge wink.

'Don't be too long. I'm cooking supper!' Odile called.

When he turned back to her, Mel had found her voice. 'François,' she began, 'I have to apologise. I completely misjudged you last night, and I didn't even give you a chance to explain. Believe me, I'm truly sorry.'

'It doesn't matter. Really. Let's just forget last night and enjoy today, live now.'

They walked and talked, and talked some more, as they walked the leafy roads lined with imposing houses. It was very peaceful in this little-known part of Harrow. Some owners only used their smart houses here for weekends. Mel relaxed in his company. He was warm and funny and she hadn't felt this happy in years.

Of course François' work kept him very busy. There were times during the weeks they were apart when he had to cancel their arrangements. Others when he arrived looking exhausted and defeated.

She decided to ask him about it.

'Most times I can deal with it, I have to.

There's bound to be failures.'

'But it's not your fault,' Mel stressed.

'Sometimes it just feels I've missed something. That I could have done more. Like with Chloe for example. Especially for Chloe.'

'But...' Mel didn't know what to say. She felt the pain just as keenly as she had then, and it must have shown on her face.

'You see...can you ever forgive me?'

A sense of guilt crept through Mel at his words. How often does anyone think of doctors and specialists feeling so deeply about their patients? They project this image of strength, of being in charge - of their treatments and their emotions. But what do they really feel?

It was humbling to have François trust her with his pain. 'Forgive you? I never blamed you.'

'Then can you forgive Chloe?'

His question startled her. 'What on earth do you mean?'

'For dying'

'That's different. It wasn't her fault. It wasn't anybody's fault.'

'But you were so angry – with her, with me.'

'That was pure selfishness on my part. It was all about me, if I'm honest. I wanted to blame everyone for taking away someone so precious to me, my last chance of motherhood.'

'You don't know that.'

Once again Mel was shaken. In four words he had thrown her into chaos. She tried to wrest her mind back from her churning thoughts.

'As you see, with the help of good friends I have got over the anger. And I wasn't really angry with you anyway. You were kind to me, and I needed kindness badly.' She wondered if she had said too much.

She looked at Francçois and saw a broad smile on his face.

'I love your honesty,' he said.

'I hope you won't mind but there's something I have to do.' Bending towards him, she kissed him slowly, tenderly.

'Mind?' he asked. 'It's very good therapy. Try it.'

He returned her kiss, at first gently and then more urgently.

But she didn't mind. She didn't mind it at all.

Reluctantly, they retraced their steps, beckoned by Odile's promised supper. For the first time that day Mel was ravenous. Reaching the flat, they opened the door on the most delicious of aromas.

'Ah bon. Here you are. Supper is ready, I will bring it.'

The food was superb, and they all tucked in, chatting companionably between mouthfuls. When they were all satisfied, Odile disappeared into the kitchen once more. Returning with a tray of coffee and petits fours laid only for two, she suggested to Bella that they go to the snug and watch a TV programme they had recorded.

Her intention was so obvious that Mel found herself blushing all over again. But she didn't object to being left alone with François and when he put his arm around her and pulled her close she didn't object to that either. Nor to the feel of his lips on hers.

There was no stopping her now. She was going to finish what she'd started. 'I think I fell a little bit in love with you back then,' you know.'

'Back when?'

'You know, when Chloe died.'

'Oh. I'm humbled. You were so sad and you thought of me. But wait - only a little bit?' He was teasing her.

'That was then. And you need to push off now. You have work tomorrow.'

It was bad timing and she was mortified when she saw the confused look he gave her. 'Push off? I don't know that.'

'It just means you have to leave now.'

'Oh.' He was still looking puzzled.

Mel knew she was making a mess of things. Words were no good. She would just have to show him. Taking his face in her hands, she gently gave him a lingering kiss.

'Everything is alright then?'

'Of course it is.'

There was no need for words. Actions were much better. And it was some time later they said their goodnights. She watched him walk away until he was out of sight, and part of her went with him.

*****

Back in the flat, Mel was having a troubled night. She tried in vain to sort out the questions hammering in her head. Did she love him? Oh yes! But if he should ask, could she spend the rest of her life with him? What about the friends who'd stood by her all this time? She'd hate them to think she'd just been making use of them. She must make sure they knew she wouldn't let them down. There was no problem as far as the bookshop was concerned. She loved it and was proud of the success they'd made of it.

Hang on, he hasn't asked you yet, a warning voice whispered. But Mel knew the signs. She'd always been like this: longing so much for something to happen that she began to act like it had. Making plans, getting prepared. Hoping, praying. Oh yes, she wanted him to. The thing she'd thought would never happen again had hit her full on: exciting, exhilarating, leaving her breathless.

Chapter 37

Sleep, which had eluded her while all these questions hammered in her brain, gradually crept up on her, and she drifted off to delicious thoughts of seeing François again.

It seemed only minutes later that she was disturbed. Coming out of a deep sleep, at first, she was puzzled by what had woken her. Then she became aware of an insistent noise, one she feared above all other. A fire alarm. It was faint, but instantly recognizable. She got out of bed and cautiously opened the door. There was no sign of a fire. No noise, no whiff of smoke.

Oh please, not the bookshop!

She ran to the window. What she saw confirmed her worst nightmare. She must alert the others. Turning, she saw a bleary-eyed Bella coming towards her.

'What's going on?' she asked. Then, 'seeing the look of terror on Mel's face, 'Oh my God! The bookshop. Odile!' she shrieked, 'allez vite!'

Together, they raced down the stairs and along to the shop, pulling on dressing gowns as they went. There were drifts of smoke, but no visible flames. Mel was already on her mobile to the Fire Service.

'With you ASAP,' the voice reassured her. I've logged where you are. Close all the doors and try not to worry.'

'They're on their way,' she told Bella and Odile. And then she prayed: that the warning had come early, the waiting would be short and there wouldn't be too much damage. They were all silent, unable to vocalize their anxieties.

In the immediate panic, thoughts of François had been pushed into the background. Now Mel longed for him, hoped he'd be proud of the way she'd taken control in the face of her greatest fears. Fire brought the vivid memories rushing back; that last time had caused her to have a nervous breakdown. But now she was strong enough to banish the negative thoughts and deal with what needed to be done, strengthening her self-belief.

'We need to leave the door unlocked ready for the firemen,' she said. But don't open it. We don't want to feed the fire.'

She snatched some tea towels from the shop's kitchen area, soaked them in water and, having wrung out the excess, passed one each to Bella and Odile. 'Hold this over your mouth and nose to protect you from the smoke,' she ordered as they began to splutter and cough.

Mel seized the fire extinguisher from the wall and was about to aim the jet of foam when the door burst open. Two firefighters hurried in and quickly found the cause of the fire. A badly wired power point had been quietly shorting, and eventually started to smoulder. This was what had been responsible for all the smoke. But it had been caught before it had burst into flames.

'You've been very lucky. We've caught it early and will soon have things under control. But we'll have to turn the electricity off until you can get an electrician in to check all the wiring. Should have done that before.'

'We did,' Mel stated firmly. Clearly, he had noticed the absence of men and was of the opinion mere women wouldn't have thought of such a thing.

'Oh. Sorry.' He had the grace to acknowledge that he'd been hasty in his judgment. 'I'd get someone different to do it this time,' he said with a grin.

'Oh, we will,' they chorused. 'And please try to make as little mess as possible. These books are irreplaceable,' added Mel.

'We'll do our best.' Turning to his mate he said, 'Get Josh to bring in the foam extinguisher Mick. I just want to make sure we haven't missed anything.'

'Will do.'

'And get the lads in to do a clean-up job when we've finished.'

'OK.'

They all got stuck in and within half an hour the job was done. The clean-up had been thorough and there was very little left for Mel and the others to do.

'I'd offer you a cup of tea,' she said, 'but we have no electrics.' She smiled sweetly.

*****

When all the excitement had subsided, Mel took herself thankfully back to bed. Exhausted, she thought she would sleep for a week, but it was still eluding her, kept at bay by her troubled thoughts. Although she berated herself for having let François go, she still had concerns about what to do for the best. She wanted to be fair to everyone and hated that her friends might think she had just been making use of them while she needed their support and, now she'd had a better offer, she would leave them to man the bookshop without any input from her. But she loved the bookshop and was proud of the success they had made of it. She must make sure they knew she wouldn't let them down.

She really applied herself to it, and there was really no problem as far as the bookshop was concerned. Except, there was one small thing that had worried her lately. Karl seemed to have lost his initial enthusiasm for what he was doing and had become a little careless. Several times she had caught him with earphones clamped to his head and guessed he was listening to music when he was supposed to be working. She took to checking up on him, asking questions about their orders and the expected delivery dates. When she asked Karl to show her around some of the sites he used it seemed to revive his energy, gave him a sense of importance. Armed with this knowledge Mel felt more relaxed.

Although the real problem was that, if she were honest, she had been looking for reasons to delay her answer should François ask her to marry him. And she so hoped he would. But perhaps she was reading too much into their burgeoning friendship. Recognizing that playing for time, attempting to cover her abiding lack of confidence in her own decision-making capabilities, was unfair, she vowed to have more faith in herself. He wasn't going to wait forever, even though he was the most understanding of men.

There was also the question of where François' work would require him to live. She loved France, in spite of all that had happened there, but she'd come alive again with the challenge of setting up the new venture and seeing it do so well. It had boosted her morale and given her something to look forward to each day. It was only with men that she felt less sure of herself. Perhaps François would understand and they could reach some sort of compromise.

They clearly needed to talk it over, take things slowly. She badly wanted to come to the right conclusion for everybody.

Chapter 38

Next morning, Bella and Odile were discussing the events of the evening before when Mel joined them.

'Well I'm glad it's over,' Mel said. 'I've done with dramas.'

'It's a good job you woke when you did,' Bella said. 'A few minutes could have made all the difference.'

'Mais oui, you did well mon amie.'

'It was good to have you with me,' Mel replied, embarrassed, 'and I know you would have done just as well.'

'I'm not sure I would have acted so promptly', Bella replied. 'Wait till I tell François how you took control. He'll be so proud of you. You've come a long way, you know.'

'You don't need to tell him. It's no more than anyone would have done.'

'But another fire? You could have completely freaked out. Instead, you held it together and did what needed to be done.'

'I didn't even think about it at the time,' Mel admitted. 'I just desperately wanted to save the books.'

'Then that in itself is amazing progress. I really admire the way you've fought your way back.'

'Moi aussi.'

'Thanks.' It had been a long haul, but Mel didn't want to be reminded of the weak, frightened girl she was back then. Things were different now. She had François and he'd believed in her from the start. It was he who had helped her turn a tragedy into a triumph.

Suddenly, she needed to see him: hold him, tell him that, with his help, everything was going to be all right. Why, oh why, hadn't she been able to tell him that last night? She'd sent him away, knowing he was uncertain of her feelings for him although she'd done her best to reassure him. Perhaps he thought that, at almost 50 she thought him too old for her. But Mel was not a teenager. The time had flown by unnoticed while she fought to be a mother and she was passed the age when life begins. His age had never been a problem. She was the problem.

Even as these thoughts were going around in her head she was keying in his number. Normally, she tried not to ring him at the hospital, but felt this was urgent. He'd said he would come and see her tonight, but could she still count on his proposal?

'Mr Millais' secretary. Can I help you?'

'Is he there please? It's Amelie Dubois. I won't keep him long.'

'Yes, he said to put you through if you rang.'

'Millais.' His voice was brisk, gave nothing away.'

'It's Mel.'

'Yes, Miss Astley acquainted me of that fact.'

Mel was thrown by his attitude. Was he playing with her, or purposely keeping his voice neutral? Supposing she'd blown it, sending him away once too often. She decided he was just being business-like for the benefit of the patient he obviously had with him.

Now she felt guilty for interrupting him. 'I just wanted to say please come tonight.'

'I will do that.'

Such a few words. Was she deluding herself with the thought that his tone had perceptibly lightened, as if concealing a smile? She heard the click that signified the end of the call and was immediately impatient. There was so much she'd wanted to say. It seemed the hours between them lengthened to eternity in an instant. But she must resign herself to the wait, just as he had had to do. Perhaps sleep had eluded him last night as it had her.

She filled the time shopping for, and preparing, the food for the meal they would share. It served to pass the time, but she had great difficulty concentrating on the task she'd set herself.

She was in the shower when she heard the ring of the doorbell. Surely he wasn't here yet? She'd so wanted to look good for him.

There were voices in the hall; and one of them was definitely his. She would recognize it anywhere. Don't panic, she told herself as she took a towel to her hair. He's waited all day, a few more minutes won't hurt.

Dragging a comb through her still-damp locks, she pulled on the new rose-coloured sweater and a pair of grey linen jeans. She did a hasty and minimal job of her make-up, more anxious to see

François than to look like some retouched celebrity in Hello Magazine.

Feeling suddenly nervous, she walked into the sitting room where he was in conversation with Bella and Odile. 'Hello,' she said. 'Sorry, I was in the shower when you arrived.'

'It doesn't matter. Really.'

'Shall I go and see how the cooking's going Cherie?' Odile said tactfully.

'I'll help you,' added Bella as they left the room.

There was an awkward silence. Now they were alone, neither of them knew what to say. And yet there was so much.

'It's so good to see you,' Mel began at last. 'I want to apologize for last night. It was unfair of me to treat you like that.'

'It's OK. But you seemed uncertain of my feelings for you, so I have one more question.'

'Another question? Is something bothering you?'

Ignoring her questions, he asked, 'Will you marry me?'

She'd dreamed of this moment, but the suddenness of his proposal robbed her of speech for a moment. Needing confirmation, she finally spluttered, 'What did you just say?'

'I said, will you marry me.' He was looking worried. 'You don't like the idea? Is it too soon? Then I will wait.'

'You surprised me, that's all. I...' In truth she didn't know what she felt about his sudden proposal and her senses reeled. In her dreams it was all she wanted and it's true her initial reaction had been elation, but it was followed by a kind of panic that she was about to make another rash decision. After all, her track record with men hadn't been too good so far.

François waited patiently for her answer, his expression flicking from anxiety to a nervous smile of encouragement. The silence lengthened.

Reminding herself that, only minutes before, she'd promised herself she could handle anything from now on, she made a decision. 'Please don't misinterpret my answer,' she began, 'I'm thrilled that you asked me, but I'd like to accept your offer of time to think before taking such a big step.'

'I understand,' François replied quietly.

'There are lots of things to be addressed,' Mel continued. 'Like where we would be living, I don't even know how long you are in England. And I wouldn't want to let my friends down when they have both supported me by investing money in the bookshop and it's doing so well. Besides, it was my idea and I love working there.'

'I've been very selfish,' François admitted. 'I can see we need to talk through all these things that concern you. I don't want to rush you. I can wait, I'm a patient man.' He attempted a smile of reassurance.

Mel's panic evaporated and only joy remained. He was such a gorgeous man. She found herself returning his smile. 'Thank you for understanding,' she said. Her answer was already made, if only she could believe in the wonderful future that beckoned. What a fool she was. How could she risk losing him? 'I…' she began, uncertain how to phrase what she needed to say.

François misinterpreted her hesitation. 'This has been a tiring evening for you.

It was the wrong time to throw another big problem at you.'

'Don't apologise. And it's not a problem really but I…'

'It's OK. I must go now, it's late. Tomorrow we will talk – yes?'

Mel hated to see his uncertainty. 'Oh yes! Yes please.' And I will have an answer ready. Just in case he was still worried, she planted a long, convincing kiss on his lips.

Chapter 39

Once again, the questions chased each other around in Mel's head all night. There was no perfect solution. Whatever decision she made it seemed that she and François would have to divide their lives between England and France. It was bound to take its toll on their relationship.

As the dawn broke through the June sky, she gave in to her exhaustion and slept. But the shriek of the alarm woke her far too soon. Wearily, she staggered out of bed and made for the shower. Hopefully, it would make her feel more refreshed.

Arriving at the bookshop she was surprised to hear loud music thrumming through the premises. It was the last thing she needed. She was already fighting a headache caused by sleep deprivation. Besides, their clients liked to enjoy peace while they perused the books. Many had said it was like a little oasis of calm when they walked in. For that reason, the popular café area was set away from the reading section. The café was where they could chat quietly and enjoy a bit of relaxation.

So what on earth was happening? Mel had thought she was the first to arrive but, as she approached the small office where Karl manned the website the noise grew louder, as if it were hitting the walls and reverberating back and forth.

Furious, Mel opened the door. Karl span round in his chair, startled and guilty.

'Turn that off immediately,' Mel shouted above the din. 'What on earth do you think you're doing?' She glanced round the room. It was a wreck. Empty cider bottles decorated the desk; the ashtray overflowed with rather amateur looking spliffs and a bundle of bedding was thrown in a corner.

'Please tell me what's been going on here. From the evidence, it's obvious you haven't been here alone. For God's sake, you surely haven't been using these premises as a drug den? Please not.'

The poor effort to cover his guilt said it all. Mel's fears were right. She was stunned. But it took only a few seconds for her fury to ignite. 'And you have been sleeping here, too,' she shouted. 'I've thought for some time that you have been looking crumpled and had lost your initial enthusiasm for the job you're paid to do.' She looked around. The place was filthy and looking like a squat.. Mel's anger rose. It hasn't gone beyond my notice that you've been wearing earphones and obviously listening to music on the shop's equipment, I turned a blind eye because you still seemed to be doing a good job.'

'I've done what I've been asked to do,' Karl said defiantly.

'That's as maybe. But there have been mistakes that others have had to put right. Clients have been disappointed when we haven't met the times we've quoted to them.'

'Well at least I've been here on time.' He consulted his watch and made a show of looking for the others, pleased with his idea of humour.

Mel was not amused. 'What upsets me most is that you've taken advantage of my friends and me, betrayed our trust. What have you to say for yourself?'

'I had nowhere else to go. I got thrown out of my flat.'

'I'm not surprised if you treated it like this.' Mel indicated the chaos around her.

'And, funnily enough, people aren't too keen on having drug users on their premises. It won't surprise you to know that I don't like it either.'

'Sorry. I should have told you I was homeless.' It was a last-ditch effort to win Mel over, but his forlorn expression didn't work.

'Well you didn't. And now I can't trust you. You'd better take your things and leave.'

'What now? You can't do that.'

'I think you'll find I can. Go!' Mel's head was pounding now: from indignation, and fury.

She watched as he collected his few meagre possessions and then ushered him to the door just as Bella and Odile arrived. One look at Mel's expression told them something was seriously wrong.

'What's going on?' Bella asked.

'The Cow's sacked me.'

'Go! Or I'll call the police.' She watched him slouch off down the road before turning to her friends to explain. She sank into the nearest chair. Now that it was over, the unpleasantness of what had happened began to sink in. She was exhausted.

'Let me make you a coffee, you're white as a sheet.' Bella was all attention. Odile stood by, anxious and unsure what to do.

'What did the boy do? Did he hurt you Cherie?'

'No, not physically, but…' Mel didn't know where to start.

Returning with the coffee, Bella took over. 'Tell us all about it. I've put a note on the door and locked it for a few minutes, so we won't be interrupted.'

'I didn't sleep well last night. I had a few things on my mind. Naturally, I overslept when I eventually got to sleep. So I had a quick shower and came straight here. As I opened the door I was deafened by music thumping from Karl's room. It turns out he's been living there.'

'Mon Dieu! I don't understand.'

'And that's not all. I found drugs and empty bottles in there. He's obviously had his mates round. The thought of them getting high on these premises doesn't bear thinking about. Anything could have happened.'

'Well it didn't, and he won't be troubling us again by the sound of it.' Bella was practical, as ever. 'What a day to be late! I'm so sorry you were here on your own.'

'It's OK.'

'Well, you seem to have handled it well. I'm proud of you.'

'Thanks, but I didn't have much choice.' Mel managed a weak smile.

Odile looked puzzled. 'If Karl has gone,' she ventured, 'who will look after the internet for us?'

'I was going to talk to you both about that. But perhaps tonight. We ought to let our customers in.'

'Are you sure you're OK?'

'Yes, I'm fine.' She fixed an almost convincing smile on her face and went to sort out the many requests with her usual warmth.

The day went by in a blur. So many thoughts were running through Mel's mind as she battled to give her customers her full attention. The headache she's woken with threatened to burst into a full-blown migraine as she re-lived the scene with Karl over and over again, castigating herself for not acting on the clues she'd noticed for a while. Her trouble was she was too trusting: too excited by the success of their business venture, thinking that everyone involved was as committed as herself.

Having to dispatch Karl on the spot had been hard without a doubt but, as the day progressed, she began to see that, out of this disaster, had come a resolution to the dilemma she had faced. She hoped her friends would accept the solution she would present to them this evening.

She thought of François and longed to tell him of her plan. His regular absences made times like this so difficult. She knew he should come first, but Bella and Odile had been such a support to her she felt she must discuss it with them first. She was pretty sure they would agree. They wanted her to be happy, had told her she deserved it after all that life had thrown at her, and yet Mel still worried that they may not be sure that her idea would work.

For Mel, it was the answer to all her prayers. It solved the one remaining problem about her situation with François. Surely, they wouldn't object? But doubts crept in and she became more and more nervous about putting her suggestion to her friends. Her head throbbed, her stomach churned and she was nauseous with fatigue.

'Why don't you go home,' Bella coaxed. 'You look dreadful. Go and get some rest. The busiest period is over and we can cope.'

'And I will come and cook you something light and delicious, and you will feel better.' Food, as ever, was Odile's answer to everything.

Reluctantly, Mel gave in and dragged herself back to the flat they shared. Absurdly, she felt a kind of severance, a separation from her friends and from the business that had meant so much to her when she'd needed a new project to throw herself into, a new life to explore.

It came to her then that, if they accepted her planned solution, this is how it would be. She would be repeatedly relinquishing her personal hold on the business. The mechanics hadn't hit her until that moment, and it felt strange. She knew she had to weigh up the benefit – to her relationship and to the bookshop. Put like that there was no real conflict. François was her priority.

Chapter 40

Away from the shop and the questions raised by the scene with Karl, Mel began to relax. Chamomile tea soothed her; her headache eased and her stomach settled. She even accepted that the decision she had made then was the only way to go. Thus calmed, she slipped into a deep and restoring sleep.

Awoken by the sound of voices, she realized Bella and Odile were back. She went shakily to meet them at the door. 'I'm so sorry, I fell asleep. I meant to have some tea waiting.'

'Don't worry, sleep was just what you needed, you were exhausted.'

'I didn't sleep much last night,' Mel admitted. 'I…' How to explain the worries that had kept her awake? How best to put across the subsequent solution that had come out of Karl's betrayal of their kindness?

'Do not worry yourself now,' Odile cut in. 'Let's have something to eat and then talk.'

Mel was grateful for her friend's ability to bring peace into any situation, to make it seem that no matter what the problem was, it was there to be solved with some good food and a glass of wine. How she was going to miss these friends. But the rewards are so worthwhile she told herself, and a smile lit her face for the first time that day.

'That's better,' Bella said, 'I was beginning to think you had something dreadful to tell us.'

'Not dreadful, but difficult for me to say to you.'

'No point in waiting until after supper then, you'd better get it over with. But it can't be that bad, we're your friends.'

As they tucked in to the fragrant mushroom tart and fresh salad Odile had prepared for them, Mel began. 'You will have realized, I'm sure that, without Karl, we are short of someone to man the website. I have thought about it and, with your agreement, I would like to be that person.' There, she'd said it and it hadn't been too hard.

'We thought you'd never get around to saying it!' Bella and Odile looked at each other and laughed. 'That's just what we hoped you would say.' Bella was, as usual speaking for both of them. 'We'd love you to do it. We've seen your interest and heard you asking Karl about how the website works. You'd be a much better choice than either of us.'

'But wait a moment,' Mel broke in. 'There's more – and you may not like what I have to say.' Mel swallowed hard as she felt tears threatening at the thought of leaving the friends who had been so good to her. But she consoled herself with knowing that she would still see them regularly.

Bella and Odile were waiting, puzzled as to what it was Mel had to tell them that she was finding so hard to put into words.

'I will have to do it from France.' It came out all wrong. Not a bit like she had rehearsed.

'There was a stunned silence.

'Oh dear, I knew it wouldn't go down well,' Mel said, 'it's not the perfect solution is it?'

'It's a surprise, that's all Cherie.'

'You are going to marry François?' It had only taken Bella a few seconds to work out the reason for Mel's decision.

'I hope so. I haven't given him my answer yet! I wanted to talk to you first.'

'Why? Your happiness is more important.'

'But I owe you so much. Without your friendship, I don't think I would have survived. We certainly wouldn't have this thriving business. I feel bad to be leaving you when you were kind enough to humour me with my idea of the bookshop.'

'We love it too. It's ideal. I am immersed in books and still have time to write. What could be better.'

'I love it here too, and I can please people with my cooking,' said Odile, not to be outdone.

'You're both very kind. Shall I tell you what I had in mind?'

'There's more?'

'Don't you want to know how I'll manage the website?'

'I imagine you can man a website wherever you are. It doesn't even matter what country you're in. It'll be fine.'

'But…'

'But what?'

'I rather wanted to…'

'Let's have it.'

'I thought I could fly over once a month to see you. To catch up with how things are going. I don't want to lose touch with you both.'

'You silly chump. That would be great. But what does François say?'

Mel laughed. 'I confess I haven't discussed it with him yet,' she owned. 'But I'm pretty sure it will be OK with him.'

'You must talk to him tonight.'

'I intend to. He's ringing at eight. There's so much I have to tell him now.' The next bit was difficult to voice. 'I even feel grateful to Karl for inadvertently giving me the answer to the problem of splitting my life between England and France. I'm so happy.'

It seemed incredible that a day that had started so badly could bring such rewards. All her past trials had faded, as if a series of bad dreams. If only Chloe were here to share in it all. Mel allowed herself to think of the child she'd grown to love so much and whose young life had been snatched from her. But though she felt sad, even without Chloe her life was almost perfect. Eight o'clock couldn't come fast enough. She needed so much to speak to François: to tell him about her day, the early drama followed by the gradual realization that it had solved all their problems.

The evening dragged, and Mel tried to concentrate on the thriller she was currently reading. But her mind kept wandering and she couldn't keep up with the plot. Reading a section for the third time, she was jolted into action by the opening bars of the Marseillaise. It had been François idea of a joke to download it as Mel's ringtone.

'Bonsoir mon Cherie.' His deep French accent still sent a thrill through her.

'Good evening to you, too,' Mel replied. 'I have so much to tell you darling.' The word slipped out as though it felt at home in her vocabulary and the lilt in her voice betrayed her unadulterated happiness.

'You're well?'

'Oh yes! Everything's wonderful. Today started badly though. I had so much on my mind.'

'The thought of marrying me caused this?'

'No. I want that badly. But there is the bookshop to consider. I didn't want to let my friends down, you see. But then something wonderful happened.'

'Tell me.'

'It was awful to start with. I had slept badly and then I had to sack Karl.'

'Why?'

'It's a long story. I'll tell you all about that when we meet. What I want to tell you now is that the problem we had with my coming to France with you is resolved.'

'Oh.'

'You don't sound very happy about it.'

'I... '

'You will when I tell you. It was when I had sacked Karl that the idea came to me. As you know, he looked after the Internet side of things for us and now we had no one to do it. But then I thought why can't I do it?'

'But you'll be in France.'

'I know. But the good thing about computers is that it doesn't matter where the website is operated from, because it's world-wide.'

'Of course. And so?'

'So I can be with you in France. But there is one more thing. I would like to come to England once a month to see my good friends who supported and encouraged me when my life fell apart. Also, to keep my eye on the business which has now become my 'baby'. I have seen my idea flourish beyond my expectations and, with the help of my friends, feel confident again.'

'Oh.'

'Are you unhappy with that François? You don't sound as pleased as I'd hoped.'

'I'm a bit confused that's all, because I have some exciting news of my own.'

'What is it?'

'I applied for a post at Great Ormond Street Hospital. The interview went well. I'm pretty sure I have the job.'

'You've done that for me?'

'I didn't want us to be parted again so I asked Alexander McNab, the consultant I'm working with in Birmingham to give me a reference. He's the reason I will get the job, I'm sure.'

'Your own reputation counts for a great deal I bet. But it's marvellous anyway, why are you sounding so uncertain?'

'You've made your own plans. I don't want to spoil things for you.'

'Spoil things for me? You're incredible, and far too kind to me.'

'But…'

'But nothing. I'm so proud of you and we can sort something out. When do you start?'

'I haven't been told I have the position yet.'

'That's just a formality.' Mel was determined to be upbeat about this latest development. 'Let's set a date for the wedding,' she said, and was rewarded with a laugh from François and a cheer from her friends.

'You're saying yes then?' he said.

Printed in Great Britain
by Amazon